A Book Of

RECENT TRENDS IN IT

B.B.A. (Computer Application) Semester - VI
Formerly known as B.C.A.

As Per Revised Syllabus
Effective from June 2015

Gautam Bapat
MCA (Sci.), PGDBM (Mkt.), MMS (Mkt.)
Asst. Professor, Computer Science & Applications
MITSOM College
Pune

Price ₹ 170.00

NIRALI PRAKASHAN
ADVANCEMENT OF KNOWLEDGE

N3474

RECENT TRENDS IN IT

ISBN 978-93-5164-853-6

Second Edition : January 2017

© : Author

Published By :   Polyplate
NIRALI PRAKASHAN
Abhyudaya Pragati, 1312, Shivaji Nagar
Off J.M. Road, PUNE – 411005
Tel - (020) 25512336/37/39, Fax - (020) 25511379
Email : niralipune@pragationline.com

➢ DISTRIBUTION CENTRES

PUNE

Nirali Prakashan : 119, Budhwar Peth, Jogeshwari Mandir Lane, Pune 411002, Maharashtra
Tel : (020) 2445 2044, 66022708, Fax : (020) 2445 1538
Email : bookorder@pragationline.com, niralilocal@pragationline.com

Nirali Prakashan : S. No. 28/27, Dhyari, Near Pari Company, Pune 411041
Tel : (020) 24690204 Fax : (020) 24690316
Email : dhyari@pragationline.com, bookorder@pragationline.com

MUMBAI

Nirali Prakashan : 385, S.V.P. Road, Rasdhara Co-op. Hsg. Society Ltd.,
Girgaum, Mumbai 400004, Maharashtra
Tel : (022) 2385 6339 / 2386 9976, Fax : (022) 2386 9976
Email : niralimumbai@pragationline.com

➢ DISTRIBUTION BRANCHES

JALGAON

Nirali Prakashan : 34, V. V. Golani Market, Navi Peth, Jalgaon 425001,
Maharashtra, Tel : (0257) 222 0395, Mob : 94234 91860

KOLHAPUR

Nirali Prakashan : New Mahadvar Road, Kedar Plaza, 1st Floor Opp. IDBI Bank
Kolhapur 416 012, Maharashtra. Mob : 9850046155

NAGPUR

Pratibha Book Distributors : Above Maratha Mandir, Shop No. 3, First Floor,
Rani Jhanshi Square, Sitabuldi, Nagpur 440012, Maharashtra
Tel : (0712) 254 7129

DELHI

Nirali Prakashan : 4593/21, Basement, Aggarwal Lane 15, Ansari Road, Daryaganj
Near Times of India Building, New Delhi 110002 Mob : 08505972553

BENGALURU

Pragati Book House : House No. 1, Sanjeevappa Lane, Avenue Road Cross,
Opp. Rice Church, Bengaluru – 560002.
Tel : (080) 64513344, 64513355,Mob : 9880582331, 9845021552
Email:bharatsavla@yahoo.com

CHENNAI

Pragati Books : 9/1, Montieth Road, Behind Taas Mahal, Egmore,
Chennai 600008 Tamil Nadu, Tel : (044) 6518 3535,
Mob : 94440 01782 / 98450 21552 / 98805 82331,
Email : bharatsavla@yahoo.com

niralipune@pragationline.com | www.pragationline.com

Also find us on www.facebook.com/niralibooks

Preface ...

I take this opportunity to present this book entitled as **"Recent Trends in IT"** to the students of Sixth Semester of B.B.A. (Computer Application). The object of this book is to present the subject matter in a most concise and simple manner. The book is written strictly according to the Revised Syllabus.

The book has its own unique features. It brings out the subject in a very simple and lucid manner for easy and comprehensive understanding of the basic concepts, its intricacies, procedures and practices. This book will help the readers to have a broader view on E-commerce. The language used in this book is easy and will help students to improve their vocabulary of Technical terms and understand the matter in a better and happier way.

I sincerely thank Shri. Dineshbhai Furia and Shri. Jignesh Furia of Nirali Prakashan, for the confidence reposed in me and giving me this opportunity to reach out to the students of management studies.

I thank Mrs. Aabha Athavale, Mrs. Anita Panajkar for their important inputs time to time and Mr. Akbar Shaikh and Ms. Chaitali Takale, who painstakingly attended to all the details to make this book appear good.

I have given my best inputs for this book. Any suggestions towards the improvement of this book and sincere comments are most welcome on niralipune@pragationline.com.

Author

Syllabus ...

1. Software Process and Project Metrics, Analysis Concepts and Principles [06]

Measures, Metric indicators, Metric in process and the project domains, Software measurement, Metrics for software quality, Software quality assurance, Requirement analysis, Communication techniques, Analysis principles, Software prototyping, Case Study.

2. Distributed Databases [08]

Standalone v/s Distributed databases, Replication, Fragmentation, Client/Server architecture, Types of distributed databases.

Object - Relational Databases

Abstract Data types, Nested Tables, Varying Arrays, Large Objects, Naming Conventions for Objects, Case Study.

3. Data Warehouse [08]

What is Data Warehouse? A Multidimensional Data Model, Data Warehouse Architecture, Data Warehouse Implementation, Data Cube Technology, From Data Warehousing to Data Mining, Data Mining, Functionalities, Data Cleaning, Data Integration and Transformation, Data Reduction.

4. Network Security [14]

Cryptography, Introduction to Cryptography, Substitution Ciphers, Transposition Ciphers, One-Time Pads, Two Fundamental Cryptographic Principles; Symmetric Key Algorithms' DES - The Data Encryption Standards, AES - The Advances Encryption Standard; Public Key algorithms; RSA - Other Public Key algorithms, Digital Signature, Symmetric - Key Signature, Public Key Signature, Message Digests.

5. Computing and Informatics [08]

Introduction to Computing and Informatics, Types of Computing Cloud, Green, Soft, Mobile, Case Study.

Contents ...

Chapter 1...

Software Process and Principles

Contents ...

1.1 Introduction

Software process and product metrics are quantitative measures that enable software people to gain insight into the efficiency of the software process and the projects that are conducted using the process as a framework. Basic quality and productivity data are collected. These data are then analyzed, compared against past averages, and assessed to determine whether quality and productivity improvements have occurred. Metrics are also used to pinpoint problem areas so that remedies can be developed and the software process can be improved.

1.2 Measures   [Oct. 16]

Measure: A standard or unit of measurement; the extent, dimensions, capacity, etc., of anything, especially as determined by a standard; an act or process of measuring; a result of measurement.

Measurement: Measurement is the act or process of measuring. A figure, extent, or amount obtained by measuring. Also a result, such as a figure expressing the extent or value that is obtained by measuring.

An example of measure: five centimeters. The centimeter is the standard, and five identifies how many multiples or fractions of the standard are being appraised. With the centimeter, someone measuring something in the United States is going to get the same measure as someone in Europe.

Let's relate this to software, such as lines of code. Currently, there really isn't a universal standard for lines of code. Someone measuring a program's lines of code in one office will probably not get the same count as someone measuring the same program in a different office. Therefore, it is imperative that each organization determine a single standard for what is meant by a line of code and ensure that everyone in the organization understands and uses that standard. Thus, a measure may be universally standard or locally standard, but it needs to be a standard.

Software measurement plays an increasingly important role in Software Engineering. Currently, software metrics are proving to be very effective for building high-quality prediction systems for large database projects for:

- Understanding and improving software development and maintenance projects,
- Assessing and maintaining system quality by highlighting problematic areas,
- Determining the best ways to help practitioners and researchers in their work, etc. Furthermore, software metrics are important tools to help assess and institutionalize Software Process Improvement in software-intensive organizations.

In software development and software testing, most commonly used measures are:

- Number of Defects found in a system or component.
- Lines of Code (LOC, KLOC).
- Number of Test Cases.

Reasons to use measure in software process:

- To characterize in order to:
  - o Gain an understanding of processes, products, resources, and environments.
  - o Establish baselines for comparisons with future assessments.
- To evaluate in order to:
  - o Determine status with respect to plans.
- To predict in order to:
  - o Gain understanding of relationships among processes and products.
  - o Build models of these relationships.
- To improve in order to:
  - o Identify roadblocks, root causes, inefficiencies, and other opportunities for improving product quality and process performance.

1.3 Metric Indicators   [April 16]

The importance of measurement in software development has been highlighted this past year, largely because of the new Air Force policy on software metrics. At the same time, there seems to be a good deal of confusion on the terminology involved, specifically measure, metric and indicator. It's important to understand differences between these terms.

Metric: A quantitative measure of the degree to which a system, component, or process possesses a given attribute. A calculated or composite indicator based upon two or more measures. A quantified measure of the degree to which a system, component, or process possesses a given attribute.

An example of a metric would be that there were only two user-discovered errors in the first 18 months of operation. This provides more meaningful information than a statement that the delivered system is of top quality.

A metric, in contrast, is a derived value which cannot be measured directly. It is a number derived from one or more measures by a formula Best known metrics in software development and software testing are:

- Number of defects found per KLOC, which serves as an estimation of quality of code.
- Productivity, i.e. Size / Effort.
- Defect Density, i.e. number of defects related to size.

There are two types of metrics, objective and subjective.

Objective metrics can be quantized and are readily available, subjective metrics rely on opinions, gut feelings, personal attitudes etc. An example is CSAT (customer satisfaction), though the former is more reliable, than the later, the reliability of subjective metrics can be improved by having checklists and guidelines.

For example, survey question need to have, probe areas, facet, scale definitions before an option can be chosen.

Effective metrics must be simple, objective, measurable, meaningful and have easily accessible underlying data.

Important attributes of a metric:

1. **Simple:** So that errors in computation or interpretation are avoided, and also that the metric can be comprehended.
2. **Objective:** Based on goals and objectives of the company.
3. **Measurable:** Based on things which can be reliably measured, not estimated or guessed.
4. **Meaningful:** So that they can help the managers to understand important aspects of their projects.
5. **Easy to collect:** Metric shall be automated and non-intrusive, i.e. not interfere with other activities of the developers.

6. **Easy to interpret:** So that it is easy to comprehend it, understand the causes which affect it.

7. **Hard to misinterpret:** Even when the metric may be easy to interpret, there may be cases leading to wrong conclusions. Metrics shall be designed with caution so that such cases are avoided.

8. **Valid:** To ensure, whether the metric really measures what it is supposed to; prevent systematic errors.

9. **Reliable:** They must perform their required functions under stated conditions for a specified period of time, providing consistent results; prevent random deviations in measurement.

Indicator: A device or variable that can be set to a prescribed state based on the results of a process or the occurrence of a specified condition.

For example, a flag or semaphore. A metric that provides insight into software development processes and software process improvement activities concerning goal attainment.

As the definition notes, a flag is one example of an indicator. An indicator is something that draws a person's attention to a particular situation. Another example of an indicator is the activation of a smoke detector in your home; it is set to a prescribed state and sounds an alarm if the number of smoke particles in the air exceeds the specified conditions for the state for which the detector is set.

In software terms, an indicator may be a substantial increase in the number of defects found in the most recent release of code.

An indicator is "a thing that indicates the state or level of something", thus it can be simply just a number showing value of a particular measure or metric. A better indicator could be a chart comparing two measures/metrics or projecting how a measure/metric developed during a time period. Also, a semaphore where red means bad and green means good is also a very simple indicator, which can be helpful in particular class of situations.

Thus, indicator is most general of these terms:

*   Software process and project metrics are quantitative measures.
*   They are a management tool.
*   They offer insight into the effectiveness of the software process and the projects that are conducted using the process as a framework.
*   Basic quality and productivity data are collected.
*   These data are analyzed, compared against past averages, and assessed.
*   The goal is to determine whether quality and productivity improvements have occurred.
*   The data can also be used to locate problem areas.
*   Remedies can then be developed and the software process can be improved.

In software project management, we are primarily concerned with productivity and quality metrics. There are four reasons for measuring software processes, products, and resources (to characterize, to evaluate, to predict, and to improve).

Role of Management in Software Development

The management of software development is heavily dependent on four factors: People, Product, Process and Project.

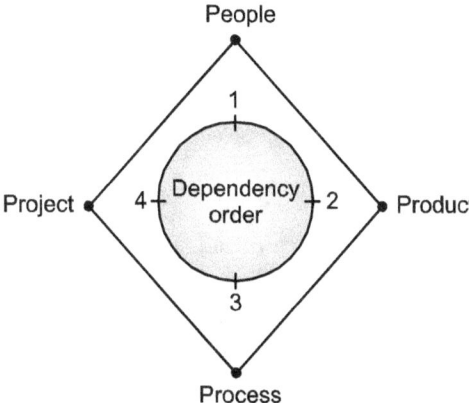

Fig. 1.1: Factors of Management Dependancy

Software development is a people centric activity. Hence, success of the project is depends on the people who are involved in the development.

The People

Software development requires good managers who can understand the psychology of people and provide good leadership. A good manager can not ensure the success of the project, but can increase the probability of success. The areas to be given priority are: proper selection, training, compensation, career development, work culture etc.

Managers face challenges. It requires mental toughness to endure inner pain. We need to plan for the best, be prepared for the worst, expect surprises, but continue to move forward anyway.

Hence, manager selection is most crucial and critical. After having a good manager, project is in safe hands. It is the responsibility of a manager to manage, motivate, encourage, guide and control the people of his/her team.

The Product

We deliver a product to the customer which is a solution to his/her problems. Hence, objectives and scope of work should be defined clearly to understand the requirements. Alternate solutions should be discussed which help the managers to select a "best" approach within constraints imposed by delivery deadlines, budgetary restrictions, personnel availability, technical interfaces etc. Without well defined requirements, it may be impossible to define reasonable estimates of the cost, development time and schedule for the project.

The Process

The process is the way in which we produce software. It provides the framework from which a comprehensive plan for software development can be established. If the process is weak, the end product will undoubtedly suffer. There are many life cycle models and process improvements models. Depending on the type of project, a suitable model is to be selected. Now-a-days CMNI (Capability Maturity Model) has become almost a standard for process framework. The process priority is after people and product, however, it plays very critical role for the success of the project. A small number of framework activities are applicable to all software projects, regardless of their size and complexity. A number of different task sets, tasks, milestones, work products, and quality assurance points, enable the framework activities to be adopted to the characteristics of the project and the requirements of the project team.

A proper planning is required to monitor the status of development and to control the complexity. In order to manage a successful project, we must understand what can go wrong and how to do it right. We should define concrete requirements and freeze these requirements. Changes should not be incorporated to avoid software surprises. Software surprises are always risky and we should minimise them. We should have a planning mechanism to give warning before the occurrence of any surprise.

All four factors (People, Product, Process and Project) are important for the success of the project. Their relative importance helps us to organise development activities in more scientific and professional way.

1.4 Metrics in Process and the Project Domains

Metrics should be collected so that process and product indicators can be confirmed. Process indicators enable a software engineering organization to gain insight into the efficacy of an existing process (i.e., software engineering tasks, work products, and milestones). They enable managers and practitioners to assess what works and what doesn't. Process metrics are collected across all projects and over long periods of time.

Their aim is to provide indicators that lead to long-term software process improvement. Project indicators enable a software project manager to:

1. Assess the status of an ongoing project.
2. Track potential risks.
3. Uncover problem areas before they go "critical".
4. Adjust work flow or tasks.
5. Evaluate the project team's ability to control quality of software work products.

In some cases, the same software metrics can be used to determine project and then process indicators. In fact, measures that are collected by a project team and converted into metrics for use during a project can also be transmitted to those with responsibility for software process improvement. For this reason, many of the same metrics are used in both the process and project domain:

- The aim of process metrics is to provide a set of process indicators that lead to long-term software process improvement.

- The only way to know how/where to improve any process is to:
  - o Measure specific attributes of the process.
  - o Develop a set of meaningful metrics based on these attributes.
  - o Use the metrics to provide indicators that will lead to a strategy for improvement.

Process and Project Metrics

Metrics should be collected so that process and product indicators can be fixed.

Process Metrics   [Oct. 16]

- Process metrics used to provide indicators that lead to long term process improvement.
- Private process metrics (e.g. defect rates by individual or module) are only known to by the individual or team concerned.
- Public process metrics enable organizations to make strategic changes to improve the software process.
- Metrics should not be used to evaluate the performance of individuals.
- Statistical software process improvement helps an organization to discover where they are strong and where they are week.

Project Metrics

- Project metrics enable project manager to:
  - o Assess status of ongoing project.
  - o Track potential risks.
  - o Uncover problem before they go critical.
  - o Adjust work flow or tasks.
  - o Evaluate the project team's ability to control quality of software work products.
- A software team can use software project metrics to adapt project workflow and technical activities.
- Project metrics are used to avoid development schedule delays, to reduce potential risks, and to assess product quality on an on-going basis.
- Every project should measure its inputs (resources), outputs (deliverables), and results (effectiveness of deliverables).

Project metrics are used to:

- Minimize the development schedule by making the adjustments necessary to avoid delays and lessen potential problems and risks.
- Assess product quality on an ongoing basis and, when necessary, to modify the technical approach to improve quality.

1.5 Software Measurement

Measurements in the physical world can be categorized in two ways:

- Direct measures (e.g., the length of a pipe) and indirect measures (e.g., the "quality" of pipes produced, measured by counting rejects).

- Software metrics can be categorized similarly. Direct measures of the software engineering process include cost and effort applied. Direct measures of the product include Lines Of Code (LOC) produced, execution speed, memory size, and defects reported over some period of time.

- Indirect measures of the product include functionality, quality, complexity, efficiency, reliability, maintainability.

- The cost and effort required to build software, the number of lines of code produced, and other direct measures are relatively easy to collect, as long as specific conventions for measurement are established in advance. However, the quality and functionality of software or its efficiency or maintainability are more difficult to assess and can be measured only indirectly. We have already partitioned the software metrics domain into process, project, and product metrics.

- Consider a simple example: Individuals on two different project teams record and categorize all errors that they find during the software process. Individual measures are then combined to develop team measures. Team A found 31^6 errors during the software process prior to release. Team B found 18^1 errors. All other things being equal, which team is more effective in uncovering errors throughout the process? Because we do not know the size or complexity of the projects, we cannot answer this question. However, if the measures are normalized, it is possible to create software metrics that enable comparison to broader organizational averages.

Types of Metrics:

- Size-oriented software metrics are derived by normalizing quality and/or productivity measures by considering the size of the software that has been produced.

- Function-oriented software metrics use a measure of the functionality delivered by the application as a normalization value. Since 'functionality' cannot be measured directly, it must be derived indirectly using other direct measures. Function-oriented metrics were first proposed by Albrecht, who suggested a measure called the function point. Function points are derived using an empirical relationship based on countable (direct) measures of software's information domain and assessments of software complexity.

- Function Points measure software size by quantifying the functionality provided to the user based only on logical design and functional specifications.

- Function point analysis is a method of quantifying the size and complexity of a software system in terms of the functions that the system delivers to the user.

- It is independent of the computer language, development methodology, technology or capability of the project team used to develop the application.

- Function point analysis is designed to measure business applications.

- Uses of Function Points: Measure productivity, Estimate development and support, Monitor outsourcing agreements, Normalize other measures such as defects, frequently require the size in function points.

1.6 Metrics for Software Quality

To produce a high-quality system, application, or product, software engineers must apply effective methods coupled with modern tools within the context of a software process. In addition, a good software engineer must measure if high quality is to be realized. A good software engineer uses measurement to assess the quality of the analysis and design models, the source code, and the test cases that have been created as the software is engineered. To accomplish this real-time quality assessment, the engineer must use technical measures to evaluate quality in objective, rather than subjective ways.

Factors assessing software quality come from three distinct points of view (product operation, product revision, product modification).

Software quality factors requiring measures include:

- **Correctness:** A program must operate correctly. Correctness is the degree to which the software performs its required function. The most common measure for correctness is the number of defects per KLOC, where a defect is defined as a verified lack of conformance to requirements. When considering the overall quality of a software product, defects are those problems reported by a user of the program after the program has been released for general use. For quality assessment purposes, defects are counted over a standard period of time, typically one year.

- **Maintainability:** Software maintenance accounts for more effort than any other software engineering activity. Maintainability is the ease with which a program can be corrected if an error is found, adapted if its environment changes, or enhanced if the customer desires a change in requirements.

  There is no way to measure maintainability directly; therefore, we must use indirect measures.

  A simple time-oriented metric is Mean-Time-To Change (MTTC), the time it takes to analyze the change request, design an appropriate modification, implement the change, test it, and distribute the change to all users.

  On average, programs that are maintainable will have a lower MTTC (for equivalent types of changes) than programs that are not maintainable. Hitachi has used a cost-oriented metric for maintainability called spoilage—the cost to correct defects encountered after the software has been released to its end-users. When the ratio of spoilage to overall project cost (for many projects) is plotted as a function of time, a manager can determine whether the overall maintainability of software produced by a software development organization is improving.

- **Integrity:** Software integrity has become increasingly important in the age of hackers and firewalls. This attribute measures a system's ability to withstand attacks to its security. Attacks can be made on all three components of software: programs, data, and documents.

  To measure integrity, two additional attributes must be defined: threat and security. Threat is the probability (which can be estimated or derived from empirical evidence) that an attack of a specific type will occur within a given time. Security is the probability (which can be estimated or derived from observed evidence) that the attack of a specific type will be repelled.

  The integrity of a system can then be defined as:

  Integrity = Summation [(1 − threat) (1 − security)]

  where threat and security are summed over each type of attack.

  Usability (easy to learn, easy to use, productivity increase, user attitude)

  If a program is not user-friendly, it is often ruined to failure, even if the functions that it performs are valuable. Usability is an attempt to quantify user-friendliness and can be measured in terms of four characteristics:

  1. The physical and or intellectual skill required to learn the system.
  2. The time required to become moderately efficient in the use of the system.
  3. The net increase in productivity measured when the system is used by someone who is moderately efficient.
  4. A subjective assessment of users attitudes toward the system.

- **Defect Removal Efficiency (DRE):** A quality metric that provides benefit at both the project and process level is Defect Removal Efficiency (DRE).

  DRE is a measure of the filtering ability of quality assurance and control activities as they are applied throughout all process framework activities. When considered for a project as a whole, DRE is defined in the following manner:

  DRE = E/(E + D)

  where   E is the number of errors found before delivery of the software to the end-user and

  D is the number of defects found after work product delivery. The ideal value for DRE is 1.

  That is no defects are found in the software.

  Realistically, D will be greater than 0, but the value of DRE can still approach 1. As E increases (for a given value of D), the overall value of DRE begins to approach 1. In fact, as E increases, it is likely that the final value of D will decrease (errors are filtered out before they become defects). If used as a metric that provides an indicator of the filtering ability of quality control and assurance activities, DRE encourages a software project team to institute techniques for finding as many errors as possible before delivery. DRE can also be used within the project to assess a team's ability to find errors before they are passed to the next framework activity or software engineering task.

Establishing A Software Metrics Program

A software metrics program includes following steps:

1. Identify your business goals.
2. Identify what you want to know or learn.
3. Identify your sub goals.
4. Identify the entities and attributes related to your sub goals.
5. Formalize your measurement goals.
6. Identify quantifiable questions and the related indicators that you will use to help you achieve your measurement goals.
7. Identify the data elements that you will collect to construct the indicators that help answer your questions.
8. Define the measures to be used, and make these definitions operational.
9. Identify the actions that you will take to implement the measures.
10. Prepare a plan for implementing the measures.

Software Quality

Definition:

IEEE definition of Software quality is:

1. The degree to which a system, component, or process meets specified requirements.
2. The degree to which a system, component, or process meets customer or user needs or expectations.

OR

Pressman's definition Software quality is defined as: Conformance to explicitly stated functional and performance requirements, explicitly documented development standards, and implicit characteristics that are expected of all professionally developed software.

1.7 Software Quality Assurance (SQA)   [April 16, Oct. 16]

The function of software quality that assures that the standards, processes, and procedures are appropriate for the project and are correctly implemented.

Software quality assurance (IEEE definition) is:

1. A planned and systematic pattern of all actions necessary to provide adequate confidence that an item or product conforms to established technical requirements.
2. A set of activities designed to evaluate the process by which the products are developed or manufactured. Contrast with quality control.

The objectives of SQA activities Software development (process-oriented):

1. Assuring an acceptable level of confidence that the software will conform to functional technical requirements.
2. Assuring an acceptable level of confidence that the software will conform to managerial scheduling and budgetary requirements.
3. Initiating and managing of activities for the improvement and greater efficiency of software development and SQA activities.

This means improving the prospects that the functional and managerial requirements will be achieved while reducing the costs of carrying out the software development and SQA activities.

Software Maintenance (Product-Oriented):

1. Assuring with an acceptable level of confidence that the software maintenance activities will conform to the functional technical requirements, managerial scheduling and budgetary requirements.
2. Initiating and managing activities to improve and increase the efficiency of software maintenance and SQA activities.

This involves improving the prospects of achieving functional and managerial requirements while reducing costs.

Software quality assurance (SQA) consists of a means of monitoring the software engineering processes and methods used to ensure quality. The methods by which this is accomplished are many and varied, and may include ensuring conformance to one or more standards, such as ISO 9000 or a model such as CMMI.

SQA encompasses the entire software development process, which includes processes such as requirements definition, software design, coding, source code control, code reviews, change management, configuration management, testing, release management, and product integration. SQA is organized into goals, commitments, abilities, activities, measurements, and verifications.

*   A planned and systematic pattern of all actions necessary to provide adequate confidence that a software work product conforms to established technical requirements.
*   A set of activities designed to evaluate the process by which software work products are developed and/or maintained.

For the purpose of this Software quality assurance (SQA) is considered a process for the measurement of deliverables and activities during each stage of the development lifecycle. The objective of SQA is to quantify the quality of the products and the activities giving rise to them and also to guide a quality improvement effort. It is advantageous to integrate it into the software development process. SQA should also take into consideration the maintenance of a product, the technical solution, product budget and scope.

Quality assurance differs from quality control in that quality control is a set of activities designed to evaluate the quality of a developed or manufactured product. The evaluation is conducted during or after the production of the product. Quality assurance however reduces the cost of guaranteeing quality by a variety of activities performed throughout the development and manufacturing process. For the purpose of this we will focus on the following aspects to SQA.

The SQA activities take place at each developmental stage of the development lifecycle. The stages are categorised into areas for requirements capture, system design and coding and testing and finally release.

1. **Verification:** The process of evaluating a system or component to determine whether the products of a given development phase satisfy the conditions imposed at the start of that phase.

2. **Validation:** The process of evaluating a system or component during or at the end of the development process to determine whether it satisfies specific requirements

3. **Qualification:** The process used to determine whether a system or component is suitable for operational use.

During the analysis, design and coding stages of product development the outputs of each stage need to be measured, monitored and managed so that each output can be verified against its predefined exit criteria. When the final product has completed the coding and integration stages, it must be validated against the original user requirements and signed off by senior team members as passed validation testing. At each stage of this product development, the efforts during the development must be improved upon where possible in order to cut costs and remain competitive. This is not an easy task when what is being produced is a program, which in itself is intangible. This is where the complications of software quality assurance lie.

Advantages:

1. Domain-specific languages allow solutions to be expressed in the expression and at the level of abstraction of the problem domain. Consequently, domain experts themselves can understand, validate, modify, and often even develop domain-specific language programs.

2. Self-documenting code.

3. Domain-specific languages enhance quality, productivity, reliability, maintainability, portability and reusability.

4. Domain-specific languages allow validation at the domain level. As long as the language constructs are safe any sentence written with them can be considered safe.

Disadvantages:

1. Cost of learning a new language vs. its limited applicability.

2. Cost of designing, implementing, and maintaining a domain-specific language as well as the tools required to develop with it (IDE).

3. Finding, setting, and maintaining proper scope.

4. Difficulty of balancing trade-offs between domain-specificity and general-purpose programming language constructs.

5. Potential loss of processor efficiency compared with hand-coded software. Proliferation of similar non-standard domain specific languages, i.e. a DSL used within insurance company A versus a DSL used within insurance company B.

6. Non-technical domain experts can find it hard to write or modify DSL programs by themselves.

Selecting a Software Quality Assurance Tool:

A Software Quality Assurance Automation Tool shall be selected such that it:

- Manages requirements
- Aligns testing priorities based on risk
- Defines test plans
- Monitors quality across releases and cycles
- Schedules and runs tests
- Tracks defects
- Uses versioning and base lining

Processes could be:

- Software Development Methodology
- Project Management
- Configuration Management
- Requirements Development/Management
- Estimation
- Software Design
- Testing

Once the processes have been defined and implemented, Quality Assurance has the following responsibilities:

- Identify weaknesses in the processes.
- Correct those weaknesses to continually improve the process.

The quality management system under which the software system is created is normally based on one or more of the following models/standards:

1. CMMI (Capability Maturity Model Integration):

- CMMI stands for Capability Maturity Model Integration. It is a process improvement approach that provides companies with the essential elements of an effective process. CMMI can serve as a good guide for process improvement across a project, organization, or division. CMMI was formed by using multiple previous CMM processes.

- The following are the areas which CMMI addresses:

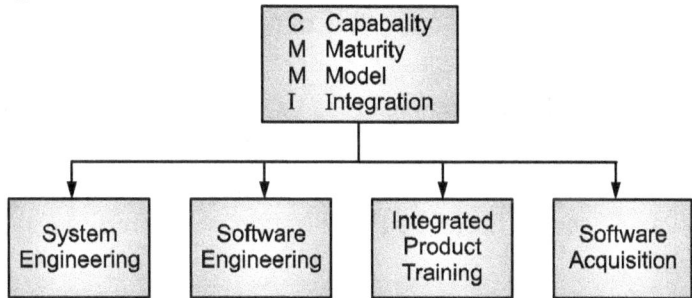

Fig. 1.2: Capability Maturity Model Integration

- **Systems Engineering:** This covers development of total systems. System engineers concentrate on converting customer needs to product solutions and supports them throughout the product lifecycle.

- **Software Engineering:** Software engineers concentrate on the application of systematic, disciplined, and quantifiable approaches to the development, operation, and maintenance of software.

- **Integrated Product and Process Development (IPPD):** Integrated Product and Process Development (IPPD) is a systematic approach that achieves a timely collaboration of relevant stakeholders throughout the life of the product to better satisfy customer needs, expectations, and requirements. This section mostly concentrates on the integration part of the project for different processes. For instance, it's possible that your project is using services of some other third party component. In such situations the integration is a big task itself, and if approached in a systematic manner, can be handled with ease.

- **Software Acquisition:** Many times an organization has to acquire products from other organizations. Acquisition is itself a big step for any organization and if not handled in a proper manner means a disaster is sure to happen.

2. Six Sigma:

Six Sigma is a accurate and proven business methodology that uses data and statistical analysis to improve business performance. With the goal of increasing profits by eliminating mistakes, waste, and rework. Six Sigma provides a means to identify and prevent process variation or defects to improve predictability and success of business processes.

Six Sigma certification confirms a level of training, practice, and capability with respect to specific competencies. Though requirements for each Six Sigma certification level are different, each requires training, and each participant, called a "Belt", is required to have a leadership-approved project prior to Six Sigma certification training.

- **Six Sigma Green Belts** have received two weeks of training on the Six Sigma road map and essential elements of statistical methodologies supporting Six Sigma projects. Green Belts allocate up to 50% of their time on Six Sigma projects, and Black Belts assist them with projects as needed.

- **Six Sigma Black Belts** are technical leaders who have received four weeks of training focusing on the Six Sigma road map and extensive statistical methodologies. Black Belts normally dedicate up to 75% of their time to Six Sigma projects, and they assist Green Belts as needed. Green Belt certification is required for Black Belt certification eligibility.

- **Six Sigma Master Black Belts** represent the highest level of technical and organizational proficiency. They have received six weeks of training on the Six Sigma methodology, and they've learned the skills and tools required to teach Six Sigma philosophies and implement Six Sigma within an organization. Master Black Belts lead all levels of Six Sigma projects, and they help Black Belts apply methodology when necessary. Their jobs are completely devoted to Six Sigma. Black Belt certification is necessary for Master Black Belt certification eligibility.

3. ISO 9000:

ISO 9000 is a series of standards, developed and published by the International Organization for Standardization (ISO), that define, establish, and maintain an effective quality assurance system for manufacturing and service industries. The ISO 9000 standard is the most widely known and has perhaps had the most impact of the 13,000 standards published by the ISO. It serves many different industries and organizations as a guide toquality products, service, and management.

An organization can be ISO 9000-certified if it successfully follows the ISO 9000 standards for its industry. In order to be certified, the organization must submit to an examination by an outside assessor. The assessor interviews staff members to ensure that they understand their part in complying with the ISO 9000 standard, and the assessor examines the organization's paperwork to ensure ISO 9000 compliance. The assessor then prepares a detailed report that describes the parts of the standard the organization missed. The organization then agrees to correct any problems within a specific time frame. When all problems are corrected, the organization can then be certified. Today, there are approximately 350,000 ISO 9000-certified organizations in over 150 countries.

Software Quality Assurance encompasses the entire software development life cycle and the goal is to ensure that the development and/or maintenance processes are continuously improved to produce products that meet requirements.

1.8 Requirement Analysis   [April 16, Oct. 16]

Requirements analysis is the first stage in the systems engineering process and software development process. Requirements analysis in systems engineering and software engineering, encompasses those tasks that go into determining the needs or conditions to meet for a new or altered product, taking account of the possibly conflicting requirements of the various stakeholders, such as beneficiaries or users. Requirements analysis is critical to the success of a development project. Requirements must be actionable, measurable, testable, related to identified business needs or opportunities, and defined to a level of detail sufficient for system design. Requirements can be functional and non-functional.

Overview conceptually, requirements analysis includes three types of activity:

- **Eliciting requirements:** The task of communicating with customers and users to determine what their requirements are. This is sometimes also called requirements gathering.

- **Analyzing requirements:** Determining whether the stated requirements are unclear Incomplete, ambiguous, or contradictory, and then resolving these issues.

- **Recording requirements:** Requirements might be documented in various forms, such as Natural-language documents, use cases, user stories, or process specifications.

Requirements analysis can be a long and difficult process during which many delicate psychological skills are involved. New systems change the environment and relationships between people, so it is important to identify all the stakeholders, take into account all their needs and ensure they understand the implications of the new systems. Analysts can employ several techniques to elicit the requirements from the customer. Historically, this has included such things as holding interviews, or holding focus groups (more aptly named in this context as requirements workshops) and creating requirements lists. More modern techniques include prototyping, and use cases. Where necessary, the analyst will employ a combination of these methods to establish the exact requirements of the stakeholders, so that a system that meets the business needs is produced.

- **Requirements analysis:** This is a process of discovery, refinement, modeling, and specification.

  During the process, both the developers and customers take an active role. This process focus on: "what" instead of "how"

  Input of the requirements analysis process:- Software Project Plan and System specification

- **Output:** Software requirements specification document
  - Provides the software engineer with models that can be translated in to data, architectural, interface, and procedure design.

- o   Customer and developer can check the quality of the software and provide the feedback.
- o   Who perform requirements analysis: system analysts.

Requirement Engineering Process:

- **Feasibility study:** Identify and guess to see if user needs can be satisfied using current techniques and technologies.
- **Requirements analysis:** The process of deriving the system requirements through observation of existing systems, discussion with users and customers, task analysis, and so on.
- **Requirements definition:** Translating the information into a REQ. document.
- **Requirements specification:** Define system requirements using a consistent precise, and complete way.

Using some requirements specification method:

Requirement Analysis Process:

- **Domain understanding:** Understanding of application domain.
- **Requirements collections:** The process of interacting with customers, users to discover the requirements for the system.
- **Requirements classification:** Group and classify the gathered requirements.
- **Conflict resolution:** Resolve the conflict requirements.
- **Prioritization:** Identify and list requirements according to their importance.
- **Requirements validation:** Check and validate the gathered requirements to see if they are complete, correct, and sound.

Software Prototyping:

In some cases, it is possible to apply operational analysis principles and derive a model of software from which a design can be developed.

Selecting the prototyping approach:

The closed-ended approach is called throwaway prototyping.

- a prototype serves only as a rough demonstration of requirements.

The open-ended approach is called evolutionary prototyping.

- a prototype serves as the first evolution of the finished system.

Prototyping Methods and Tools:

- Fourth Generation Techniques
- Reusable Software Components
- Formal Specification and Prototyping Environments

1.9 Communication Techniques

Especially during the early phases of software development, cognitive psychology (concerning the mind), linguistic aspects and communication theory are in focus, because thinking and talking are highly connected. For problems like software development, psychology provides the following three concepts which explain why people behave as we can observe in many typical software projects:

Systemic Thinking focuses on dynamics and causal relations within social systems like teams, customers, producers, companies. Systemic thinking means that any action within a system has effects on the system itself.

For example, if there is a planning, talk with a stakeholder to get his requirements, the outcome of this talk will be influenced by the way this talk is conducted.

Radical Constructivisim explains that knowledge is the self-organized cognitive process of the human brain. That is, the process of constructing knowledge regulates itself, and since knowledge is a construct rather than a compilation of empirical data, it is impossible to know the extent to which knowledge reflects an ontological reality. This means, without exception that any knowledge is subjective and thus there is nothing objective we can rely on.

Autopoiesis deals with the self-referentiality of living systems. This means, that people always act based on the experiences they have made earlier in their life. This explains for example the behavior of people who work with a certain software and now define the requirements for a new version - the observed behavior, that the old version always acts as reference point, is due to autopoiesis.

In **Systemic Coaching** psychology also provides communication and creativity techniques for dealing with these effects. For example the effects of autopoicsis can be dealt with special questioning techniques where the person being interviewed is made to change his viewpoint on the system being discussed.

We now consider it typical software life-cycle as shown in Fig. 1.3. Initially, there are ideas and considerations on the customer's side together with intentional as well as unintentional expectations, Even if the customer is already thinking in technological categories, it is not always transparent approach to describe the actual problem space.

To transform these concepts into a structured and complete problem understanding (ontology), adequate ways of interaction are required. If such domain knowledge is complete, it can be transformed in a structured and technical oriented solution knowledge with tools and languages like UML.

The later steps of the software process, transforming the solution knowledge into software and validating that the software is in line with the customer's expectations is left out at this Point.

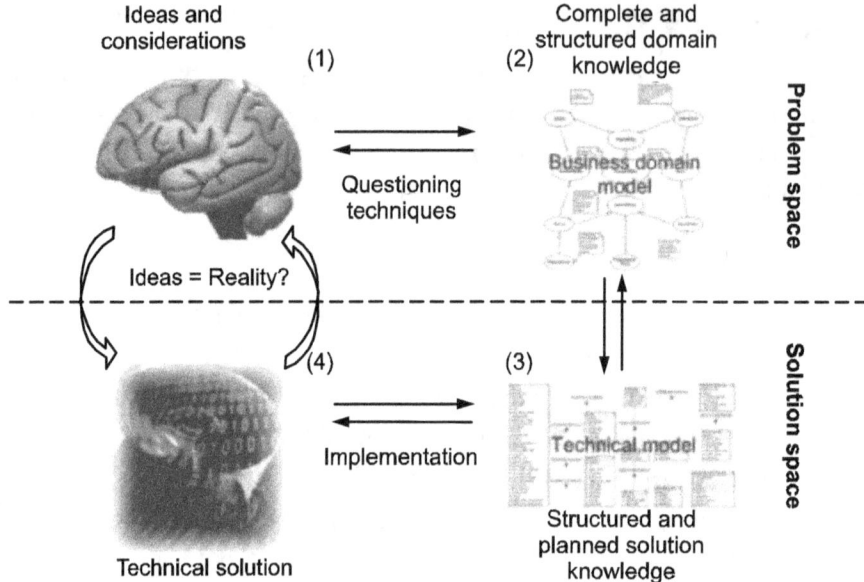

Fig. 1.3: Software life-cycle: from ideal to technical implementation

Case Study

Now depict how 4' ps of a typical software project can look like if the insights gained from psychology are used for the early stages of a project. We depict how the initial ideas and concepts can be elicited and how the structured and complete domain knowledge can be established.

Starting Situation

In a typical situation two groups of experts work together. One group consists of the IT architects. They are supplier of the future system and their task is to gather the requirements for the system and to define the resulting IT architecture. Their motto could be described as 'how to build software, and we want to learn what kind of software is necessary in this case here'.

The other group of experts comes from the customer and has deep knowledge about the actual business problem and demand. Their motto could be 'We have solved these business problems in the past in certain ways and for the future we want a suitable software for this'.

To achieve an solution which is optimal for both groups and fulfills all management requirements (like time, budget, quality), it is necessary that both groups of experts exchange their knowledge in an interactive process and incrementally develop requirements for the future software solution. This process consists of the following steps.

Step 1: Understanding Customer Needs

The customer presents his business problem (i.e. not wishes about certain technology), the background, why he thinks that software is a suitable means for solving this problem and the improvements he expects from software usage. The task of the IT experts is to question and to understand the viewpoint of the customer, but also to explore the context in which the demand for such an IT solution is of special importance.

During this process the customer - and not the provider - subjectively defines the significance of his problem areas. It is the provider's duty at this stage to explore this subjective problem space and to understand the problem areas and if there are adjacent areas which should be considered in this context as well.

It is also part of this process step to elaborate which parts should change from a customer perspective, in which way they should change, which parts have explicitly to stay as, they are, and what the probable reasons for current shortcomings are. These topics provide a plethora of detailed insights for the system provider, which are of extreme importance for the later planning stages.

Step 2: Consolidating Problem Areas

The next stage is about consolidating the problem areas which have been elicited so far. It is of special importance what kind of measures have been taken by the customer so far to overcome the business problems or shortcomings addressed by the future software. Even if this has happened with 'onboard-means' only, this information can contain important hints for unnamed mutual dependencies or other required resources. Therefore, this step is not only about technology- or process-related issues. The approach of systems thinking provides other also important questions which allow to assess how certain changes, shortcomings or solutions will be perceived by the customer's employees or management. This also provides important boundary information.

Step 3: Developing Technical Ideas

This is the first time technology gets onto the scene. Of course, normally the customer always has certain ideas, expectations or specifications related to technological solutions. These need to be considered and discussed. Since usually no system is built oil tile green field, this step is in first order about including elements of the technological solution (on a high abstraction level) into the discussion and to discuss with the customer, how a certain system would behave under the constraints of the already given IT application landscape. By means of this dialog, the existing and planned infrastructure is evaluated in order to detect possible influences and interfaces to he covered for the future software solution.

Step 4: Developing the Ideal Solution

Usually projects cannot be realized in all ideal manner due to monetary and/or time con-straints. However, during the later software life-cycle features are added, which have been omitted in the initial project. In reality this leads to continually extended software which in long terms turns out to be ineffective and of deteriorating effect for the software system. During this step we therefore strive for developing a holistic view on the application. In this larger context we explore - assuming an ideal world - how the developed system in a later stage behaves in contexts like other systems or company strategies.

The reason for this is obvious: Many systems grow generically. In the beginning there is the demand for a small solution. However, if the small solution exists, wishes and requirements start to grow. By partial considering possible wishes in advance, there is a much clearer technological planning base, which is a probate means against uncontrolled growth of the later software system.

Step 4: Defining the Further Proceeding

So far concepts for the ideal solution have been developed. Now the next step is to go back to reality with all the insights, at hand. Based on the knowledge which has been created, the optimal target for the development project can be defined to satisfy the primary goals of the customer within a given cost and time range - and also to set up the technological infrastructure broad enough to cater for later requirements.

Even during this step discussions must not only revolve around aligning business and technical issues, but also must ensure that the chosen approach is accepted by all stakeholders of the project.

Step 5: Detailing and Documenting Content

Now the project has reached a stage where classical requirements engineering techniques can take place. The coarse frames of requirements are defined and need to be refined in close cooperation with the customer. The insights that have been gathered during the earlier steps need to be documented in appropriate ways and structures.

1.10 Analysis Principles

Today analysis modeling can be accomplished by applying one of a number of different methods that populate the three regions of the software engineering methods landscape. Yet all methods conform to a set of analysis principles:

1. **The data domain of the problem must be modeled.** To accomplish this, the analyst must define the data objects (entities) that are visible to the user of the software and the relationships that exist between the data objects. The content of each data object (the objects attributes) must also be defined.

2. **The functional domain of the problem must be modeled.** Software functions transform the data objects of the system and can be modeled as a hierarchy (conventional methods), as services to classes within a system (the object oriented view), or as a brief set of mathematical expressions (the formal view).

3. **The behavior of the system must be represented.** All computer based systems respond to external events and change their state of operation as a consequence. Behavioral modeling indicates, the externally observable states of operation of a system and how transition occurs between these states.

4. **Models of data, function, and behavior must be partitioned.** All engineering problem solving is a process of collaboration. The problem (and the models described above) are first represented at a high level of abstraction. As problem definition progresses, detail is refined and the level of abstraction is reduced. This activity is called partitioning.

5. **The overriding trend in analysis is from essence toward implementation.** As the process of elaboration progresses, the statement of the problem moves from a representation of the essence of the solution toward implementation specific detail. This progression leads us from analysis toward design.

1.11 Software Prototyping   [April 16, Oct. 16]

In some cases, it is possible to apply operational analysis principles and derive a model of software from which a design can be developed.

Selecting the prototyping approach:

- The closed-ended approach is called Throwaway Prototyping.
  - o   a prototype serves only as a rough demonstration of requirements.
- The open-ended approach is called Evolutionary Prototyping.
  - o   a prototype serves as the first evolution of the finished system.
- Prototyping Methods and Tools:
  - o   Fourth Generation Techniques
  - o   Reusable Software Components
  - o   Formal Specification and Prototyping Environments

The Software Prototyping refers to building software application prototypes which display the functionality of the product under development but may not actually hold the exact logic of the original software. Software prototyping is becoming very popular as a software development model, as it enables to understand customer requirements at an early stage of development. It helps to get valuable feedback from the customer and helps software designers and developers understand about what exactly is expected from the product under development.

What is Software Prototyping?

- Prototype is a working model of software with some limited functionality.
- The prototype does not always hold the exact logic used in the actual software application and is an extra effort to be considered under effort estimation.

- Prototyping is used to allow the users evaluate developer proposals and try them out before implementation.
- It also helps understand the requirements, which are user specific and may not have been considered by the developer during product design.

Following is the stepwise approach to design a software prototype:

1. **Basic Requirement Identification:** This step involves understanding the very basics product requirements especially in terms of user interface. The more complex details of the internal design and external aspects like performance and security can be ignored at this stage.

2. **Developing the initial Prototype:** The initial Prototype is developed in this stag e, where the very basic requirements are showcased and user interfaces are provided. These features may not exactly work in the same manner internally in the actual software developed and the workarounds are used to give the same look and feel to the customer in the prototype developed.

3. **Review of the Prototype:** The prototype developed is then presented to the customer and the other important stakeholders in the project. The feedback is collected in an organized manner and used for further enhancements in the product under development.

4. **Revise and enhance the Prototype:** The feedback and the review comments are discussed during this stage and some negotiations happen with the customer based on factors like, time and budget constraints and technical feasibility of actual implementation. The changes accepted are again incorporated in the new prototype developed and the cycle repeats until customer expectations are met.

Prototypes can have horizontal or vertical dimensions.

- Horizontal prototype displays the user interface for the product and gives a broader view of the entire system, without concentrating on internal functions.
- Vertical prototype on the other side is a detailed elaboration of a specific function or a sub system in the product.

The purpose of both horizontal and vertical prototype is different. Horizontal prototypes are used to get more information on the user interface level and the business requirements. It can even be presented in the sales demos to get business in the market. Vertical prototypes are technical in nature and are used to get details of the exact functioning of the sub system.

Software Prototyping Types

There are different types of software prototypes used in the industry. Following are the major software prototyping types used widely:

- **Throwaway/Rapid Prototyping:** A software process model based on an initial throwaway prototyping stage is illustrated in Fig. 1.4. The throwaway prototyping approach extends the requirements analysis process with the intention of reducing overall life cycle costs. The principal function of the prototype is to clarify requirements and provide additional information for managers to assess process risks. After evaluation, the prototype is thrown away. It is not used as a basis for further system development.

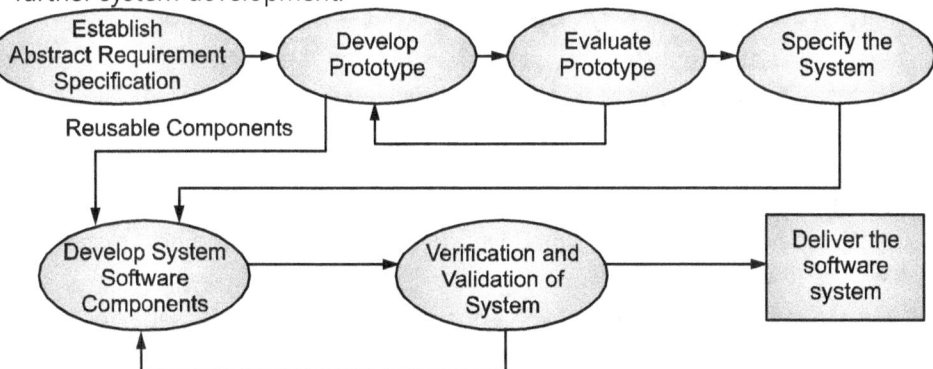

Fig. 1.4: Throwaway prototyping

The process model in above figure assumes that the prototype is developed from an outline or abstract system specification, delivered for experiment and modified until the stakeholder or user is satisfied with its functionality. At this stage, a conventional software process model is entered; a specification is derived from the prototype and the system re-implemented in a final production version. Components from the prototype may be reused in the production-quality system.

The stakeholders and end-users should resist the temptation to turn the throwaway prototype into a delivered system. The reasons for this are:

1. Important system characteristics such as performance, security, robustness and reliability may have been ignored during prototype development so that a rapid implementation could be developed. It may be impossible to tune the prototype to meet these nonfunctional requirements.

2. During the prototype development, the prototype will have been changed to reflect user needs. It is likely that these changes will have been made in an uncontrolled way. The only design specification is the prototype code. This is not good enough for long-term maintenance.

3. The changes made during prototype development will probably have degraded the system structure. The system will be difficult and expensive to maintain.

It is sometimes suggested that the system specification should be the prototype implementation itself. The instruction to the software contractor should simply be "write a system like this one".

There are also several problems with this approach:

1. Important features may have been left out of the prototype to simplify rapid implementation. It may not be possible to prototype some of the most important parts of the system such as safety-critical elements.

2. A prototype implementation has no legal standing as a contract between customer and contractor.

3. Non-functional requirements such as those concerning reliability, robustness and safety cannot be adequately tested in a prototype implementation.

A general problem with throwaway prototyping is that the mode of use of the prototype may not correspond with the way that the final delivered system is used. The tester of the prototype may be particularly interested in the system and may not be typical of system users. The training time during prototype evaluation may be insufficient. If the prototype is slow, the evaluators may adjust their way of working and avoid those system features, which have slow response times. When provided with better response in the final system, they may use it in a different way.

- **Evolutionary Prototyping:** Evolutionary prototyping is based on the idea of developing an initial implementation, exposing this to user comment and refining this through many stages until an adequate system has been developed as shown in Fig. 1.5.

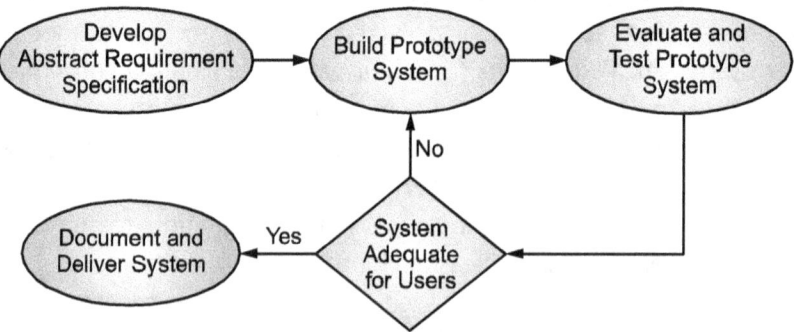

Fig. 1.5: Evolutionary Prototyping

Evolutionary prototyping is one realistic way to develop systems where it is difficult or impossible to establish a detailed system specification document. The key to success in the evolutionary prototyping approach is to use techniques, which allow for rapid system iterations. Suggested changes may be incorporated and demonstrated as quickly as possible. This may mean using high level programming language such for software development. Special-purpose environments and integrated software tools may be used to support and accelerate the development process.

An important difference between evolutionary prototyping and a specification-based approach to development is in verification and validation. Verification is only meaningful when a program is compared to its specification. If there is no specification, verification is impossible. The validation process should demonstrate that the program is suitable for its intended purpose rather than its conformance to a specification.

The systems adequacy is not measurable and only a subjective judgment of a program can be made. This does not invalidate its usefulness; human performance cannot be guaranteed to be correct but we are satisfied if performance is adequate for the task in hand.

There are three problems with evolutionary prototyping, which are particularly important when large, long-lifetime systems are being developed:

1. Existing software management structures are set up to deal with a software process model that generates regular deliverables to assess progress. Prototypes usually evolve so quickly that it is not cost-effective to produce a great deal of system documentation and schedules.

2. Continual change tends to corrupt the structure of the prototype system. Maintenance is therefore likely to be difficult and costly. This is particularly likely when the system maintainers are not the original developers. The development teams are hardly ever responsible for system maintenance.

3. It is not clear how the range of skills, which is normal in software engineering teams, can be used effectively for this mode of development. Small teams of highly skilled and motivated individuals have implemented the systems developed in this way.

These three problems do not mean that evolutionary prototyping should not be used. It allows systems to be developed and delivered rapidly. System development costs are reduced. If the stakeholders and users are involved in the development, the system is likely to be appropriate for their needs. However, organizations that use this approach must accept that the lifetime of the system will be relatively short. As its structure becomes un maintainable, it must be completely rewritten.

- **Incremental Prototyping:** An incremental development model combines the advantages of evolutionary prototyping with the control required for large-scale development projects was developed by Mills et al (1980). This incremental development model (Fig. 1.6) involves developing the requirements and delivering the system in an incremental fashion. As a part of the system is delivered, the user may experiment with it and provide feedback to the system developers. Incremental development is a key part of the Clean room development process.

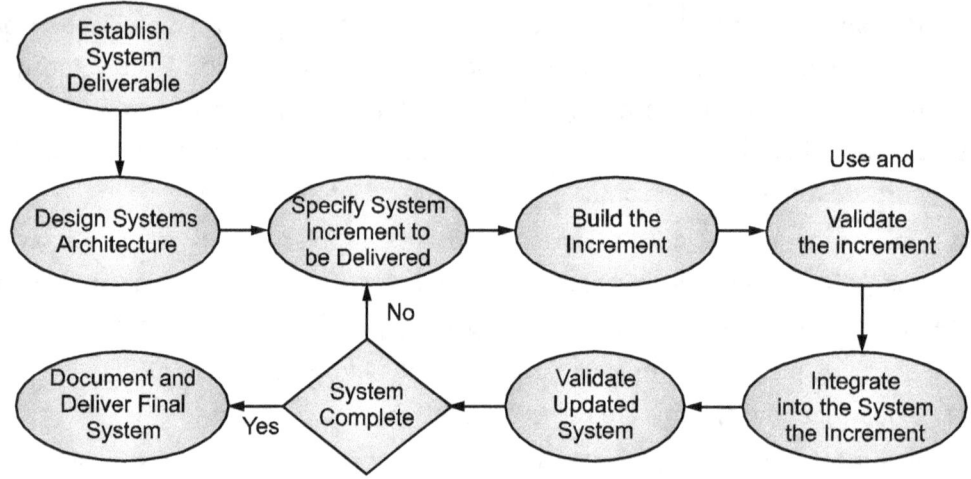

Fig. 1.6: Incremental Development Model

Incremental development avoids the problems of constant change, which characterize evolutionary prototyping. An overall system architecture is established early in the process to act as a framework. System components are incrementally developed and delivered within this framework. Once these have been validated and delivered, neither the framework nor the components are changed unless errors are discovered. User feedback from delivered components however can influence the design of components scheduled for later delivery.

Incremental development is more manageable than evolutionary prototyping as the normal software process standards are followed. Plans and documentation must be produced for each system increment. It allows some user feedback early in the process and limits system errors, as the development team is not concerned with interactions between quite different parts of the software system. Once an increment has been delivered. its interfaces are frozen. Later increments must adapt to these interfaces and can be tested against them.

A problem with incremental development is that the system architecture has to be established before the requirements are complete. Another, non-technical problem is that this approach to development does not fit well with established contractual models for software developers. Contracts for the development must be flexible and established before the requirements are fixed. Many organizations that use traditional engineering models for software procurement find it impossible to adapt to the form of contract, which this approach requires.

- **Extreme Prototyping:** Extreme prototyping is used in the web development domain. It consists of three sequential phases. First, a basic prototype with all the existing pages is presented in the html format. Then the data processing is simulated using a prototype services layer. Finally the services are implemented and integrated to the final prototype. This process is called Extreme Prototyping used to draw attention to the second phase of the process, where a fully functional UI is developed with very little regard to the actual services.

Software Prototyping Application

Software Prototyping is most useful in development of systems having high level of user interactions such as online systems. Systems which need users to fill out forms or go through various screens before data is processed can use prototyping very effectively to give the exact look and feel even before the actual software is developed.

Software that involves too much of data processing and most of the functionality is internal with very little user interface does not usually benefit from prototyping. Prototype development could be an extra overhead in such projects and may need lot of extra efforts.

Prototyping Techniques

System prototyping techniques should allow the rapid development of a prototype system. As staff costs are the principal software costs, rapid development means that prototype costs are minimized. It also means that feedback from the stake holder's users can be obtained early in the overall software process.

There are a number of techniques, which have been used for system prototyping. These include:

- Executable specification languages
- Very high-level languages
- Application generators and fourth-generation languages
- Composition of reusable components.

These prototyping techniques are not mutually exclusive. They can be used in combination. One part of the system may be generated using an application generator and linked to reusable components that have been taken from existing systems. Luqi (1992) describes this mixed approach, which was used to create a prototype of a command and control system.

Software Prototyping Pros and Cons

Software prototyping is used in typical cases and the decision should be taken very carefully so that the efforts spent in building the prototype add considerable value to the final software developed. Following table lists out the pros and cons of Software Prototyping:

Pros	Cons
• Increased user involvement in the product even before implementation. • Since a working model of the system is displayed, the users get a better understanding of the system being developed. • Reduces time and cost as the defects can be detected much earlier. • Quicker user feedback is available leading to better solutions. • Missing functionality can be identified easily. • Confusing or difficult functions can be identified.	• Risk of insufficient requirement analysis owing too much dependency on prototype. • Users may get confused in the prototypes and actual systems. • Practically, this methodology may increase the complexity of the system as scope of the system may expand beyond original plans. • Developers may try to reuse the existing prototypes to build the actual system, even when it is not technically feasible. • The effort invested in building prototypes may be too much if not monitored properly.

1.12 Case Study

Appendix A

Case Study: The Rainforest Book Company Problem

The following four events are services provided by the Rainforest Book Company:

Event I: A customer wishes to set up an account to purchase books. The Sales Department at the Rainforest Book Company receives the request and sends out a blank Account Request form. The form has space for the following information:

- Customer Name
- Customer Address
- Customer Phone Number
- Customer Fax Number
- Credit Card Information (if applicable)
- Credit Card Number
- Type of Credit Card
- Expiration Date
- Cardholder's Name
- ZIP or postal code of the billing address for this card

The customer sends back a completed Account Request form. The "for office use only" section is filled out by the Sales Group. This information includes the processor's identification, the date the account is opened, and a customer account number that is assigned. The customer account file is updated, and the Account Request form is filed. The Account Processing Department receives notification of the new account and sends the customer a confirmation letter. This letter notifies the customer of their customer account number. This number can be used to expedite the ordering process.

Event II: A customer makes a book inquiry. The customer can request a book by giving any of the following information: (book title and book author) or ISBN number. The Sales Department first verifies that the customer has a valid account. If the book is found based upon the information that was given, the customer receives the following information about the book:

- Title of the book
- Author of the book
- Paperback/Hardcover
- Price
- Date Published
- Availability
- Reviews

If the book is not available in stock, all of the above information is returned and an out-of-stock notice is sent specifying the approximate date the book will be in stock. If the book is no longer in print and has been discontinued, an out-of-print notice is sent to the customer. This out-of-print notice includes a list of Used Book Stores in the customer's country.

Event III: A customer decides to purchase books, places the order for the books, and requests a book order form from the Sales Department. A blank book order form is forwarded to the customer. The customer account number and the date the order is being placed is entered. The following information is included in the book order:

- Customer Account Number
- Date Order is placed
- Title of the Book
- Author
- Paperback or Hardcover
- ISBN, if available

In addition, the customer indicates the shipping option by entering the following information: Standard Shipping or Second Day Air or Next Day Air.

Placed orders are sent to the warehouse, and the customer account file is updated. The warehouse issues an order confirmation when the books are shipped. The invoice is generated and then sent to the customer. The customer then sends the invoice slip and a payment or authorizes the use of a credit card on file to the Accounting Department. The Accounting Department processes the payment and updates the customer account.

Event IV: The Sales Department generates a monthly sales report and forwards it to Management.

* Case Study created by Cynthia Hernandez.

Appendix B

Case Study: The CGT Rental Service Problem

The following five events represent the services provided by the CGT rental agency:

I Events:

1. Potential renters call CGT and ask them if apartments are available for either beachfront or mountainside views. All callers have their information recorded and stored in an information folder. The most important information for CGT to obtain is the caller's maximum monthly rent limit.

2. CGT examines their database and searches for potential matches on the properties requested.

3. People call the agency to inform them that they have an apartment for rent. The agency only deals with rentals for beach fronts and mountain sides. All other calls are forwarded to their sister organization that handles other requests.

4. Fifteen days before rent is due, CGT sends renters their monthly invoices.

5. Sixty days before the lease is up, CGT sends out a notice for renewal to the renter

II: High Level Data Elements: The following data elements should be broken down to their elementary level and added, if necessary.

- Renter Name
- Renter Address
- Renter Phone Number

- Maximum Monthly Rent
- Rental Property
- Rental Monthly Rent
- Rental Number Bedrooms
- Rental Dates
- Rental Owner Information
- Rental Number of Blocks from Beach
- Rental Beach Side
- Rental Mountain Range
- Rental Mountain Ski Area
- Rental Mountain Lake Site

Appendix C

Case Study: The Collection Agency Problem

I.   Background

Statement of Purpose: The purpose of the ABC organization is to process customer payments on credit cards. ABC processes these payments for banks and other financial institutions. Currently, the operation is done manually, and you have been called in as a consultant to do the analysis for an automated system.

The Event List: During your analysis, you have met with departments and determined that there are essentially 8 events as follows:

Event 1: Mary gets a delivery of mail every morning from a messenger who picks up the mail at the local Post Office. Mary starts her day by opening and processing the mail. There are, however, a number of types of information contained in an envelope:

1. A check with a payment form
2. Cash only
3. Check only
4. Cash with a payment form
5. Payment form only

Note: All of the above can sometimes be accompanied with correspondence from the customer.

The information on the payment form is necessary to process the payment. The payment form is shown on Attachment I.

Mary fills in the "FOR OFFICE USE ONLY" portion and sends the Payment Form and cash/check to Joe, the Bookkeeper. Correspondence is forwarded to the Support Dept (including forms with no payment).

Payments made without a form are sent to Janet in the Research Department.

ATTACHMENT I

```
┌─────────────────────────────────────────────────────────────┐
│                       PAYMENT FORM                          │
│ DATE INVOICED:_/_/_ PERIOD COVERED: _/_/_ TO_/_/_           │
│ ACCOUNT NO.:_____(30/NUMERIC)                            │
│ NAME:_____(30/ALPHANUMERIC)                      │
│ ADDRESS:_____(30/ALPHANUMERIC)               │
│ _____(30/ALPHANUMERIC)                        │
│ STATE:___(SELF-DEFINING) CITY:_____(15/ALPHANUMERIC)       │
│ ZIPCODE:_____(9/NUMERIC)                                    │
│ ___ADDRESS CORRECTION (Y/BLANK)                             │
│ ============================================                │
│ (A) (B) (C)                                                 │
│ PREVIOUS BAL:$___.__ NEW PURCH:$___.__                      │
│ PAYMENTS:$___.__                                            │
│ OUTSTANDING BALANCE:$_____.__(A+B-C)                        │
│ MINIMUM PAYMENT DUE:$_____.__                               │
│ PAST AMOUNT DUE: $_____.__                                  │
│ PAYMENT DUE THIS PERIOD: $_____.__                          │
│ AMOUNT ENCLOSED $_____.__                                   │
│ ============================================                │
│ FOR OFFICE USE ONLY                                         │
│ OPERATOR CODE:___(4/NUMERIC)                                │
│ DATE RECEIVED:_/_/_ AMOUNT PAID:$_____.__                   │
│ CORRESPONDENCE:___(Y/N) CASH:___(Y/N)                       │
└─────────────────────────────────────────────────────────────┘
```

Event 2: Janet receives payments from Mary and begins a process of looking up the information that the customer has provided. This can typically include Name, Address, etc. If the customer account number is located, Janet fills out a blank Payment Form to substitute for the original and forwards the form and the check to Joe, the Bookkeeper. If the account number is not found, a substitute Payment Form is still developed with whatever information is available. These payments are also forwarded to Joe in bookkeeping.

Event 3: The Support Department receives the correspondence from Mary. The correspondence requires written response. Correspondence falls into 4 categories:

1. An error in the outstanding balance or address of a customer. This will require support to fill out a balance correction form (Attachment II). This Form is forwarded to the Correction Dept.
2. A complaint about service. The complaint is researched and a written response is sent to the customer. A monthly summary report of customers with complaints is also forwarded to the department manager.
3. A client default request, stating that the customer cannot pay due to a hardship. The Technician will send the customer a request for default form (Attachment III).
4. A request for default form (3) is received for processing. These are sent to the Correction Department.

Event 4: Joe, the bookkeeper receives payments. Payments are posted to the account master ledger. A deposit slip is prepared for identified account payments. Unknown account payments are deposited into a separate bank account called "Unapplied Payments." The payment forms are filed by account number. A daily report of payments by customer (including unapplied payments) is produced.

Event 5: The Correction Department receives balance correction forms or requests for default notices; the appropriate adjustments are made to the account master ledger. The forms are filed by type and account number. A daily and monthly report of adjustments is produced.

ATTACHMENT II

BALANCE CORRECTION FORM

DATE:_/_/_

SUPPORT TECHNICIAN:_____(30/ALPHANUMERIC)

ACCOUNT NO.:_____(30/NUMERIC)

___ADDRESS CORRECTION (Y/BLANK)

NAME:_____(30/ALPHANUMERIC)

ADDRESS:_____(30/ALPHANUMERIC) _____(30/ALPHANUMERIC)

STATE:___(SELF-DEFINING) CITY:_____(15/ALPHANUMERIC)

ZIPCODE:_____(9/NUMERIC)

===

CURRENT BALANCE:$_____.___ (A)

ADJUSTMENT AMT:$_____.___ (B)

NEW BALANCE:$_____.___ (A+/−B)

===

AUTHORIZATION CODE:_____(10/NUMERIC)

SUPERVISOR NO:_____(8/NUMERIC)

SIGNATURE:_____

Event 6: The department manager receives the monthly complaint report. After analyzing the information, a summary report is produced by Complaint Type (e.g., unhappy with service, credit card problem, and wrong outstanding balance) and the department manager issues a report to management. A quarterly client survey questionnaire on service is sent to customers. This report includes statistics on client satisfaction which resulted from the previous questionnaire.

ATTACHMENT III

REQUEST FOR DEFAULT

DATE:__/__/__

SUPPORT TECHNICIAN: _____(30/ALPHANUMERIC)

ACCOUNT NO.:_____(30/NUMERIC)

NAME:_____(30/ALPHANUMERIC)

ADDRESS:_____(30/ALPHANUMERIC)

_____(30/ALPHANUMERIC)

STATE:___(SELF-DEFINING) CITY:_____(15/ALPHANUMERIC)

ZIPCODE:_____(9/NUMERIC)

===

REASON FOR DEFAULT

(CHECK ONE)

1.   ___ DEATH (ATTACH DEATH CERTIFICATE) NO PAYMENT REQUIRED

2.   ___ BANKRUPTCY (ATTACH LEGAL DOCUMENT) 180 DAY TERMS

3.   ___ REQUEST FOR NEW PAYMENT TERMS 60 OR 90 DAY TERMS

===

FOR OFFICE USE ONLY

OPERATOR CODE:___(4/NUMERIC)

DATE RECEIVED:__/__/__ ACTION CODE:__(1/2/3)

Event 7: Joe, the bookkeeper, receives bounced checks from the bank. He fills out a balance correction form and forwards it to the Correction Department such that the outstanding balance can be corrected. Joe sends a bounced check letter to the customer requesting another check plus a $15.00 penalty (this is now included as part of the outstanding balance). Checks are never re-deposited.

Event 8: Joe, the bookkeeper, issues a weekly update report on the balance of each account where there was a transaction during that week.

Appendix D

Case Study: The Mobile Telephone Company Problem

A Global System for Mobile communications (GSM) cellular telephone company provides wireless telephone equipment and services for customers. GSM telephones are packaged for sale in the form of a "pre-sale-distribution-kit" at the company's product assembly center. Each kit consists primarily of a Telephone Handset and a SIM card. (A "Subscriber Identity Module" is a credit card-like device that is inserted into digital cellular phones and identifies each customer to the telephone system.) The telephone handset manufacturer assigns each and every handset a unique International Mobile-communications Equipment Identifier (IMEI) number.

An individual may own more than one SIM, but must own at least one SIM to be considered a Customer. A customer may own more than one telephone handset; however, handset ownership is not a requisite. The SIM is interchangeable among the various handset models sold by the company. (In practice, nearly all customers own at least one telephone handset. Following the initial sale, some customers chose to "upgrade" their handset to a smaller, lighter, more functional model.)

In the back office, the company maintains an inventory of available, yet unassigned, telephone numbers. To make the technological leap from wiredtelephone-number to wireless-telephone-number, each conventional Telephone Number is assigned to a Mobil Identification Number (MIN). Each unique MIN will ultimately be associated with a specific customer's SIM card when a new account is activated. A unique International Mobile SIM Identifier (IMSI) number identifies each SIM.

For billing purposes, the company maintains a record of each Call Delivery Notification (CDN) event. The unique identifier for the CDN is a concatenation of the CDN_id + IMSI.

Case Study created by Greg Vimont.

Note: All case studies are taken from :

http://library.atgti.az/categories/ict/Langer%20-
%20Analysis%20and%20Design%20of%20Information%20Systems%203e%20(Springer,%202008).
pdf

Practice Questions

1. What are the Measures in Software Process?

2. What is Metric? Describe Metric Indicator.

3. Explain role of Metric in software process and project domain.

4. Explain Software Measurement in software process.

5. Describe Metrics for Software Quality.

6. What is Software Quality Assurance (SQA)? State Advantages and Disadvantages of SQA.

7. Describe the role of Requirement Analysis in software process.

8. Which Communication Techniques are used in Software Process?

9. Write a short note on Analysis principle in Software Process.

10. What is Software Prototyping? Explain in brief.

■■■

Chapter 2...

Distributed Databases

Contents ...

2.1 Introduction

In recent years, the availability of database and computer networks has promoted the development of a new field known as distributed databases.

A distributed database is stored in more than one physical location. Parts of the database are stored physically in one location, and other parts are stored and maintained in other locations.

Many enterprises consider the distributed databases as a best platform for their services that spread over a wide geographical area.

2.2 Standalone v/s Distributed Database [April 16]

A standalone device is able to function independently of other hardware. This means it is not integrated into another device. For example, a fax machine is a stand-alone device because it does not require a computer, printer, modem, or other device. A printer, on the other hand, is not a stand-alone device because it requires a computer to feed it data.

Standalone database servers used to be popular earlier when networks were local inside a company. The internet technology connects the standalone servers together to let clients explore information inside the standalone database. That makes them become multiple-connected databases. When they are connected, the term of multi-connected databases had been defined such as Centralized database systems, distributed systems, parallel databases and distributed databases.

Since early 1980's, database technology allowed for concurrent access. Many clients could connect to a database server via a server of a local area network in a company. Each client used an interface built by programmers who wrote embedded - SQL programs. The embedded programs connected to a database and allowed clients to log in to a database server. Clients can manipulate - insert, update and delete information from the databse.

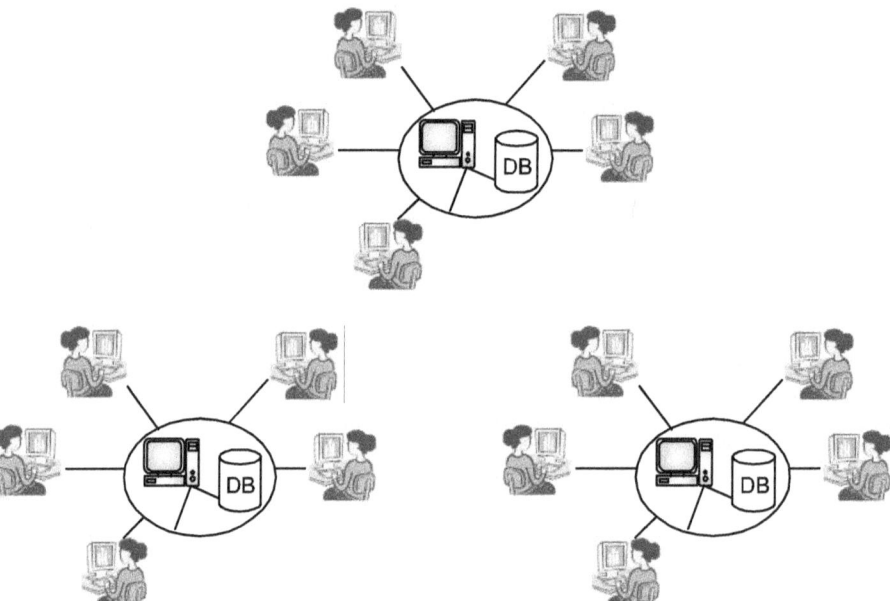

Fig. 2.1: Standalone Databases

The information can be shared if it is inside the same LAN sharing network, databases anti application server. At the same time, the technology of storage was growing. The information of many departments can be stored and used together. The relational database of information among departments was design together as one database system of a company.

The expansion of a company has grown outside one location of a company. Companies had many branches. Each branch has their own LAN's and database systems. The information needed to be shared not just inside a branch but across their local networks. Also one information was stored in more than one place. That was leading to data redundancy. At the same time, advances in computer technology led to better Processors, memory, storage and importantly, networks. Business demanded the connecting of all databases together or combining their databases together. So the business can share the information across branches.

Distributed database: **[Oct. 16]**

A database that consists of two or more data files located at different sites on a computer network. Because the database is distributed, different users can access it without interfering with one another. However, the DBMS must periodically synchronize the scattered databases to make sure that they all have consistent data.

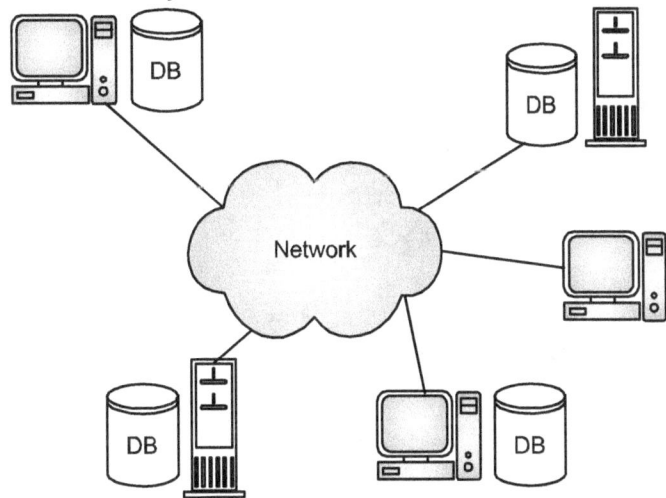

Fig. 2.2: Distributed Database

Functions of a DDBMS (Distributed Database Management System):

- **Application interface:** It Allows the interaction with the end user or application programs and with other DBMS's within the distributed database.
- **Validation:** Able to analyze data requests.
- **Transformation:** To determine which data request components are distributed and which ones are local.
- **Query-optimization:** To find the best access strategy.
- **Mapping:** To determine the data location of local and remote fragments.
- **I/O interface:** To read or write data from or to permanent local storage.
- **Formatting:** To prepare the data for presentation to the end user or an application program presentation.
- **Security:** To provide data privacy at both local and remote databases.
- **Backup and recovery:** To ensure the availability and recoverability of the database in case of a failure.
- **DB administration:** To allow the Database Administrator to maintain the databases.
- **Concurrency control:** To manage simultaneous data access and ensure data consistency across database fragments in the DDBMS.
- **Transaction management:** To ensure that the data move from on consistent state to another – synchronizing transactions.

Types of distributed database are Homogeneous and heterogeneous database.

Homogeneous Distributed Databases: In a homogeneous distributed database:

- All sites have identical software.
- Sites are aware of each other and agree to cooperate in processing user requests.
- Each site surrenders part of its autonomy in terms of right to change schemas or software.
- Appears to user as a single system.

Heterogeneous Distributed Database:

In a heterogeneous distributed database:

- Different sites may use different schemas and software "Difference in schema is a major problem for query processing". Difference in software is a major problem for transaction processing.
- Sites may not be aware of each other and may provide only limited facilities for cooperation in transaction processing.
- Whether the database is centralized or distributed, the design principles and concepts are same. However, the design of a distributed database introduces three new issues:
- How to partition the database into fragments.
- Which fragments to replicate.
- Where to locate those fragments and replicas.

Data fragmentation and data replication deal with the first two issues and data allocation deals with the third issue.

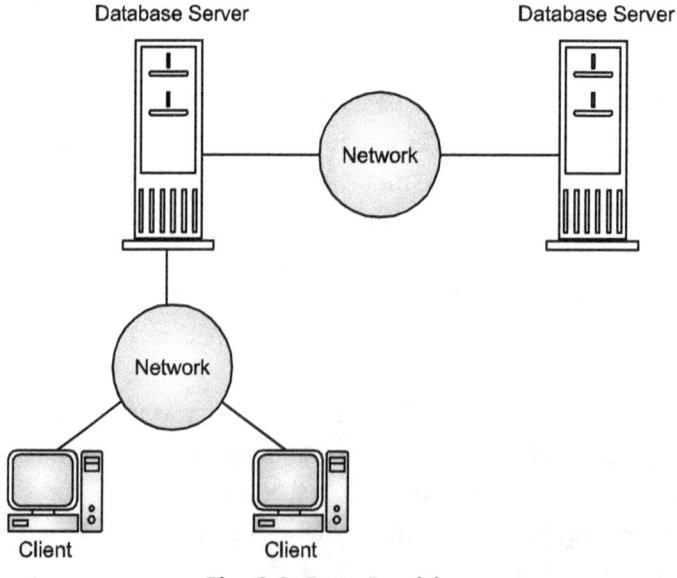

Fig. 2.3: Data Partition

Data Partition:

The central database can be partitioned so that each remote processor has the necessary data to serve its local area. Changes in local files can be justified with the central database on a batch basis.

Data Replication: Another strategy is to replicate the central database at all remote locations. This strategy requires updating of the central database off hours.

In a distributed database system (DDS), multiple Database Management Systems run on multiple servers (sites) connected by a network.

Data may be split up among the different servers or it may be replicated.

Distributed systems reduce the weakness of a single, massive central site. They permit increases in systems power by purchasing smaller less expensive computers. Finally, they increase service and responsiveness to local users.

Distributed systems, however, are dependent on high quality telecommunication lines, which themselves are vulnerable. Moreover, local databases can sometimes depart from central data standards and definitions, and they pose security problems by widely distributing access to sensitive data. The economies of distribution can be lost when remote sites buy more computing power than they need. Despite these drawbacks, distributed processing is growing rapidly.

The distributed database offers several advantages to users and designers of databases.

Advantages of distributed database: [Oct. 16]

1. **Local Autonomy:** Since data is distributed, a group of users that commonly share such data can have it placed at the site where they work, and thus have local control. By this way, users have some degree of freedom as accesses can be made independently from the global users.

2. **Improved Performance:** Data retrieved by a transaction may be stored at a number of sites, making it possible to execute the transaction in parallel. Besides, using several resources in parallel can significantly improve performance.

3. **Improved Reliability/Availability:** If data is replicated so that it exists at more than one site, a crash of one of the sites, or the failure of a communication line making some of these sites inaccessible, does not necessarily make the data impossible to reach. Furthermore, system crashes or communication failures do not cause total system not operable and distributed DBMS can still provide limited service.

4. **Economics:** If the data is geographically distributed and the application are related to these data, it may be much more economical, in terms of communication costs, to partition the application and do the processing at each site. On the other hand, the cost of having smaller computing powers at each site is much more less than the cost of having an equivalent power of a single mainframe.

5. **Expandibility:** Expansion can be easily achieved by adding processing and storage power to the existing network. It may not be possible to have a linear improvement in power but significant changes are still possible.

6. **Shareability:** If the information is not distributed, it is usually impossible to share data and resources. A distributed database makes this sharing feasible. On the other hand, distribution of the database can cause several problems.

Disadvantages of Distributed Database: [Oct. 16]

1. **Lack of Experience:** Some special solutions or prototype systems have not been tested in actual operating environments. More theoretical work is done compared to actual implementations.

2. **Complexity:** Distributed DBMS problems are more complex than centralized DBMS problems.

3. **Cost:** Additional hardware for communication mechanisms are needed as well as additional and more complex software may be necessary to solve the technical problems. The trade-off between increased profitability due to more efficient and timely use of information and due to new dataprocessing sites, increased personnel costs has to be analyzed carefully.

4. **Distribution of Control:** The distribution creates problems of synchronization and coordination as the degree to which individual DBMSs can operate independently.

5. **Security:** Security can be easily controlled in a central location with the DBMS enforcing the rules. However, in distributed database system, network is involved which it has its own securityrequirements and security control becomes very complicated.

6. **Difficulty of Change:** All users have to use their legacy data implemented in previous generation systems and it is impossible to rewrite all applications at once. A distributed DBMS should support a graceful transition into a future architecture by allowing old applications for obsolete databases to survive with new applications written in current generation DBMSs.

In spite of the problems and its complexity, the users that will mostly benefit from the distributed DBMSs.

2.3 Replication

Database replication is the frequent electronic copying data from a database in one computer or server to a database in another so that all users share the same level of information. The result is a distributed database in which users can access data relevant to their tasks without interfering with the work of others. The implementation of database replication for the purpose of eliminating data inconsistency among users is known as normalization.

In most implementations of database replication, one database server maintains the master copy of the database and the additional database servers maintain slave copies of the database. The two or more copies of a single database remain synchronized.

The original database is called a Design Master and each copy of the database is called a Replica. Together, the Design Master and the replicas make up a replica set. There is only one Design Master in a replica set.

Synchronization is the process of ensuring that every copy of the database contains the same objects and data. When you synchronize the replicas in a replica set, only the data that has changed is updated.

You can also synchronize changes made to the design of the objects in the Design Master. Database writes are sent to the master database server and are then replicated by the slave database servers. Database reads are divided among all of the database servers, which results in a large performance advantage due to load sharing. In addition, database replication can also improve availability because the slave database servers can be configured to take over the master role if the master database server becomes unavailable.

Methods of performing Database Replication

Database replication can be performed in at least three different ways:

1. Snapshot Replication:

Data on one database server is plainly copied to another database server, or to another database on the same server.

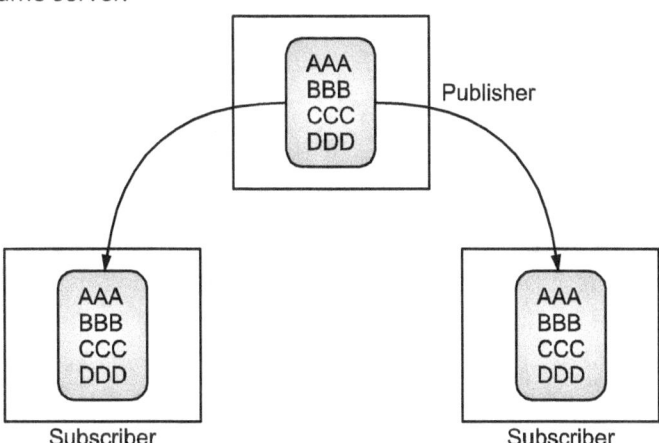

Fig. 2.4: Snapshot Replication

As the name "snapshot" says, it takes a snapshot of the published database and moves it to a subscriber database. Snapshot replication completely overwrites the transactions/data at the subscriber database every time as it drops the tables and recreates it again. A snapshot is best when the data frequency is a bit low or the subscriber needs data on a certain interval rather than very frequently. For example Snapshot Replication is for updating a list of items that only change periodically or at certain intervals like end of business day. A snapshot is bit slower than transactional because on each attempt it moves multiple records, perhaps millions of records, from one end (the publisher) to the other end(the subscriber).

Snapshot replication is helpful when:
- Data is mostly static and does not change often.
- It is acceptable to have copies of data that are out of date for a period of time.
- Replicating small volumes of data in which an entire refresh of the data is reasonable.

2. Merging Replication:

Data from two or more databases is combined into a single database.

As the name implies "Merge" joins publisher and subscriber databases, it is one of the complex replications and helps to keep data consistent among multiple ends. Merge replications work in an integrated manner with a publisher and a subscriber. Every time the Merge Agent traces each change that has occurred at both ends and sends those changed transactions to the distributor database for further propagation.

The Merge Agent runs either at the distributor end for push subscriptions or the subscriber for pull subscriptions. Merge replication best fits into the retail market like Pantaloons, BigBazar Lifestyle and many more. Where it's helpful in synchronizing the records among multiple stores as per the inventory increased or decreased.

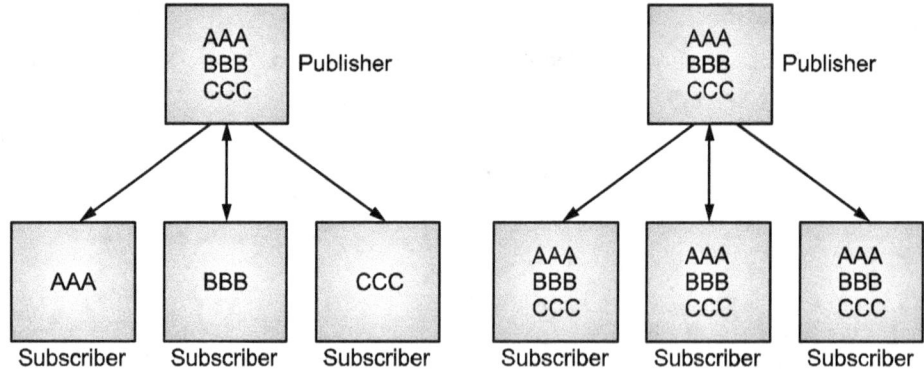

Fig. 2.5: Merging Replication

Merge Replication is helpful when:
- Multiple Subscribers need to update data at various times and propagate those changes to the Publisher and to other subscribers.
- Subscribers need to receive data, make changes offline, and later synchronize changes with the Publisher and other subscribers.
- You do not expect many conflicts when data is updated at multiple sites (because the data is filtered into partitions and then published to different Subscribers or because of the uses of your application). However, if conflicts do occur, violations of ACID (Automicity, Consistency, Isolation, Durability) properties are acceptable.

3. Transactional Replication:

Users obtain complete initial copies of the database and then obtain periodic updates as data changes.

Transactional replication replicates each transaction from a publisher to a subscriber for the article/table being published. Initially transactional replication takes a snapshot of the publisher database and applies to the subscriber to synchronize the data. As we know replication is helpful for synchronizing the data among the publisher and subscriber databases.

A Log Reader Agent reads transactions from the transaction log and writes it to the distribution database and then to the subscriber database. Each database published using transactional replication keeps a Log Reader agent and moves transactions from the publisher to the distributor. Transactional replication is helpful where real time data is required such as online trading and bank-specific transactions to keep a live data backup of each debit or credit transaction.

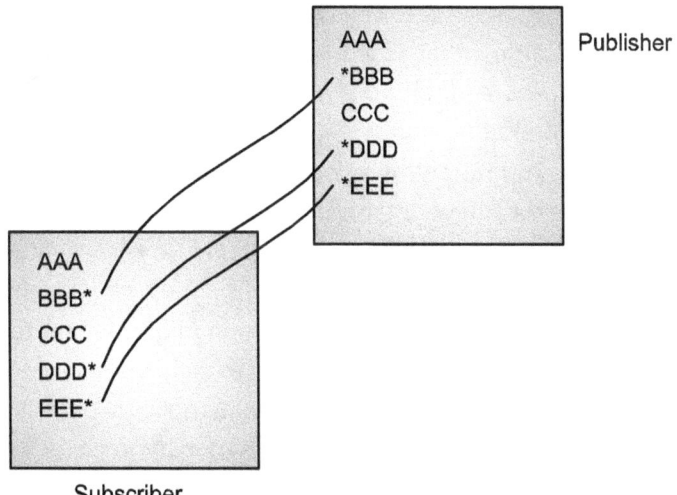

Fig. 2.6: Transactional Replication

Transactional replication is helpful when:

- You want incremental changes to be propagated to subscribers as they occur.
- You need transactions to adhere to ACID properties.
- Subscribers are reliably and/or frequently connected to the publisher.

When to chose Database Replication?

Database replication is well suited to business solutions that need to:

- **Share data among remote offices:** You can use database replication to create copies of a corporate database to send to each satellite office across a wide area network (WAN). Each location enters data in its replica, and all remote replicas are synchronized with the replica at corporate headquarters. Individual replicas can maintain local tables that contain information not included in the other replicas in the set.

- **Share data among dispersed users:** New information that is entered in the database while users are out of the office can be synchronized any time the users establish an electronic link with the corporate network. As part of their workday routine, users can dial in to the network, synchronize the replica, and work on the most current version of the database. Because only the incremental changes are transmitted during synchronization, the time and expense of keeping up-to-date information are minimized. By using partial replicas, you can synchronize only specified parts of the data.

- **Make server data more accessible:** If your solution does not need to have immediate updates to data, you can use database replication to reduce the network load on your primary server. Introducing a second server with its own copy of the database improves response time. You determine the schedule for synchronizing the replicas, and you can adjust that schedule to meet the changing needs of your users. Replication requires less centralized administration of the database while offering greater access to centralized data.

- **Distribute solution updates:** When you replicate your solution, you automatically replicate not only the data in your tables, but also your solution's objects. If you make changes to the design of the database, the changes are transmitted during the next synchronization; you don't have to distribute complete new versions of the software.

- **Back up data:** At first glance, database replication might appear to be very similar to copying a database. However, while replication initially makes a complete copy of the database, thereafter it simply synchronizes that replica's objects with the original objects at regular intervals. This copy can be used to recover data if the original database is destroyed. In addition, users at any replica can continue to access the database during the entire backup process.

- **Provide Internet or intranet replication:** You can configure an Internet or intranet server to be used as a hub for propagating changes to participating replicas. When Database Replication should not be used Although database replication has many benefits and can solve many problems in distributed-database processing, we should recognize the fact that in some situations replication is less then ideal.

Advantages:

1. **Increased reliability and availability:** We have many copies of same data in several different locations (usually different geographical locations). Hence, failure of any sites (servers) will not affect the transactions.

2. **Queries requesting replicated copies of data are always faster (especially read queries):** Distributed database ensures the availability of data where it is needed much. In case of replication, this is one step ahead. Yes, the complete table itself loaded locally. Hence, those queries can be answered quickly from the local site where they are initiated.

3. **Less communication overhead:** When more number of read queries is generated in a site, all of them can be answered locally. Only the queries involving different table or the queries try to write something need to use the communication links to contact other sites.

Disadvantages:

1. **More storage space is needed when compared to a centralized system:** Replication would mean to duplicate any tables and store them in every site. This need more space in every site.

2. **Update operation is costly:** If we have more copies of same data loaded in different sites, obviously we need to update all the replicas whenever we would like to change data. Hence, write operation is always costly.

3. **Maintaining data integrity is complex:** It involves complex procedures to maintain consistent database.

Asynchronous Versus Synchronous Replication

There are two basic ways to replicate data between a source database and a target database – asynchronously and synchronously.

With asynchronous replication, changes to the source database are queued and are sent to the target system after the fact. Asynchronous replication is generally transparent to the application. With synchronous replication, a change cannot be made to the source database unless it is also made at the same time to the target database. Synchronous replication impacts application performance since the application must wait for each change to complete across the application network. Both methods are subject to data conflicts in an active architecture. This is because of the delay in signaling between the nodes due to communication latency and replication delays.

With asynchronous replication, simultaneous changes will be replicated to the other node and will overwrite the change originally made at that node. Now the databases are different and both are wrong. This is a data collision. A data conflict in a synchronous replication environment occurs when the application instance in two different nodes lock their local copies of the same data item at the same time. When each attempts to gain a lock on the remote copy of the data item, neither can. A distributed deadlock has occurred. Distributed deadlocks are generally resolved via timeouts. Asynchronous replication suffers from problem of data loss . Source data changes may not be reflected in the target database for two reasons. Should the source node fail, changes in the replication pipeline may not make it to the target system. Secondly, there is no guarantee that the target node will be able to apply changes that it receives from the source system. If it cannot for some reason, the changes made to the source database will not appear in the target database. It is for these reasons that a verification and validation utility should be periodically run to compare the databases and to repair them if necessary. Synchronous replication does not have this problem – either all database copies are changed or none are. With respect to data conflicts, data collisions under asynchronous replication can present a much more difficult problem than distributed deadlocks under synchronous replication.

2.4 Data Fragmentation (Partitioning)   [April 16, Oct. 16]

Data can be stored in different computers by fragmenting the whole database into several pieces called fragments. Each piece is stored at a different site. Fragments are logical data units stored at various sites in a distributed database system.

Types of Fragmentation:

Data may be split up (or partitioned) in several ways:

1. **Horizontal:** Rows in a table are split up across multiple sites. i.e.Horizontal fragmentation refers to the division of a relation into subsets (fragments) of tuples (rows). Each fragment is stored at a different node, and each fragment has unique rows. However, the unique rows all have the same attributes (columns).

2. **Vertical:** Columns in a table are split across multiple sites. In other words,Vertical fragmentation refers to the division of a relation into attribute (column) subsets. Each subset (fragment) is stored at a different node, and each fragment has unique columns—with the exception of the key column, which is common to all fragments.

3. **Mixed:** Mixed fragmentation refers to a combination of horizontal and vertical strategies. In other words, a table may be divided into several horizontal subsets (rows), each one having a subset of the attributes (columns).

Splitting up data can improve performance by reducing contention for tables.

Distributed Database Design:

Whether the database is centralized or distributed, the design principles and concepts are same. However, the design of a distributed database introduces three new issues:

*   **Data fragmentation:** How to partition the database into fragments?
*   **Data replication:** Which fragments to replicate?
*   **Data collection:** Where to locate those fragments and replicas?

Data Fragmentation:

Data fragmentation allows you to break a single object into two or more segments, or fragments. The object might be a user's database, a system database, or a table. Each fragment can be stored at any site over a computer network. Information about data fragmentation is stored in the distributed data catalog (DDC), from which it is accessed by the TP to process user requests.

Data fragmentation strategies, are based at the table level and consist of dividing a table into logical fragments. Three types of data fragmentation strategies are horizontal, vertical, and mixed.

Horizontal Fragmentation refers to the division of a relation into subsets (fragments) of tuples (rows). Each fragment is stored at a different node, and each fragment has unique rows. However, the unique rows all have the same attributes (columns).

Vertical Fragmentation refers to the division of a relation into attribute (column) subsets. Each subset (fragment) is stored at a different node, and each fragment has unique columns—with the exception of the key column, which is common to all fragments.

Mixed Fragmentation refers to a combination of horizontal and vertical strategies. In other words, a table may be divided into several horizontal subsets (rows), each one having a subset of the attributes (columns).

To illustrate the fragmentation strategies, let's use the CUSTOMER table for the ABC Company. The table contains the attributes cust_id, cust_name, cust_address, state, limit, balance, rating, due_amt.

Table 2.1: Customer Table

CUS_ID	CUS_NAME	CUS_ADDRESS	STATE	LIMIT	BALANCE	RATING	DUE_AMT
10	Syntax Inc.	12, East street	MH	3500.00	2700.00	3	1245.00
11	George Corp.	321, Sunrise Bldg.	AP	6000.00	1200.00	1	0.00
12	Mayur Corp.	901, Seagull Station,	MH	4000.00	3500.00	3	3400.00
13	ABC Inc.	Mainstreet, Camp	AP	5000.00	5890.00	3	1090.00
14	Jay Inc.	123 Oak Street	AP	1200.00	550.00	1	0.00
15	MBT Corp.	909 Park Ave.	AP	2000.00	350.00	2	50.00

Horizontal Fragmentation:

Suppose that ABC Company's corporate management requires information about its customers in all three states, but company locations in each state (MH, MP, and AP) require data regarding local customers only. Based on such requirements, you decide to distribute the data by state. Therefore, you define the horizontal fragments to conform to the structure shown in the following table.

Table 2.2: Horizontal Fragmentation of the Customer Table by State

Fragment name	Location	Condition	Node Name	Customer Numbers	Number of Rows
CUST_H1	Maharashtra	CUST_STATE='MH'	NAS	10, 12	2
CUST_H2	Madhya Pradesh	CUST_STATE='MP'	ATL	15	1
CUST_H3	Andhra Pradesh	CUST_STATE='AP'	TAM	11, 13, 14	3

Fragment name: CUST_H1   **Location: Maharashtra**   **Node: NAS**

CUS_ID	CUS_NAME	CUS_ADDRESS	STATE	LIMIT	BALANCE	RATING	DUE_AMT
10	Syntax Inc.	12, East street	MH	₹ 3500.00	₹ 2700.00	3	₹ 1245.00
12	Mayur Corp.	901, Seagull Station,	MH	₹ 4000.00	₹ 3500.00	3	₹ 3400.00

Fragment name: CUST_H2   **Location: Madhya Pradesh**   **Node: ATL**

CUS_ID	CUS_NAME	CUS_ADDRESS	STATE	LIMIT	BALANCE	RATING	DUE_AMT
15	MBT Corp.	909 Park Ave.	MP	₹ 2000.00	₹ 350.00	2	₹ 50.00

Fragment name: CUST_H3   **Location: Andhra Pradesh**   **Node: TAM**

CUS_ID	CUS_NAME	CUS_ADDRESS	STATE	LIMIT	BALANCE	RATING	DUE_AMT
11	George Corp.	321, Sunrise Bldg.	AP	₹ 6000.00	₹ 1,200.00	1	₹ 0.00
13	ABC Inc.	Mainstreet, Camp	AP	₹ 5000.00	₹ 5,890.00	3	₹ 1090.00
14	Jay Inc.	123 Oak Street	AP	₹ 1200.00	₹ 550.00	1	₹ 0.00

Vertical Fragmentation:

You may also divide the CUSTOMER relation into vertical fragments that are composed of a collection of attributes. For example, suppose that the company is divided into two departments: the service department and the collections department. Each department is located in a separate building, and each has an interest in only a few of the CUSTOMER table's attributes. In this case, the fragments are defined as shown in the following table.

Table 2.2: Vertical Fragmentation of the Customer Table

Fragment name	Location	Node Name	Attribute Names
CUST_V1	Service Bldg	SVC	cust-id, cust_name, cust_addr, state
CUST_V2	Collection Bldg	ARC	cust-id, limit, balance, rating, due_amt

Fragment name: CUST_V1   **Location: Service Bldg**   **Node: SVC**

cust_id	cus_name	cust_address	State
10	Syntex Inc.	12, East street	MH
11	Georg Corp.	321, Sunrise Bldg	MP
12	Mayur Corp.	910, Seagull State	MH
13	ABC Inc.	Mainstreet, Camp	MP
14	Jay Inc.	123, Oak St.	MP
15	MBT Corp.	909, Park Avenue	AP

Fragment name: CUST_V2   **Location: Collection Bldg**   **Node: ARC**

cust_id	cus_name	Balance	Rating	due_amt
10	₹ 3500.00	₹ 2700.00	12, East street	MH
11	₹ 6000.00	₹ 1200.00	321, Sunrise Bldg	MP
12	₹ 4000.00	₹ 3500.00	910, Seagull State	MH
13	₹ 6000.00	₹ 5890.00	Mainstreet, Camp	MP
14	₹ 1200.00	₹ 550.00	123, Oak St.	MP
15	₹ 2000.00	₹ 350.00	909, Park Avenue	AP

Mixed Fragmentation:

The ABC Company's structure requires that the CUSTOMER data be fragmented horizontally to accommodate the various company locations; within the locations, the data must be fragmented vertically to accommodate the two departments (service and collection). In short, the CUSTOMER table requires mixed fragmentation. Mixed fragmentation requires a two-step procedure. First, horizontal fragmentation is introduced for each site based on the location within a state (CUS_STATE). The horizontal fragmentation yields the subsets of customer tuples (horizontal fragments) that are located at each site. Because the departments are located in different buildings, vertical fragmentation is used within each horizontal fragment to divide the attributes, thus meeting each department's information needs at each sub site. Mixed fragmentation yields the results displayed in the following Table.

Table 2.3: Mixed Fragmentation of the customer table

Fragment name	Location	Horizontal criteria	Mode name	Resulting Rows at Site	Vertical criteria attributes at each fragment
CUST_M1	TN_Service	CUS_STATE='TN'	NAS-S	10, 12	CUS_NUM, CUS_NAME, CUS_ADDRESS, CUS_STATE
CUST_M2	TN_Collection	CUS_STATE='TN'	NAS-C	10, 12	CUS_NUM, CUS_LIMIT, CUS_BAL, CUS_RATING, CUS_DUIE
CUST_M3	TN_Service	CUS_STATE='GA'	ATL-S	15	CUS_NUM, CUS_NAME, CUS_ADDRESS, CUS_STATE
CUST_M4	TN_Collection	CUS_STATE='GA'	ATL-C	15	CUS_NUM, CUS_LIMIT, CUS_BAL, CUS_RATING, CUS-DUE
CUST_M5	TN_Service	CUS_STATE='FL'	TAM-S	11, 13, 14	CUS_NUM, CUS_NAME, CUS_ADDRESS, CUS_STATE
CUST_M6	FL_Collection	CUS_STATE='FL'	TAM-C	11, 13, 14	CUS_NUM, CUS_LIMIT

Data Replication:

Data replication refers to the storage of data copies at multiple sites served by a computer network. Fragment copies can be stored at several sites to serve specific information requirements. Because the existence of fragment copies can enhance data availability and response time, data copies can help to reduce communication and total query costs.

Suppose database A is divided into two fragments, A1 and A2. Within a replicated distributed database, the scenario depicted in the following Figure is possible: fragment A1 is stored at sites S1 and S2, while fragment A2 is stored at sites S2 and S3.

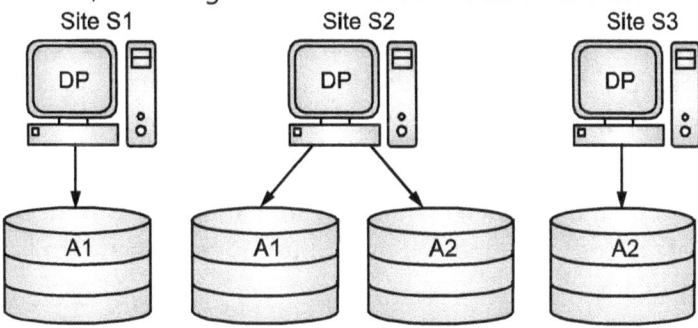

Fig. 2.7: Data Replication

Replicated data are subject to the mutual consistency rule. The mutual consistency rule requires that all copies of data fragments be identical. Therefore, to maintain data consistency among the replicas, the DDBMS must ensure that a database update is performed at all sites where replicas exist.

The different replica overheads imposed on DDBMS are as follows.

- If the database is fragmented, the DDBMS must decompose a query into sub queries to access the appropriate fragments.
- If the database is replicated, the DDBMS must decide which copy to access. A READ operation selects the nearest copy to satisfy the transaction. A WRITE operation requires that all copies be selected and updated to satisfy the mutual consistency rule.
- The TP sends a data request to each selected DP for execution.
- The DP receives and executes each request and sends the data back to the TP.
- The TP assembles the DP responses.
- The problem becomes more complex when you consider additional factors such as network topology and communication throughputs.

Three replication scenarios exist: a database can be fully replicated, partially replicated, or unreplicated.

- A fully replicated database stores multiple copies of each database fragment at multiple sites. In this case, all database fragments are replicated. A fully replicated database can be impractical due to the amount of overhead it imposes on the system.

- A partially replicated database stores multiple copies of some database fragments at multiple sites. Most DDBMSs are able to handle the partially replicated database well.
- An unreplicated database stores each database fragment at a single site. Therefore, there are no duplicate database fragments.

Several factors influence the decision to use data replication:

Database Size:

The amount of data replicated will have an impact on the storage requirements and also on the data transmission costs. Replicating large amounts of data requires a window of time and higher network bandwidth that could affect other applications.

Usage Frequency:

The frequency of data usage determines how frequently the data needs to be updated. Frequently used data needs to be updated more often, for example, than large data sets that are used only every quarter.

Costs:

Including those for performance, software overhead, and management associated with synchronizing transactions and their components vs. fault-tolerance benefits that are associated with replicated data.

Data Allocation:

Data allocation describes the process of deciding where to locate data. Data allocation strategies are as follows:

- With centralized data allocation, the entire database is stored at one site.
- With partitioned data allocation, the database is divided into two or more disjointed parts (fragments) and stored at two or more sites.
- With replicated data allocation, copies of one or more database fragments are stored at several sites.
- Data distribution over a computer network is achieved through data partitioning, through data replication, or through a combination of both. Data allocation is closely related to the way a database is divided or fragmented. Most data allocation studies focus on one issue: which data to locate where.

Data allocation algorithms take into consideration a variety of factors, including:

- Performance and data availability goals.
- Size, number of rows, and number of relations that an entity maintains with other entities.
- Types of transactions to be applied to the database and the attributes accessed by each of those transactions.

Disconnected operation for mobile users. In some cases, the design might consider the use of loosely disconnected fragments for mobile users, particularly for read-only data that does not require frequent updates and for which the replica update windows (the amount of time available to perform a certain data processing task that cannot be executed concurrently with other tasks) may be longer.

Advantages of Fragmentation

1. **Usage:** In general, applications work with views rather than entire relations. Therefore, for data distribution, it seems appropriate to work with subsets of relation as the unit of distribution.

2. **Efficiency:** Data is stored close to where it is most frequently used. In addition, data that is, not needed by' local applications is not stored.

3. **Parallelism:** With fragments as the unit of distribution, a transaction can be divided into several sub queries that operate on fragments. This should increase the degree of concurrency, or parallelism, in the system.

4. **Security:** Data not required by local applications is not stored, and thus not available to unauthorized users.

Disadvantages of fragmentation

Fragmentation has two primary disadvantage:

1. **Performance:** The performance of global application that requires data from several fragments located at different sites may be slower.

2. **Integrity:** Integrity control may be more difficult if data and functional dependencies are fragmented and located at different sites.

2.5 Client/Server Architecture

Client-server architecture (client/server) is a network architecture in which each computer or process on the network is either a client or a server.

Servers: A server is a computer system that receives the request, processes it and returns the requested information back to the client. Servers can be several types, for example, file servers, printer servers, web servers, database server etc.

Clients: A client is a computer system that sends request to the server connected to the network. Client and server are usually present at different sites. The end users (remote database users) work on client computer system and database system runs on the server.

Clients rely on servers for resources, such as files, devices, and even processing power. Client-server architectures are sometimes called two-tier architectures.

The client machines have user interfaces that help users to utilize the server. It also provides users the local processing power to run local applications on the client side.

There are two approaches to implement client/server architecture.

Two Tier Client-Server Architecture:

In the first approach, the user interface and application programs are placed on the client side and the database system on the server side. It divides the application logic, data and processing between client and server devices. This architecture is called 2-tier architecture. 2-tier are typical because there are clients and servers users that cooperate each other; In a two-tier client/server r computing architecture, an entire application is distributed as two distinct layers or tiers. A two-tier client/server works when most or all of the application logic and data is hosted on a server. The client integrates with the presentation layer and accesses the server for application specific tasks and processing.

For example, the core application and data are installed at a central server. One or more client devices uses its client-end application to request data or processes from the server. The server sends the required data or performs a process to fulfill the query.

In another two-tier client/server instance, such as a data backup architecture, the application access and logic may be with the client device, whereas the server stores and provides the core data.

The Fig. 2.8 shows 2-tier clinet/server architectecture.

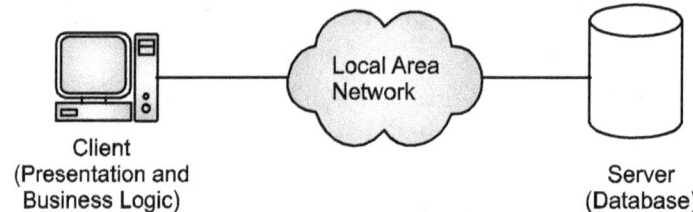

Client
(Presentation and
Business Logic)

Server
(Database)

Fig 2.8: Two Tier Client Server Architecture

Three Tier Client-Server Architecture:

The second approach, 3-tier architecture is primarily used for web based applications. It adds intermediate layer known as application server (web server) between the client and the database server. The client communicate with the application server which in turn communicate with the database server. The application server stores the business rules used for accessing data from database users

When a client requests for information, the application layer accepts the request, processes it and sends corresponding database commands to database server. The database server sends to result back to application server which is converted into GUI format and presented to the client. Fig. 2.9 shows 3-tier client/server architecture.

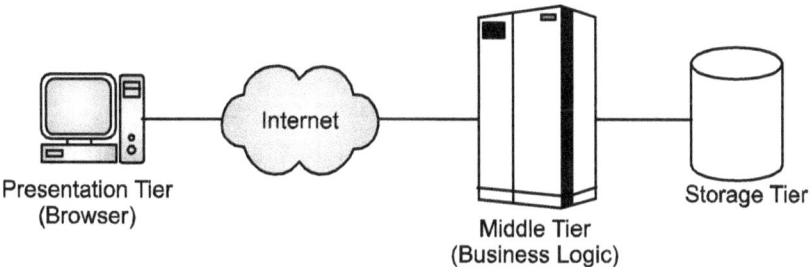

Fig. 2.9: Three Tier Client Architecture

Thin Clients:

Thin clients are computer terminals (rather than desktop computers) that do little or no data processing. The client processes only keyboard input and screen output. All application processing tasks are done in the server. Thin clients are used in a client/server environment to lower the cost of PCs or Macs used in a network. One can combine thin clients with a "thick" or "fat" client in a network. Thin clients may be used as e-mail stations, Web access stations, and/or OPAC stations, for example, whereas "thick" or "fat" clients may be utilised for access and use of application software, such as word processing, home page development and other tasks that require use of hard disk storage.

Examples of Client/Server Architecture:

- **Oracle Server** RDBMS running on a server.
- **BEA Tuxedo** Transaction Processing System running on the "Middle tier"
- **Sybase-PowerSoft PowerBuilder** running on a client PC.
- **Oracle Server** RDBMS running on a server.
- **Oracle Fusion** running on the "Middle tier"
- **MS Internet Explorer** (web browser) running on a client PC.
- **Microsoft SQL Server** running on a Windows Server
- **Microsoft Transaction Server (MTS)** running on the Middle tier
- **Microsoft Visual Basic application** running on the client PC

Advantages of Client/Server:

1. Processing of the entire Database System is spread out over clients and server.
2. DBMS can achieve high performance because it is dedicated to processing transactions (not running applications).
3. Client Applications can take full advantage of advanced user interfaces such as Graphical User Interfaces.

Disadvantages of Client/Server:

1. Implementation is more complex because one needs to deal with middleware and the network.

2. It is possible the network is not well suited for client/server communications and may become a blockage.

3. Additional burden on DBMS server to handle concurrency control, etc.

4. As more business rule logic is programmed into the client side applications, they can become heavy.

Example: Oracle RDBMS running on a server. Sybase PowerBuilder or a Java application running on a client PC.

2.6 Types of Distributed Databases

Distributed database is classified into two types: Homogeneous and Heterogeneous database

1. Homogeneous:

Every site runs same type of DBMS. All sites of the database system have identical setup i.e. same database system software. Much easier to design and maintain. In other words, the same DBMS is used at each node.

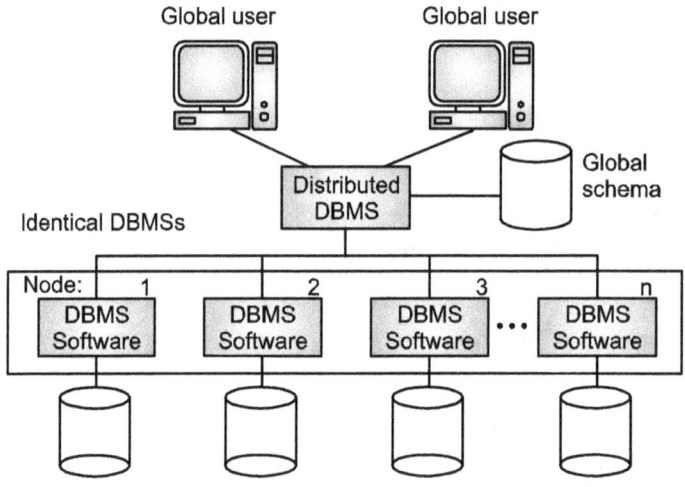

Fig. 2.10: Homogeneous Databases

For example, library information systems by the same vendor, such as Geac Computer Corporation, use the same DBMS software which allows easy data exchange between the various Geac library sites.

(a) Autonomous Each DBMS works independently, passing messages back and forth to share data updates.

(b) Nonautonomous A central, or master, DBMS coordinates database access and updates across the nodes.

2. Heterogeneous:

In a heterogeneous distributed database system, different sites might use different DBMS software, but there is additional common software to support data exchange between these sites.

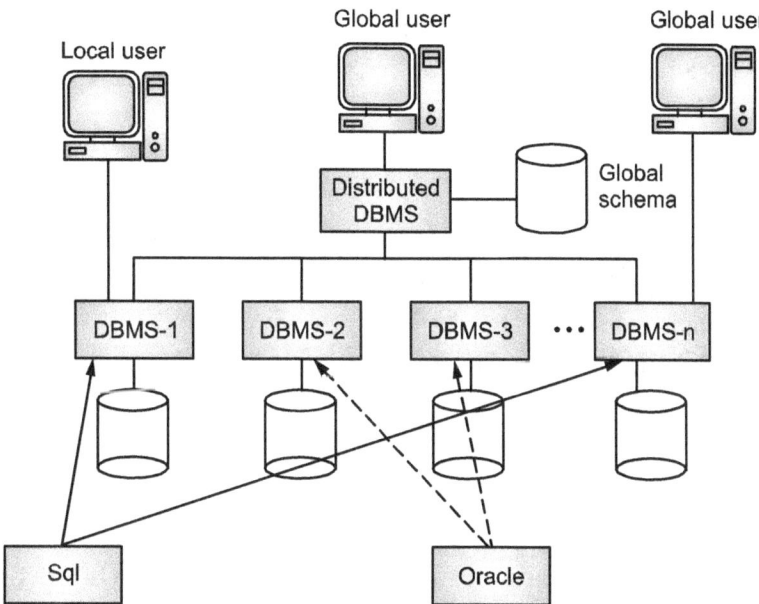

Fig. 2.12: Heterogeneous Distributed Databases

For example, the various library database systems use the same machine-readable cataloguing (MARC) format to support library record data exchange.

Different sites run different DBMSs (different RDBMSs or even nonrelational DBMSs). DBMS1 DBMS2 DBMS3

The ability to create a distributed database has existed since at least the 1980s. The range of distributed database environments are briefly explained as follows:

Heterogeneous Potentially different DBMSs are used at each node. A. Systems Supports some or all of the functionality of one logical database.

Types of Hetrogeneous DDBMS are:

(a) Systems: Supports some or all of the functionality of one logical database. (DDMS)

(b) Gateways: Simple paths are created to other databases without the benefits of one logical database.

A heterogeneous environment will be defined by the following characteristics:

- Data are distributed across all the nodes.
- Different DBMSs may be used at each node.
- Some users require only local access to databases, which can be accomplished by using only the local DBMS and schema.

(A) Full DBMS functionality

Supports all of the functionality of a distributed database.

Decentralized database: A database that is stored on computers at multiple locations; these computers are not interconnected by network and database software that make the data appear in one logical database.

(i)   Distributed database environments Source: Based on Bell and Grimson (1992)

(ii) Partial-multidatabase Supports some features of a distributed database.

(a) Federated Supports local databases for unique data requests.

   (i) **Loose integration:** Many schemas exist, for each local database, and each local DBMS must communicate with all local schemas.

   (ii) **Tight integration:** One global schema exists that defines all the data across all local databases.

(b) Unfederated Requires all access to go through a central coordinating module.

(B) Gateways:

Simple paths are created to other databases, without the benefits of one logical database. This environment is typically defined by the following characteristics (related to the nonautonomous category described previously):

- Data are distributed across all the nodes.
- The same DBMS is used at each location.
- All data are managed by the distributed DBMS (so there are no exclusively local data).

2.7 Object Relational Databases

Current and Future Database Trends In the late 1960s and early 1970s, there were two mainstream approaches to constructing Database Management System's (DBMS's).

The first approach was based on the hierarchical data model, typified by IMS (Information Management Systems) from IBM, in response to the enormous information storage requirements generated by the Apollo space program.

The second approach was based on the network data model, which attempted to create a database standard and resolve some of the difficulties of the hierarchical model, such as its inability to represent complex relationships DBMS's.

However, these two models had some fundamental disadvantages:

- Complex programs had to be written to answer even simple queries
- There was minimal data independence
- There was no widely accepted theoretical foundation.

In response to the increasing complexity of database applications, two "new" data models have emerged; the Object-Relational Database Management Systems (ORDBMS) and Object-Oriented Database Management Systems (OODBMS), which subscribes to the relational and object data models respectively. The OODBMS and ORDBMS have been combined to represent the third generation of Database Management Systems. Recent database trends include the growth of distributed databases and the emergence of object-oriented and hyper-media databases. The growth of distributed processing and networking has been accompanied by a movement towards distributed database.

Several major software companies including IBM, Informix, Microsoft, Oracle, and Sybase have all released object-relational versions of their products. These companies are promoting a new, extended version of relational database technology called object-relational database management systems also known as ORDBMSs.

Advantages:

1. The main advantages of extending the relational data model come from reuse and sharing.

2. Reuse comes from the ability to extend the DBMS server to perform standard functionality centrally, rather than have it coded in each application.

3. If we can embed the functionality in the server, it saves having to define it in each application that needs it, and consequently allows the functionality to be shared by all applications.

Disadvantages:

1. The ORDBMS's approach has the obvious disadvantage of complexity and associated increased costs.

2. There are proponents of the relational approach that believe the essential simplicity and purity of the relational model are lost with these types of extension.

3. There are also those that believe that the RDMS's is being extended for what will be a minority of applications that do not achieve optimal performance with current relational technology.

An ORDBMS supports an extended form of SQL called SQL3 that is still in the development stages. The extensions are needed because ORDBMS's have to support ADT's.

The ORDBMS has the relational model in it because the data is stored in the form of tables having rows and columns and SQL is used as the query language and the result of a query is also table or tuples (rows).

1. **Example:** Object-Relational Version of Employees Table

   Consider the Employees example. Using an ORDBMS,

   CREATE TABLE Employees (

Name	PersonName	NOT NULL,
DOB	DATE	NOT NULL,
Salary	Currency	NOT NULL,
Address	StreetAddress	NOT NULL ,
	PRIMARY KEY (Name, DOB)	

   );

For readers familiar with relational databases, this CREATE TABLE statement should be reassuringly familiar. An object-relational table is structurally very similar to its relational counterpart and the same data integrity and physical organization rules can be enforced over it. The difference between object-relational and relational tables can be seen in the section stipulating column types. In the object-relational table, readers familiar with RDBMSs should recognize the DATE type, but the other column types are completely new. From an object-oriented point of view, these types correspond to class names, which are software modules that encapsulate state and (as we shall see) behavior.

2. **Example:** Object-Relational Version of the Temporary_Employees Table

As another example of the ORDBMS data model's new functionality, consider a company supplying skilled temporary workers at short notice. Such a company would need to record each employee's resumes, the geographic location where they live, and a set of Periods (fixed intervals in the time line) during which they are available, in addition to the regular employee information.

CREATE TABLE Temporary_Employees (

Resume	DOCUMENT	NOT NULL,
LivesAt	GEOPOINT	NOT NULL,
Booked	SET(Period NOT NULL)	

) UNDER Employees;

Readers familiar with earlier RDBMS releases of Informix Dynamic Server (IDS) will also be struck by the use of the UNDER keyword. UNDER signifies that the Temporary_Employees table inherits from the Employees table. All the columns in the Employee table are also in the Temporary_Employees table, and the rows in the Temporary_Employees table can be accessed through the Employee table.

3. **Example:** Object-Relational Query against the Employees Table

Answering business questions about temporary employees requires that the information system be able to support concepts such as "Is Point in Circle," "Is Word in Document," and "Is some Period Available given some set of Booked Periods." In the IDS product such behaviors are added to the query language. Below we present a query demonstrating OR-SQL.

"Show me the names of Temporary Employees living within 60 miles of the coordinates (-122.514, 37.221), whose resumes include references to both INFORMIX and 'database administrator,' and who are not booked for the period between today and seven days ahead."

```
SELECT Print(E.Name)
FROM Temporary_Employees E
WHERE Contains (GeoCircle('(-122.514, 37.221)', '60 miles')),
E.LivesAt ) AND DocContains ( E.Resume, 'INFORMIX and Database
Administrator') AND NOT IsBooked ( Period(TODAY, TODAY + 7),
E.Booked );
```

Again, many readers will be familiar with the general form of this SELECT statement. But this query contains no expressions that are defined in the SQL-92 language standard. In addition to accommodating new data structures, an ORDBMS can integrate logic implementing the behavior associated with the objects. Each expression, or function name, in this query corresponds to a behaviorial interface defined for one of the object classes mentioned in the table's creation. Developing an object-relational database means integrating whatever the application needs into the ORDBMS.

Object-Relational DBMS Applications

Extensible databases provide a significant boost for developers building traditional business data processing applications. By implementing a database that constitutes a better model of the application's problem domain the information system can be made to provide more flexibility and functionality at lower development cost. Doing so, however, involves a more complex implementation and requires considerably more effort.

The more important effect of the technology is that it makes it possible to build information systems to address data management problems usually considered to be too difficult. In table, we present a list of applications that early adopters of ORDBMS technology have built successfully. Other technology changes are accelerating demand for these kinds of systems.

One way to characterize applications in which an object-relational DBMS is the best platform is to focus on the kind of data involved. For thirty years, software engineers have used the term "data entry" to describe the process by which information enters the system. Human users enter data using a keyboard. Today many information systems employ electronics to capture information. Video cameras, environmental sensors, and specialized monitoring equipment record data in rich media systems, industrial routing applications, and medical imaging systems. Object-relational DBMS technology excels at this kind of application.

It would be a mistake to say that ORDBMSs are only good for digital content applications. As we shall see in this book OR techniques provide considerable advantages over more low-level RDBMS approaches even in traditional business data processing applications. But as other technology changes move us towards applications in which data is recorded rather than entered, ORDBMSs will become increasingly necessary.

Application Domain	Description
Complex data analysis	You can integrate sophisticated statistical and special purpose analytic algorithms into the ORDBMS and use them in knowledge discovery or data mining applications. For example, it is possible to answer questions such as "Which attribute of my potential customers indicates most strongly that they will spend money with me?"
Text and documents	Simple cases permit to find all documents that include some word or phrase. More complex uses would include creating a network that reflected similarity between documents.
Digital asset management	The ORDBMS can manage digital media such as video, audio, and still images. In this context, manage means more than store and retrieve- It also means "convert format," "detect scene changes in video and extract first frame from new scene," and even "What MH audio tracks do I have that include this sound?"
Geographic data	For traditional applications, this might involve "Show me the lat/long coordinates corresponding to this street address." This might be extended to answer requests such as "Show me all house and contents policy holders within a quarter mile of a tidal water body." for next-generation applications, with a GIIS device integrated with a cellular phone, it might even be able to answer the perpetual puzzler "Car 54, where are you?"
Bio-medical	Modern medicine gathers lots of digital signal data such as CAT scans and ultrasound imagery. In the simplest case, you can use these images to filter out "all cell cultures with probable abnormality." in the more advanced uses, you can also answer questions such as "show me all the cardiograms which are 'like' this cardiogram."

2.7.1 Abstract Data Types (Structured Types)

The major advantage of using objects is the ability to define new data types (Abstract Data Types). In ORDBMS, the RDBMS extends the usage of objects that can be defined and stored as part of database. Like a CLASS declaration in C++ language, a new type can be defined in an ORDBMS as follows:

```
CREATE TYPE type_name AS

(Attribute1_name data_type(size),

Attribute2_name data_type(size),

Attribute3_name data_type(size),

…….

AttributeN_name data_type(size));
```

Here, data_type can be any of the following;

- It can be one of the valid data types like CHAR, VARCHAR, NUMBER, INTEGER, etc. Or

OR

- It can be another User Defined Type.

We call this kind of new User Defined Types as Structured Types / Abstract Datatypes.

For example, Structured types can be declared and used in as follows;

```
CREATE TYPE phone AS

(Country_code NUMBER(4),

STD_Code NUMBER(5),

Phone_Number NUMBER(10))
```

This type can be used in other TYPE definition or TABLE definition as follows;

```
CREATE TABLE contact

(Contact_name VARCHAR(25),

Street VARCHAR(25),

City VARCHAR(25),

Ph PHONE);
```

In this TABLE definition, PHONE is the structured type that we have defined through previous example.

Structured Types in Oracle

Let us see some examples of defining and manipulating structured types in Oracle.

```
CREATE TYPE Address AS OBJECT

(Street VARCHAR(35),

City VARCHAR(30),

State VARCHAR(30),

Pincode NUMBER(10));
```

Execution of the above statement will create a new ABSTRACT datatype named ADDRESS and store the definition as part of the database.

This new type can be used to define an attribute in any TABLEs or TYPEs as follows:

```
CREATE TABLE Person
(Person_name VARCHAR(25),
Addr ADDRESS,
Phone NUMBER(10));
```

This table Person will consist of 3 columns where the first one and the third one are of regular datatypes VARCHAR, and NUMBER respectively, and the second one is of the abstract type ADDRESS. The table PERSON will look like as follows:

Table 2.3 Person table

Person_name	Addr				Phone
	Street	City	State	Pincode	

2.7.2 Nested Tables   [Oct. 16]

Nested table is a table that is stored in database as the data of a column of the table. Nested table is like an Index-By table, but the main difference is that a nested table can be stored in the database and an Index-by table cannot. Nested table extends Index-by table by allowing the operations such as SELECT, DELETE, UPDATE and INSERT to be performed on nested table.

The following example illustrates steps related to creating and using nested table. create type project_type as object (name varchar2(50), role varchar2(20));

Now create a TABLE data type as follows:

create type ProjectTable as Table of Project_type;

Finally we use PROJECTTABLE type to create a column in EMP table as follows:

create table emp (empno number(5), ename varchar2(30), projects projecttable) nested table projects store as projects_nt;

Table EMP contains PROJECTS, which contains a table of PROJECTTABLE type for each row. NESTED TABLE option is required as we have a nested table column in the table. NESTED TABLE clause specifies the name of the table in which Oracle stores the data of the nested table. In this example PROJECTS_NT is created by Oracle and maintained by Oracle. It contains the data of PROJECTS column.

We could use a nested table type as:

- a data type in a table column.
- an object type attribute.
- a PL/SQL variable.

We should use a nested table in a design when:

- The order of the data elements is not important.
- There is a requirement to index the column specified as a collection.
- The number of elements in the collection is not know.
- The elements need to be queried.

2.7.3 Varying Arrays   [April 16]

Varrays are ordered groups of items of type VARRAY. Varrays can be used to associate a single identifier with an entire collection. This allows manipulation of the collection as a whole and easy reference of individual elements.

The maximum size of a varray needs to be specified in its type definition. The range of values for the index of a varray is from 1 to the maximum specified in its type definition. If no elements are in the array, then the array is atomically null. The main use of a varray is to group small or uniform-sized collections of objects.

Elements of a varray cannot be accessed individually through SQL, although they can be accessed in PL/SQL, OCI, or Pro*C using the array style subscript. The type of the element of a VARRAY can be any PL/SQL type except the following:

```
BOOLEAN
    TABLE
    VARRAY
    object types WITH TABLE OR VARRAY attributes
    REF CURSOR
    NCHAR
    NCLOB
    NVARCHAR2
```

Varrays can be used to retrieve an entire collection as a value. Varray data is stored in-line, in the same tablespace as the other data in its row.

When a varray is declared, a constructor with the same name as the varray is implicitly defined. The constructor creates a varray from the elements passed to it. You can use a constructor wherever you can use a function call, including the SELECT, VALUES, and SET clauses.

A varray can be assigned to another varray, provided the datatypes are the exact same type. For example, suppose you declared two PL/SQL types:

Code: sql

```sql
    TYPE My_Varray1 IS VARRAY(10) OF My_Type;
        TYPE My_Varray2 IS VARRAY(10) OF My_Type;
```

An object of type My_Varray1 can be assigned to another object of type My_Varray1 because they are the exact same type. However, an object of type My_Varray2 cannot be assigned to an object of type My_Varray1 because they are not the exact same type, even though they have the same element type.

Varrays can be atomically null, so the IS NULL comparison operator can be used to see if a varray is null. Varrays cannot be compared for equality or inequality.

The following shows how to create a simple VARRAY:

(a) First, define a object type ELEMENTS as follows:

```
SQL> CREATE TYPE MEDICINES AS OBJECT (
    2> MED_ID    NUMBER(6),
    3> MED_NAME  VARCHAR2(14),
    4> MANF_DATE DATE);
    5> /
```

(b) Next, define a VARRAY type MEDICINE_ARR which stores MEDICINES objects:

```
SQL> CREATE TYPE MEDICINE_ARR AS VARRAY(40) OF MEDICINES;
    2> /
```

(c) Finally, create a relational table MED_STORE which has MEDICINE_ARR as a column type:

```
SQL> CREATE TABLE MED_STORE (
    2> LOCATION   VARCHAR2(15),
    3> STORE_SIZE NUMBER(7),
    4> EMPLOYEES  NUMBER(6),
    5> MED_ITEMS  MEDICINE_ARR);
```

2.7.4 Large objects

Large Objects (LOBs) are a set of data types that are designed to hold large amounts of data as along text file or a graphics file. A LOB can hold up to a maximum size ranging from 8 terabytes to 128 terabytes depending on how your database is configured. Storing data in LOBs enables you to access and manipulate the data efficiently in your application.

Large Object Data types

Binary Large Object(BLOB): Stores any kind of data in binary format. Typically used for multimedia data such as images, audio, and video.A binary string that does not have a character set Example: Image BLOB (10 mb),Movie blob (2GB)

Character large object (CLOB): CLOB stores string data in the database character set format. Used for large strings or documents that use the database character set exclusively. Characters in the database character set are in a fixed width format. NLOB is a fixed-width multibyte CLOB.

Example: `Book_review  CLOB( 10Kb);`

LOB has locater that is unique id and allows to be manipulated without extensive copying. They are stored separately from data records in whose fields they appear.

 Supports lob:DB2,INFORMIX, MS-SQL,ORACLE 8, SYBASE ASE.

National Character Set Large Object(NCLOB): Stores string data in National Character Set format. Used for large strings or documents in the National Character Set. Supports characters of varying width format.It can hold up to 4 GB of character data.

```
CREATE TABLE table1(Column1 NCLOB);

INSERT INTO table1 VALUES( N'any nchar literal' );
```

External Binary File: A binary file stored outside of the database in the host operating system file system, but accessible from database tables. BFILEs can be accessed from your application on a read-only basis. Use BFILEs to store static data, such as image data, that does not need to be manipulated in applications. Any kind of data, that is, any operating system file, can be stored in a BFILE. For example, you can store character data in a BFILE and then load the BFILE data into a CLOB specifying the character set upon loading.

2.7.5 Naming Conventions for Objects   [April 16]

- Table and column names are singular (such as EMPLOYEE, Name and State).
- Abstract datatype names are singular nouns with an _TY suffix (such as PERSON_TY or ADDRESS_TY).
- Table and datatype names are always uppercase (such as EMPLOYEE or PERSON_TY).
- Column names are always capitalized (such as State and Start_Date).
- Object view names are singular nouns with an _OV suffix (such as PERSON_OV or ADDRESS_OV).
- Nested table names are plural nouns with an _NT suffix (such as WORKERS_NT).
- Varying array names are plural nouns with an _VA suffix (such as WORKERS_VA).

The name of an object should consist of two parts: the core object name and the suffix. The core object name should follow your naming standards; the suffixes help to identify special types of objects.

Teradata Conventions

The data objects that you can name in Teradata include tables, views, columns, indexes and macros. When naming a Teradata object, use the following conventions:

- A name must start with a letter unless you enclose it in double quotation marks.
- A name must be from 1 to 30 characters long.
- A name can contain the letters A through Z, the digits 0 through 9, the underscore (_), $, and #. A name in double quotation marks can contain any characters except double quotation marks.
- A name, even when enclosed in double quotation marks, is not case sensitive. For example, CUSTOMER is the same as customer.
- A name cannot be a Teradata reserved word.
- The name must be unique between objects. That is, a view and table in the same database cannot have the identical name.

SAS Naming Conventions

When naming a SAS object use the following conventions:

- A name must start with a letter or underscore.
- A name cannot be enclosed in double quotation marks.
- A name must be from 1 to 32 characters long.
- A name can contain the letters A through Z, the digits 0 through 9, and the underscore (_).
- A name is not case sensitive. For example, CUSTOMER is the same as customer.
- A name need not be unique between object types.

Naming Objects to Meet Teradata and SAS Conventions

To share objects easily between the DBMS and SAS, create names that meet both SAS and Teradata naming conventions. Make the name

- Start with a letter
- Include only letters, digits, and underscores
- Have a length of 1 to 30 characters.

2.8 Case Study

This case study examines a company that is that recently purchased a Database System. It also considers some of the issues that needed to be considered during the purchase procedure.

Problems identified with the manual process

- Paper files had to be pulled each time the client came in and sometimes they could not be found.
- There was limited space available for filing resulting in some files being located in different locations.
- There was no standard method adopted in relation to filing which resulted in multiple paper files for a client in a location.
- There was no standard approach adopted in way a file was created.
- Different groups of therapists used slightly different processes.
- Different groups of therapists used different forms across the region.
- Statistics requested on an ad-hoc basis had to be gathered by referring back to paper files. This was time consuming and laborious.
- Users had to manually write reports for other departments

New Business Processes

The new system operates as follows:

- To search for a client search via the Client Index Database or enter client details.
- Key information from a referral is entered onto the database, namely "date", "who from" and "reason for referral".
- The senior user will view all unassigned referrals and assign them to individual users electronically.
- The system automatically creates an appointment and an appointment letter will be printed on the individual user's printer.
- The user will receive an email automatically, informing them of the new referral and the suggested appointment date.
- The user can change the appointment date and create an alternate letter.
- The user will give the letters to their clerical support to be sent out or send them themselves.
- When the client presents for assessment and/or treatment, the user will:-
  1. See the client and fill out the appropriate forms.
  2. The forms will be printed with the client information, using the computer system, thus saving the therapist time filling the form.
  3. Later the user updates the database with key information from the assessment and/or treatment, namely "date, actions, presenting conditions and free text".

4. The user will make a new appointment using the computer and the client will be handed a letter leaving the clinic with the date, time and location for the next appointment. (The majority of fields are drop down boxes).

- Each week a user or manager can view open referrals that have had no activity for a specified period.

- A new referral cannot be created until the existing referral and treatments have been closed off, for any client.

- All statistics can be achieved using an ad-hoc report generator, using combinations of drop down boxes.

- All reports for other health care professionals can be generated automatically by the secretary and they just need to be signed by the user.

Benefits achieved by the New System

- The new IT system shares information electronically. This improves the service to our clients and allows us manage client interactions more effectively. Information can be shared with other departments as appropriate.

- The new IT system is aligned to the business processes and the business processes are thought out.

- The business processes are standardised across the region (4 counties)

- The IT solution supports and prescribes standardised filing and numbering across the region.

- The IT solution is a working tool with statistics as a by-product.

- The system allows the users manage and monitor appointments at client level electronically.

- The therapists can get Ad-hoc reports off the system to get information.

- The system can produce referral reports for other departments as required.

- Statistics from the system influences the service planning process.

- Credibility; the health care professionals have experienced that an information system can make their work easier, thus improving services to clients.

- The users on the project group learned a lot about developing a computer system and reengineering business processes.

Factors in Determining the Type of Database Selected

The following factors were considered in deciding the most appropriate system:

- The requirement for an integrated computer system that could link to existing computer systems.

- Security of data was a huge factor with the need to safeguard client information from being accessed by unauthorized personnel.
- Features such as manageability, availability, scalability and reliability were important factors.
- A demand for higher availability features and more functionality, which could adapt to the complex and changing environment.
- The requirement of a system that was compatible with existing systems and networks.
- A recognized and trusted supplier who understood the environment and our systems.
- There was an emphasis on the need for tried and tested technology as opposed to cutting edge technology, which carried a higher risk of failure.

Functionality of the New System

The new system is client focused, integrated and shares information across all systems across the subsidiary outlets. This client centered database ensures consistency and standardization of client data across a wide range of services.

How it works?

The object-oriented database is constructed on a modular based system with the client as the central object. Object oriented database management systems (OODBMS) integrate client details from a variety of sources. The software allows for sharing of information with other professionals, and interface with over 200,000 existing clients in the region.

This system is also useful for storing data types such as recursive data. Within the health department the system allows for recording of referrals and client interactions, and also the development of reports and statistical information.

Functionality of the New System

This system is characterised by the support of the following features:

- **Data persistence:** The ability for data to outlive the execution of a program and possibly the lifetime of the program itself.
- **Data Sharing or Concurrency:** The ability for multiple applications (or instances of the same one) to access common data possibility at the same time.
- **Reliability:** The assurance that the data in the database is protected from hardware and software failure.
- **Scalability:** The ability to operate on large amounts of data in simple ways
- **Security and Integrity:** The protection of the data against unauthorised access, and the assurance that the data conforms to specified correctness and consistency rules.

- **Distribution:** The ability to physically distribute a logically interrelated collection of shared data over a computer network, preferably making the distribution transparent to the user.

Long Term Application

In the future, this system can be used to manage various multimedia components. Medical data on clients/patients may be stored in this multimedia database.

Health care professionals will be able to access patient files including vital images to generate reports and derive the information they need to deliver quality health care quickly. It was for this reason this system was chosen over the Relational DBMS, which cannot store more complex types of information. This database will be capable of handling the projected amounts of data over an extended period of time.

Delivery of the system

The delivery of the new system was achieved by the following:-

- Feedback from workshops came up with various enhancements to be made to the system.
- Any changes made and delivered were made in conjunction with training of project groups.
- Each week a new release of the software was delivered with the changes and the project group continued to use the system for a select number of client transactions.
- At the end of a month, the project groups were satisfied that the software delivered met their expectations.

Training Requirements

Information was gathered from the senior users and IT support staff, to identify training requirements.

This training included:

- Introduction to computers
- Introduction to Microsoft Word
- Email

Further training incorporating the following aspects was also included:

- A description of this new environment.
- How information is shared across sections.
- Making changes to information that is shared with other departments.
- Workflow theory and practise.

- The new IT system used for:
    - How to find a client?
    - How to add a client?
    - How to add / update and delete a referral, assessment, treatment?
    - Appointments
    - Reporting
    - Statistics

Lessons Learned

There is a need for a data quality function to monitor data entry and data quality on an ongoing basis. This is to prevent duplication of data on the system. Standardisation of data input is vital to the success of the system e.g. Surname details such as O'Sullivan, O'Brien must be entered with space after O and no apostrophe e.g., O Sullivan.

There is also a need for an unlinked department to monitor processes and procedures and ensure that they are followed. This department should identify training and future enhancements as systems and processes evolve.

Conclusion

One of the major difficulties associated with IT systems in the health care service sector over the years has been the ad hoc approach in which systems were developed and implemented. By allowing different departments and disciplines in the organisation to maintain their own files independently, the traditional file environment created problems such as data redundancy and inconsistency, program-data dependency, inflexibility, poor security and lack of data-sharing and availability. This resulted in inconsistent and inaccurate statistical reports as well as inflexible systems that are unable to respond to the complexities of the environment in which we now operate.

The adoption of an object-based database has allowed for an integrated client centred system. This enables relevant disciplines across the services to access and share relevant data of clients on an integrated and secure basis.

This is in keeping with the objectives of the National Health Strategy which states that our health services should be client centred. It also states that client health information should be shared across all health service departments as a means to creating a holistic service to customers.

Practice Questions

1. Define Distributed Database.
2. State the Difference between Standalone and Distributed Database.
3. Explain Database Replication.
4. Define concept of Fragmentation. Explain Types of Fragmentation in Distributed database.
5. Describe Client-Server Architecture in Distributed database.
6. Which are the different types of in Distributed database?
7. Explain the term: Object-Relational Model.
8. Write a short note on:
   (a) Nested Tables
   (b) Varying Arrays
   (c) Large Objects
9. State the Naming Conventions of Objects.
10. Explain- Abstract Data types.
11. Define Distributed database. Describe any Case Study on it.

■■■

Chapter 3...

Data Warehouse

Contents ...

3.1 Introduction of Data Warehouse   [April 16]

The term "Data Warehouse" was first coined by Bill Inmon in 1990. According to Inmon, a data warehouse is a subject oriented, integrated, time-variant, and non-volatile collection of data. This data helps analysts to take informed decisions in an organization.

What is Data warehouse?

Data warehouse is a collection of data designed to support management decision-making.

Another definition is "Data warehousing is the process, whereby, organisations extract meaning from their informational assets through the use of data warehouses (Barguin, 1996").

Another definition is "A data warehouse is a subject oriented, integrated, time variant, non-volatile collection of data used in support of management decision-making processes".

A data warehouse is a database designed to enable business intelligence activities:

- It exists to help users understand and enhance their organization's performance.
- It is designed for query and analysis rather than for transaction processing.
- It contains historical data derived from transaction data, but can include data from other sources.
- Data warehouses separate analysis workload from transaction workload and enable an organization to consolidate data from several sources.

This helps in:

- Maintaining historical records.
- Analyzing the data to gain a better understanding of the business and to improve the business.

A data warehouse environment can include an extraction, transportation, transformation, and loading (ETL) solution, statistical analysis, reporting, data mining capabilities, client analysis tools, and other applications that manage the process of gathering data, transforming it into useful, actionable information, and delivering it to business users.

To achieve the goal of enhanced business intelligence, the data warehouse works with data collected from multiple sources. The source data may come from internally developed systems, purchased applications, third-party data syndicators and other sources. It may involve transactions, production, marketing, human resources and more. In today's world of big data, the data may be many billions of individual clicks on web sites or the massive data streams from sensors built into complex machinery.

Data warehouses are distinct from online transaction processing (OLTP) systems. With a data warehouse you separate analysis workload from transaction workload. Thus data warehouses are very much read-oriented systems. They have a far higher amount of data reading versus writing and updating. This enables far better analytical performance and avoids impacting your transaction systems.

There are two important terms that need to be mentioned. These are the Data Mart and the Operation Data Store (ODS).

Data Mart:

A data mart serves the same role as a data warehouse, but it is intentionally limited in scope. It may serve one particular department or line of business. The advantage of a data mart versus a data warehouse is that it can be created much faster due to its limited coverage.

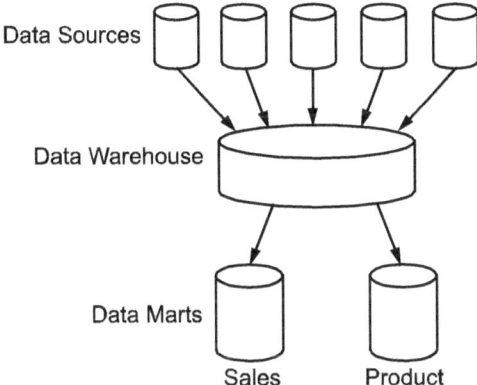

Data Sources

Data Warehouse

Data Marts

Sales   Product

Fig. 3.1: Data Warehouse

A data mart contains only those data that is specific to a particular group. For example, the marketing data mart may contain only data related to items, customers, and sales. Data marts are confined to subjects.

However, it also creates problems with inconsistency. It takes tight discipline to keep data and calculation definitions consistent across data marts. This problem has been widely recognized, so data marts exist in two styles.

- **Independent data marts** are those which are fed directly from source data. They can turn into islands of inconsistent information.

- **Dependent data marts** are fed from an existing data warehouse. Dependent data marts can avoid the problems of inconsistency, but they require that an enterprise-level data warehouse already exist.

Operational Data Stores:

The ODS gives data warehouses a place to get access to the most current data, which has not yet been loaded into the data warehouse. The ODS may also be used as a source to load the data warehouse.

Operational data stores exist to support daily operations. The ODS data is cleaned and validated, but it is not historically deep: it may be just the data for the current day. Rather than support the historically rich queries that a data warehouse can handle. As data warehousing loading techniques have become more advanced, data warehouses may have less need for ODS as a source for loading data. Instead, constant trickle-feed systems can load the data warehouse in near real time.

Layers in Data Warehouse:

In general, all data warehouse systems have the following layers:

- Data Source Layer
- Data Extraction Layer
- Staging Area
- ETL Layer
- Data Storage Layer
- Data Logic Layer
- Data Presentation Layer
- Metadata Layer
- System Operations Layer

Each component is discussed individually below:

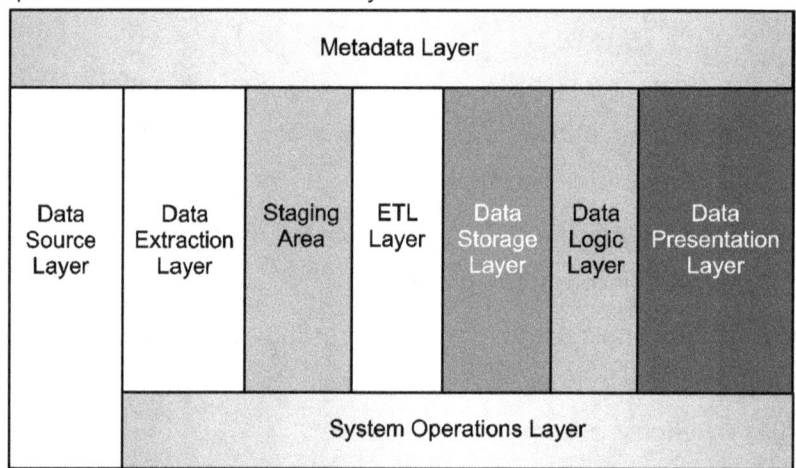

Fig. 3.2: Data Warehouse Layers

Data Source Layer: This represents the different data sources that feed data into the data warehouse. The data source can be of any format -- plain text file, relational database, other types of database, Excel file, etc. can all act as a data source.

Many different types of data can be a data source:

- Operations - Such as sales data, HR data, product data, inventory data, marketing data, systems data.
- Web server logs with user browsing data.
- Internal market research data.
- Third-party data, such as census data, demographics data, or survey data.

All these data sources together form the Data Source Layer.

- **Data Extraction Layer:** Data gets pulled from the data source into the data warehouse system. There is likely some minimal data cleansing, but there is unlikely any major data transformation.
- **Staging Area:** In this area, data ties prior to being scrubbed and transformed into a data warehouse / data mart. Having one common area makes it easier for subsequent data processing / integration.
- **ETL (Extract, Transform, Load) Layer:** In this layer data gains its "intelligence", as logic is applied to transform the data from a transactional nature to an analytical nature. Data cleansing also happens in this layer.
- **Data Storage Layer:** This is where the transformed and cleansed data lie. Based on scope and functionality, 3 types of entities can be found here: Data Warehouse, Data Mart, and Operational Data Store (ODS). In any given system, you may have just one of the three, two of the three, or all three types.
- **Data Logic Layer:** Layer stores the business rules. These rules do not affect the underlying data transformation rules, but do affect what the report looks like.
- **Data Presentation Layer:** This layer refers to the information that reaches the users. This can be in a form of a tabular / graphical report in a browser, an emailed report that gets automatically generated and sent everyday. It can be an alert that warns users of exceptions, among others. Usually an OLAP tool and/or a reporting tool is used in this layer.
- **Metadata Layer:** This is where information about the data stored in the data warehouse system. A logical data model would be an example of the metadata layer. A metadata tool is often used to manage metadata.
- **System Operations Layer:** This layer includes information on how the data warehouse system operates, such as ETL job status, system performance, and user access history.

Advantages of Data Warehouse Systems:

Advantages of an up-to-date data warehouse include four characteristics:

1. **Subject-Oriented:** A data warehouse can be used to analyze a particular subject area. For example, "sales" can be a particular subject.
2. **Integrated:** A data warehouse integrates data from multiple data sources. For example, source A and source B may have different ways of identifying a product, but in a data warehouse, there will be only a single way of identifying a product.
3. **Time-Variant:** Historical data is kept in a data warehouse. For example, one can retrieve data from 3 months, 6 months, 12 months, or even older data from a data warehouse. This contrasts with a transactions system, where often only the most

recent data is kept. For example, a transaction system may hold the most recent address of a customer, where a data warehouse can hold all addresses associated with a customer.

4. **Non-volatile:** Once data is in the data warehouse, it will not change. So, historical data in a data warehouse should never be altered.

5. **Accessible:** The primary purpose of a data warehouse is to provide readily accessible information to end users.

Applications of data warehouse:

As explained before, a data warehouse helps business executives to organize, analyze, and use their data for decision making.

Data warehouses are widely used in the following fields:

- Banking services
- Financial services
- Consumer goods
- Retail sectors
- Controlled manufacturing

3.2 A Multidimensional Data Model   [Oct. 16]

Data Warehouse uses a data model that is based on a multidimensional data model. This model is also known as a data cube which allows data to be modeled and viewed in multiple dimensions.

Dimensions are the different perspectives for an entity that an organization is interested in. For example, a store will create a soles data warehouse in order to keep track of the store' sales with respect to different dimensions such as time, branch, and location. "Sales" is an example of a central theme around which the data model is organized.

The multidimensional nature of business questions is reflected in the fact that, for example, marketing managers are no longer satisfied by asking simple one-dimensional questions such as "How much revenue did the new product generate? Instead, they ask questions such as "How much revenue did the new product generate by month, in the northeastern division, broken down by user demographic, by sales office, relative to the previous version of the product, compared the with plan ?"—A six-dimensional question.

The purpose of dimensional model is to improve performance by matching data structures to queries.

The multidimensional data model is composed of logical cubes, measures, dimensions, hierarchies, levels, and attributes. The simplicity of the model is inherent because it defines objects that represent real-world business entities. Analysts know which business measures they are interested in examining, which dimensions and attributes make the data meaningful, and how the dimensions of their business are organized into levels and hierarchies. The multidimensional data model is designed to solve complex queries in real time.

The entity-relationship data model is commonly used in the design of relational databases. However, such a schema is not appropriate for a data warehouse. A data warehouse requires a concise, subject oriented schema that facilitates on-line data analysis.

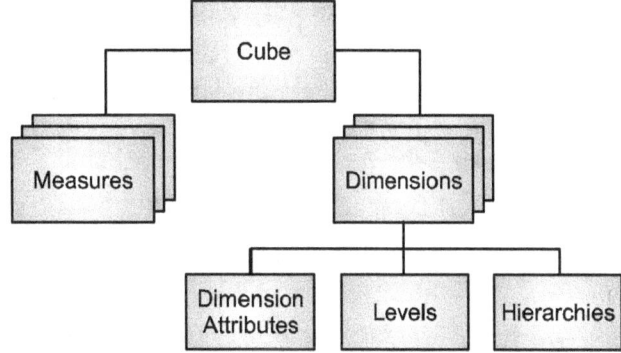

Fig. 3.3: Multidimensional Data Model

Star Schema:

The most popular data model for data warehouse is a multidimensional model. Such a model can exist in the form of a star schema. The star Schema consists of the following.

1. A large central table (fact table) containing the bulk of data.
2. A set of smaller dimension tables one for each dimension.

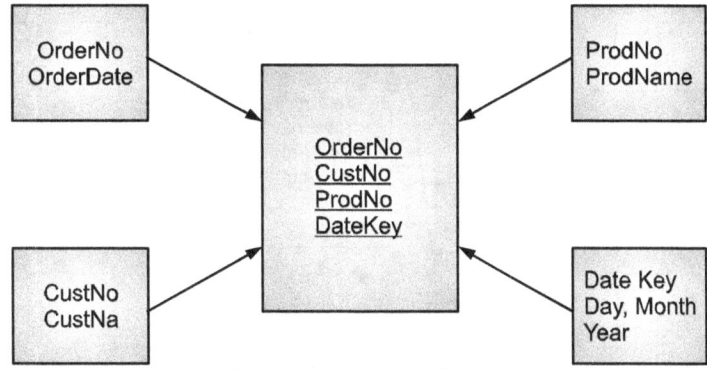

Fig. 3.4 (a): Star Schema

The schema resembles a star, with the dimension tables displayed in a radial pattern around the central fact table. An example of a sales table and the corresponding star schema is shown in the Fig. 3.4 for each dimension, the set of associated values can be structured as a hierarchy. For example, cities belong to states and states belong to countries. Similarly, dates belong to weeks that belong to months and quarters/years. The hierarchies are shown in Fig. 3.5.

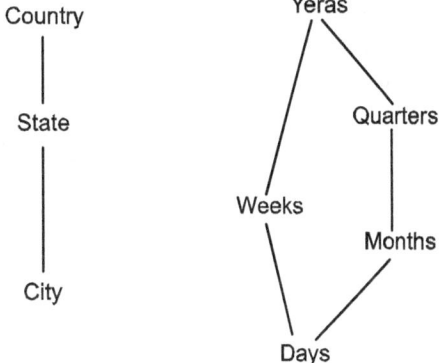

Fig. 3.5: Concept Hierarchy

In data warehousing, there is a distinction between a data warehouse and a data mart. A data warehouse collects information about subjects that span the entire organization such as customers, items, sales and personnel. Therefore, the scope of a data warehouse is enterprise wide. A data mart on the other hand is a subset of the data warehouse that focuses on selected subjects and is therefore limited in size. For example, there can be a data mart for sales information another data mart for inventory information.

Snowflake Schema: The snowflake schema is an extension of the star schema, where each point of the star explodes into more points. In a star schema, each dimension is represented by a single dimensional table, whereas in a snowflake schema, that dimensional table is normalized into multiple lookup tables, each representing a level in the dimensional hierarchy. The snowflake schema architecture is a more complex because the dimensional tables are normalized. It normalizes dimensions to reduce redundancy. The decomposed snowflake structure visualizes the hierarchical structure of dimensions very well. The snowflake model is easy for data modellers to understand and for database designers to use for the analysis of dimensions. The main advantage of the snowflake schema is the improvement in query performance due to minimized disk storage requirements and joining smaller lookup tables. The main disadvantage of the snowflake schema is the additional maintenance efforts needed due to the increase number of lookup tables. The diagram of snowflake schema is as follows:-

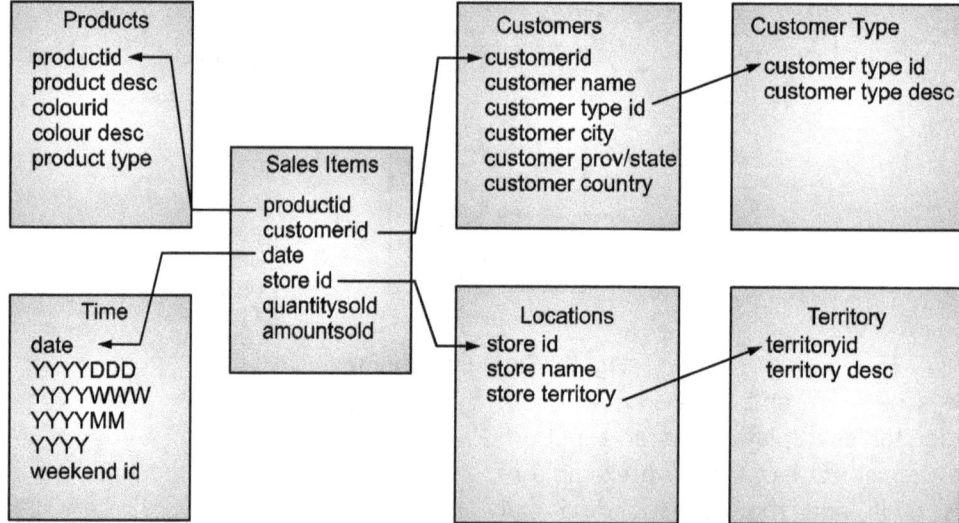

Fig. 3.4 (b): Snowflake Schema for Sales items

Characteristics:

The principal characteristic of a multidimensional model is a set of detailed business facts surrounded by multiple dimensions that describes those facts, when realized in a database, the schema for a multidimensional model contains a central fact table and multiple dimension tables.

Two types of tables are used in multidimensional modeling: Fact tables and Dimensional tables.

Fact Tables

Fact tables are used to record actual facts or measures in the business. Tracts are the numeric data items that are of interest to the business.

Below are examples of facts for different industries
- **Retail:** Number of units sold, sales amount.
- **Telecommunications:** Length of call in minutes, average number of calls.
- **Banking:** Average daily balance, transaction amount.
- **Insurance:** Claims amounts.
- **Airline:** Ticket cost, baggage weight

Facts are the numbers that users analyze and summarize to gain a better understanding of the business.

Dimension Tables

Dimension tables, on the other hand, establish the context of the facts. Dimensional tables store fields that describe the facts.

Below are examples of dimensions for the same industries:
- **Retail:** Store name, store zip, product name, product category, day of week.
- **Telecommunications:** Call origin, call destination.
- **Banking:** Customer name, account number, data, branch, account officer.
- **Insurance:** Policy type, insured policy
- **Airline:** Flight number, flight destination, airfare class.

A dimensional model may produce a star schema or snowflake schema. A multi-dimensional data model views data in the form of a data cube.

3.3 Data Warehouse Architecture   [April 16]

Data warehouse architecture is a design that includes all the facets of data warehousing for an enterprise environment. It has all reporting requirements- data management, security requirements, band width requirements and storage requirements.

There are three common types of data architecture as follows:

Data warehouses and their architectures vary depending upon the specifics of an organization's situation. Three common architectures are:
- Data Warehouse Architecture (Basic)
- Data Warehouse Architecture (with a Staging Area)
- Data Warehouse Architecture (with a Staging Area and Data Marts)

1. Data Warehouse Architecture (Basic):

Following Fig. 3.6 shows a simple architecture for a data warehouse. End users directly access data derived from several source systems through the data warehouse.

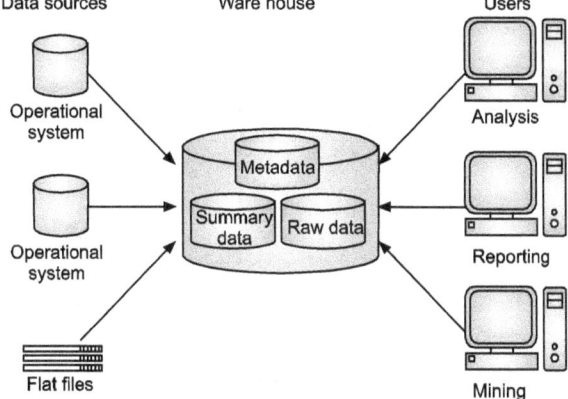

Fig 3.6: Architecture of a Data Warehouse

In following Fig. 3.6, the metadata and raw data of a traditional OLTP (Online Transaction Processing) system is present, as is an additional type of data, summary data. Summaries are very valuable in data warehouses because they pre-compute long operations in advance. For example, a typical data warehouse query is to retrieve something such as August sales.

2. Data Warehouse Architecture (with a Staging Area):

You need to clean and process your operational data before putting it into the warehouse, as shown in Fig. 3.7. You can do this programmatically, although most data warehouses use a staging area instead. A staging area simplifies building summaries and general warehouse management. Fig. 3.7 shows this typical architecture.

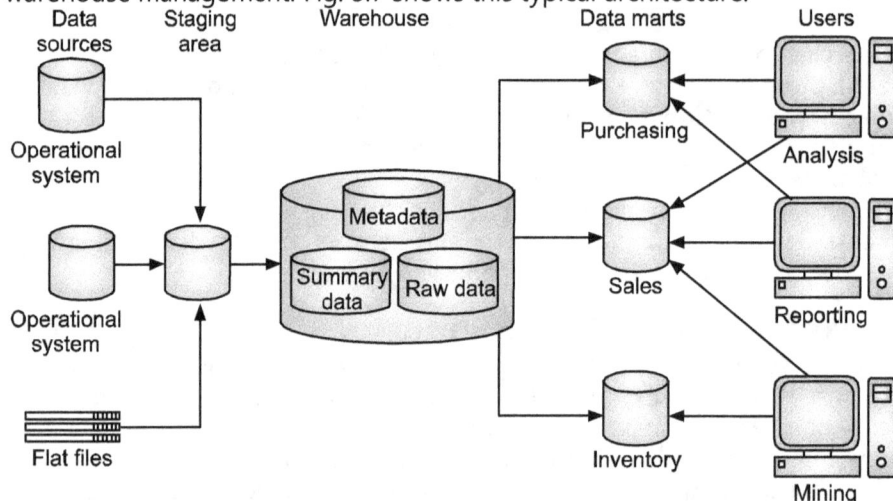

Fig. 3.7: Architecture of a Data Warehouse with a Staging Area

3. Data Warehouse Architecture (with a Staging Area and Data Marts):

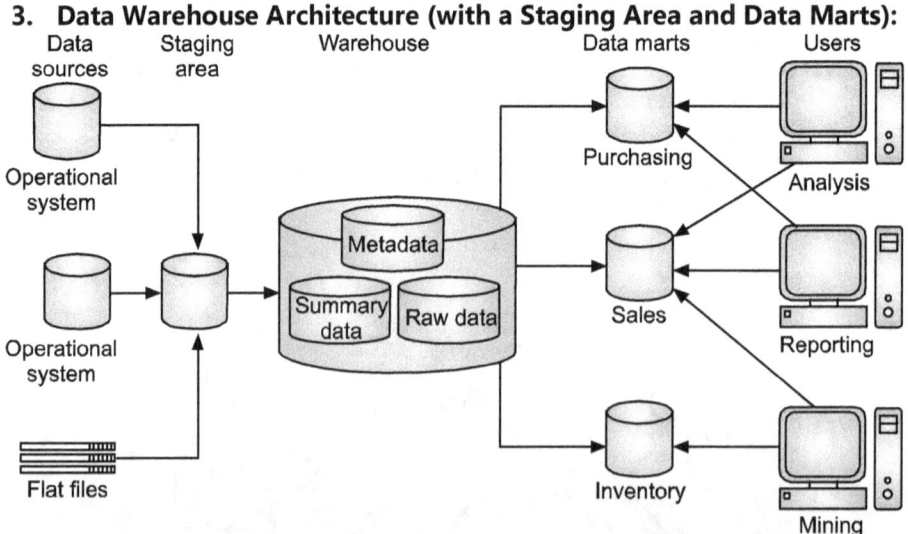

Fig. 3.8: Architecture of a Data Warehouse with a Staging Area and Data Marts

Although the architecture in Fig. 3.7 is quite common, you may want to customize the warehouse's architecture for different groups within the organization. This can be done by adding data marts, which are systems designed for a particular line of business. Fig. 3.8 illustrates an example where purchasing, sales, and inventories are separated. In this example, a financial analyst might want to analyze historical data for purchases and sales.

3.4 Data Warehouse Implementation

A Data Warehouse is a storehouse of the information gathered from multiple sources stored under a unified schema, at a single site. Data warehouse provide us a single consolidated interface to data making decision support queries easier to write.

Primary features of distributed data warehouse:

- The data copied into a data warehouse does not change (except to correct errors). The data warehouse is a historical record of the state of an organization. The frequent changes of the source OLTP systems are reflected in the data warehouse by adding new data, not by changing existing data.
- Data warehouses are subject oriented, that is, they focus on measuring entities, such as sales, inventory, and quality. OLTP systems, by contrast, are function oriented and focus on operations such as order fulfillment.
- In data warehouses, data from distinct function oriented systems is integrated to provide a single view of an operational entity. Data warehouses are designed for business users, not database programmers, so they are easy to understand and query.

Transaction processing systems:

- Support the operational level of the organization, possibly integrating needs of different functional areas (ERP).
- Perform and record the daily transactions necessary to the conduct of the business.
- Execute simple read/update operations on traditional databases, aiming at maximizing transaction throughput.

Types of Data Warehouse:

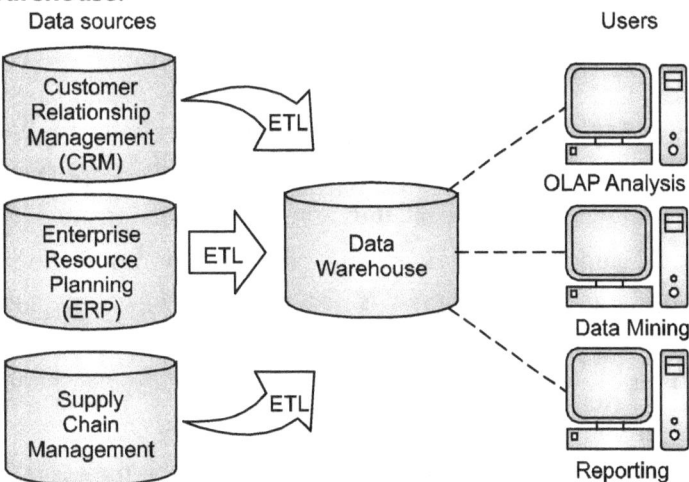

Fig. 3.9: Types of Data Warehouse

- **Information Processing:** A data warehouse allows to process the data stored in it. The data can be processed by means of querying, basic statistical analysis, reporting using crosstabs, tables, charts, or graphs.

- **Analytical Processing:** A data warehouse supports analytical processing of the information stored in it. The data can be analyzed by means of basic OLAP (Online Analytical Processing) operations, including slice-and-dice, drill down, drill up, and pivoting.

- **Data Mining:** Data mining supports knowledge discovery by finding hidden patterns and associations, constructing analytical models, performing classification and prediction. These mining results can be presented using the visualization tools.

- **Online Transaction and Processing (OLTP):** OLTP helps and manages applications based on transactions involving high volume of data. Typical example of a transaction is commonly observed in Banks, Air tickets etc. Because OLTP uses client server architecture, it supports transactions to run cross a network.

- **Online Analytical Processing (OLAP):** OLAP performs analysis of business data and provides the ability to perform complex calculations on usually low volumes of data. OLAP helps the user gain an insight on the data coming from different sources (multi dimensional).

OLAP Server Architecture

Their classification based on the underlying storage layouts:

- **MOLAP:** A more traditional way of OLAP analysis. Data is persisted in a multi-dimensional cube in MOLAP. The storage is in proprietary formats but not in the relational database. MOLAP data cubes are built in such a way that data retrieval is faster and are optimal for dicing and slicing operations.

- **ROLAP:** A methodology that is relied on manipulating the persisted data in the relational database, for providing an appearance of traditional OLAP's dicing and slicing functionality. The actions of slicing and dicing are equivalent to add the 'WHERE' clause in the SQL statement, is the essential part of ROLAP. The amount of data is not limited by ROLAP itself, thus able to handle large amounts of data.

- **HOLAP:** In a Hybrid OLAP, the database gets divided into relational and specialized storage. Specialized data storage is for data with fewer details while relational storage can be used for large amount of data. Use of virtual cubes and other different forms of HOLAP enable one to modify storage as per the needs.

Typical OLAP Operations

- **Roll-up (drill-up):** Perform aggregation on a data cube by – Climbing up a concept hierarchy for a dimension and by dimension reduction.

- **Drill-down (roll down):** The roll down operation (also called drill down) is the reverse of roll up. It navigates from less detailed data to more detailed data. It can be realized by either stepping down a concept hierarchy for a dimension or introducing additional dimensions.

- **Slice and dice:** Slice performs a selection on one dimension of the given cube, thus resulting in a subcube. The dice operation defines a subcube by performing a selection on two or more dimensions

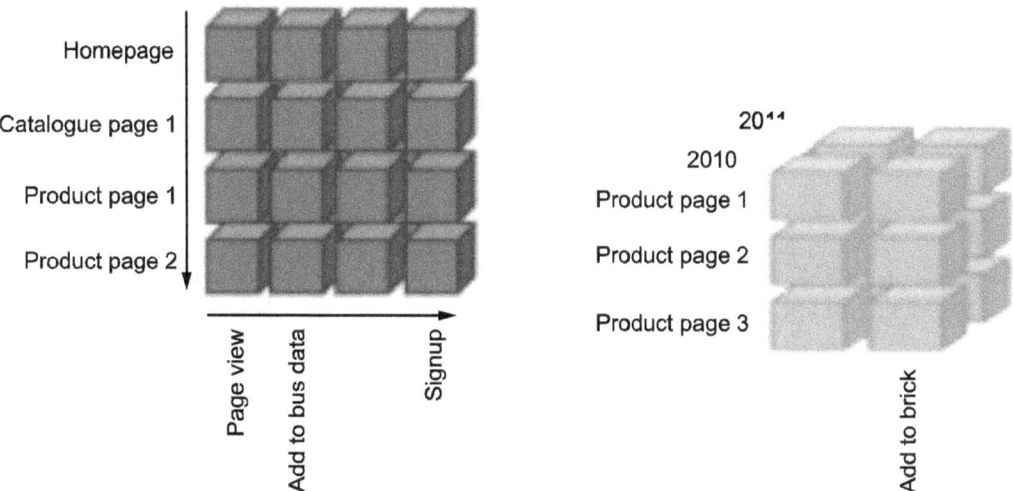

Fig 3.10: Slice and dice

- **Pivot (rotate):** Pivot otherwise known as Rotate changes the dimensional orientation of the cube, i.e. rotates the data axes to view the data from different perspectives. Pivot groups data with different dimensions.

- **Drill-across:** Accesses more than one fact table that is linked by common dimensions. It combines cubes that share one or more dimensions.

- **Drill-through:** Drill down to the bottom level of a data cube down to its back end relational tables.

3.5 Data Cube Technology

Data Cube helps us represent data in multiple dimensions. It is defined by dimensions and measures.

- **Dimensions:** The dimensions are the entities with respect to which an enterprise preserves the records.

- **Measures:** It represents some fact(or number) such as cost or units of service.

Data cubes are commonly used for easy interpretation of data. It is used to represent data along with dimensions as some measures of business needs. Each dimension of the cube represents some attribute of the database. Example, Sales per day, month or year.

Three important concept associated with data cubes are slicing, dicing, rotating.

1. Slicing:

A slice in a multidimensional array is a column of data corresponding to a single value for one or more members of the dimension. Slicing is the act of divvying up the cube to extract this information for a given slice. It is important because it helps the user visualize and gather information specific to a dimension. When you think of slicing, think of it as a specialized filter for a particular value in a dimension.

For instance, if a user wanted to know the total number of Wireless Mice sold over the whole dataset time space (2000-2003), the user would perform a horizontal slice as shown in Fig 3.11.

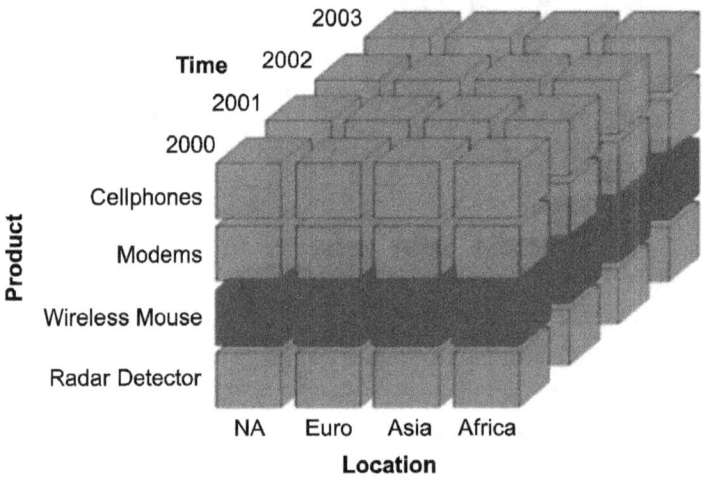

Fig. 3.11: Slicing

Key features of slicing:

- The term slice most often refers to a two-dimensional page selected from the cube.
- Subset of a multidimensional array corresponding to a single value for one or more members of the dimensions not in the subset.

2. Dicing:

Dicing is similar to slicing but it works a little bit differently. When one thinks of slicing, filtering is done to focus on a particular attribute, dicing on the other hand is more a zoom feature that selects a subset over all the dimensions but for specific values of the dimension. This tool is very useful in allowing the user to get more detailed information on what goes in on a smaller scale.

For instance, Fig. 3.12 shows a graphical representation of dicing for a particular produce, over a specific time span for a particular region. The subset shows the Cell phone market, in North America only for the year 2000.

Illustration: Suppose a company wants to keep track of sales records with the help of sales data warehouse with respect to time, item, branch, and location. These dimensions allow to keep track of monthly sales and at which branch the items were sold. There is a table associated with each dimension. This table is known as dimension table. For example, "item" dimension table may have attributes such as item_name, item_type, and item_brand.

The following table represents the 2-D view of Sales Data for a company with respect to time, item, and location dimensions.

Location = "New Delhi"

Time (Quarter)	Item (Type)			
	Entertainment	Keyboard	Mobile	Locks
Q1	500	700	10	300
Q2	769	765	30	476
Q3	987	489	18	659
Q4	666	976	40	529

But here in this 2-D table, we have records with respect to time and item only. The sales for New Delhi are shown with respect to time, and item dimensions according to type of items sold. If we want to view the sales data with one more dimension, say, the location dimension, then the 3-D view would be useful. The 3-D view of the sales data with respect to time, item, and location is shown in the table below:

Time	Location = "Gurgaon"			Location = "New Delhi"			Location = "Mumbai"		
	Item			Item			Item		
	Mouse	Mobile	Modern	Mouse	Mobile	Modern	Mouse	Mobile	Modern
Q1	788	987	765	786	85	987	986	567	875
Q2	678	654	987	659	786	436	980	876	908
Q3	899	875	190	983	909	237	987	100	1089
Q4	787	969	908	537	567	836	837	926	987

The above 3-D table can be represented as 3-D data cube as shown in the following Fig. 3.14.

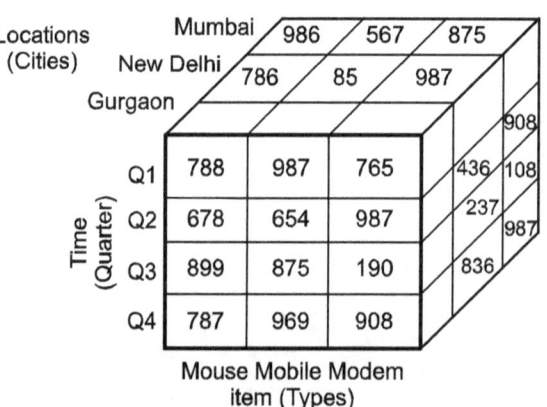

Fig. 3.14: Mouse Mobile Modem

3.6 From Data Warehousing to Data Mining

Data warehousing is merely extracting data from different sources, cleaning the data and storing it in the warehouse. Where as data mining aims to examine or explore the data using queries. These queries can be fired on the data warehouse. Explore the data in data mining helps in reporting, planning strategies, finding meaningful patterns etc.

For example, a data warehouse of a company stores all the relevant information of projects and employees. Using Data mining, one can use this data to generate different reports like profits generated etc.

Data mining is the extraction of hidden predictive information from large databases, is a powerful new technology with great potential to help companies focus on the most important information in their data warehouses.

Data mining tools predict future trends and behaviors, allowing businesses to make proactive, knowledge-driven decisions. The automated, prospective analyses offered by data mining move beyond the analyses of past events provided by retrospective tools typical of decision support systems. Data mining tools can answer business questions that traditionally were too time-consuming to resolve. They scour databases for hidden patterns, finding predictive information that experts may miss because it lies outside their expectations.

Data mining techniques can be implemented rapidly on existing software and hardware platforms to enhance the value of existing information resources, and can be integrated with new products and systems as they are brought on-line.

With the increased and widespread use of technologies, interest in data mining has increased rapidly. Companies are now utilized data mining techniques to examine their database looking for trends, relationships, and outcomes to enhance their overall operations and discover new patterns that may allow them to better serve their customers. Data mining provides numerous benefits to businesses, government, society as well as individual persons. However, like many technologies, there are negative things that caused by data mining such as invasion of privacy right.

Data mining is ready for application in the business community because it is supported by three technologies that are now sufficiently mature:

- Massive data collection
- Powerful multiprocessor computers
- Data mining algorithms

In the evolution from business data to business information, each new step has built upon the previous one. For example, dynamic data access is critical for drill-through in data navigation applications, and the ability to store large databases is critical to data mining.

Theoretical Foundation of Data Mining

Several theories for the basis of data mining include the following:

1. **Data Reduction:** In this theory, the basis of data mining is to reduce the data representation. Data reduction trades accuracy for speed in response to the need to obtain quick approximate answers to queries on very large databases. Data reduction techniques include singular value decomposition (the driving element behind principal components analysis), wavelets, regression, log-linear models, histograms, clustering, sampling, and the construction of index trees.

2. **Data Compression:** According to this theory, the basis of data mining is to compress the given data by encoding in terms of bits, association rules, decision trees, clusters, and so on. Encoding based on the minimum description length principle states that the "best" theory to infer from a set of data is the one that minimizes the length of the theory and the length of the data when encoded, using the theory as a predictor for the data. This encoding is typically in bits.

3. **Pattern Discovery:** In this theory, the basis of data mining is to discover patterns occurring in the database, such as associations, classification models, sequential patterns, and so on. Areas such as machine learning, neural network, association mining, sequential pattern mining, clustering and several other subfields contribute to this theory,

4. **Probability Theory:** This is based on statistical theory. In this theory, the basis of data mining is to discover joint probability distributions of random variables, for example, Bayesian belief networks or hierarchical Bayesian models.

5. **Microeconomic View:** The microeconomic view considers data mining as the task of finding patterns that are interesting only to the extent that they can be used in the decision—making process of some enterprise (e.g. regarding marketing strategies and production plans). This view is one of utility, in which patterns are considered interesting if they can be acted on. Enterprises are regarded as facing optimization problems, where the object is to maximize the utility or value of a decision. In this theory, data mining becomes a nonlinear optimization problem.

6. **Inductive Databases:** According to this theory, a database schema consists of data and patterns that are stored in the database. Data mining is therefore the problem of performing induction on databases, where the task is to query the data and the theory (i.e. patterns) of the database. This view is popular among many researchers in database systems.

Steps in the Evolution of Data Mining:

Evolutionary Step	Business Question	Enabling Technologies	Product Providers	Characteristics
Data Collection (1960's)	"What was my total revenue in the last five years?"	Computers, tapes, disks.	IBM, CDC	Retrospective, static data delivery.
Data Access (1980s)	"What were unit sales in India last March"?	Relational, databases (RDBMS), Structured Query Language (SQL), ODBC.	Oracle, Sybase, Informix, IBM, Microsoft	Retrospective dynamic data delivery at record level.
Data Warehousing and Decision Support (1990s)	"What were unit sales in India last March? Drill down to Mumbai."	Online analytic processing (OLAP), multidimensional databases, data warehouses.	Pilot, Comshare, Arbor, Cognos, Microstrategy.	Retrospective, dynamic data delivery at multiple levels.
Data Mining (Emerging Today)	"What's likely to happen to Mumbai unit sales next month? Why?"	Advanced algorithms, multiprocessor computers, massive databases.	Pilot, Lockheed, IBM, SGI, numerous startups (nascent industry).	Prospective, proactive information delivery.

3.7 Data Mining   [April 16]

Definitions

"Data Mining is a set of processes related to analyzing and discovering useful, actionable knowledge buried deep beneath large volumes of data stores or data sets."

OR

"Data mining is the process of discovering hidden, previously unknown, and usable information from a large amount of data. This information is represented in a compact form, often referred to as a model."

OR

Time - referenced data when analyzed can also help in spotting the hidden trends between different associative data elements, which may not be obvious to the naked eye. This exploration activity is formed "data mining."

OR

"Data mining helps and users extract useful business information from large database."

Data mining is about extraction of interesting (non-trivial, implicit, previously unknown and potentially useful) information or patterns from data in large databases.

OR

Data mining as the process of discovering meaningful new correlations, patterns, and trends by digging into (mining) large amounts of data stored in warehouses, using artificial-intelligence (AI) and statistical and mathematical techniques.

Data Mining Elements

Data Mining Consists of Five Major Elements:

1. Extract, transform, and load transaction data onto the data warehouse system.
2. Store and manage the data in a multidimensional database system.
3. Provide data access to business analysts and information technology professionals.
4. Analyze the data by application software.
5. Present the data in a useful format, such as a graph or table.

Architecture of Data Mining

Based on databases, data warehouse of a typical data mining system may have the following components:

1. **Database, Data Warehouse or Other Information Repository:** This is one or a set of databases, data warehouses, spreadsheets or other kinds of information repositories. Data cleaning and data integration techniques may be performed on the data.

2. **Database or Data Warehouse Server:** The database or data warehouse server is responsible for fetching the relevant data, based on the user's data mining request.

3. **Knowledge Base:** This is the domain knowledge that is used to guide the search or evaluate the interestingness of resulting patterns. Such knowledge can include concept hierarchies, used to organize attributes or attribute values into different levels of abstraction. Knowledge such as user beliefs, which can be used to assess a pattern's interest based on its unpredictability, may also be included.

4. **Data Mining Engine:** This is essential to the data mining system and consists of a set of functional modules for tasks such as characterization, association, classification, cluster analysis and evolution and deviation analysis.

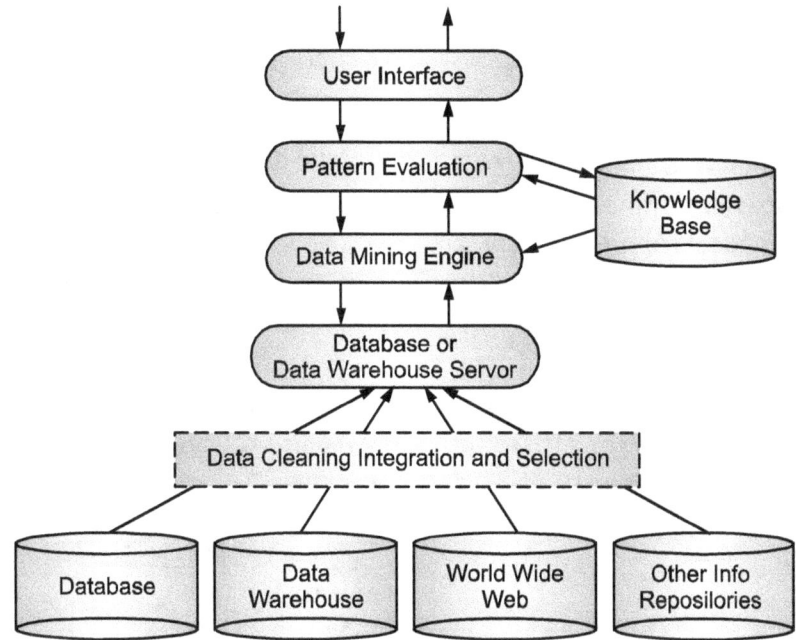

Fig. 3.15: Architecture of a typical Data Mining system

5. **Pattern Evaluation Module:** This component typically employs attractiveness which measures and interacts with the data mining modules so as to focus the search towards interesting patterns. For efficient data mining. it is highly recommended to push the evaluation of pattern attractiveness as deep as possible into the mining process so as to confine the search to only the interesting patterns.

6. **Graphical User Interface:** This module communicates between user and the data mining system, allowing the user interact with the system by specifying a data mining query or task, providing information to help focus the search and performing exploratory data mining, based on the intermediate dam mining results. In addition, this component allows the user to browse database and data warehouse schemes or data structures, evaluate mined patterns and visualize the patterns in different forms.

Data Mining Process

Data mining analysis tends to work from the data up and the best techniques are those developed with an orientation towards large volumes of data, making use of as much of the collected data as possible to arrive at reliable conclusions and decisions.

The Fig. 3.16 summarizes the some of the stages identified in data mining and knowledge discovery by Usama Fayyad and Evangelos Simoudis, two of leading exponents of this area.

The phases depicted start with the raw data and finish with the extracted knowledge, which was acquired as a result of the following stages:

1. **Selection:** Selecting or segmenting the data according to some criteria e.g., all those people who own a car; in this way subsets of the data can be determined.

2. **Preprocessing:** This is the data cleansing stage where certain information is removed which is deemed unnecessary and may slow down queries. Also the data is reconfigured to ensure a consistent format as there is a possibility of inconsistent formals because the data is drawn from several sources e.g. Sex may be recorded as f or m and also as 1 or 0.

3. **Transformation:** The data is not merely transferred across but transformed in that overlays may be added such as the demographic overlays commonly used in market research. The data is made useable and navigable.

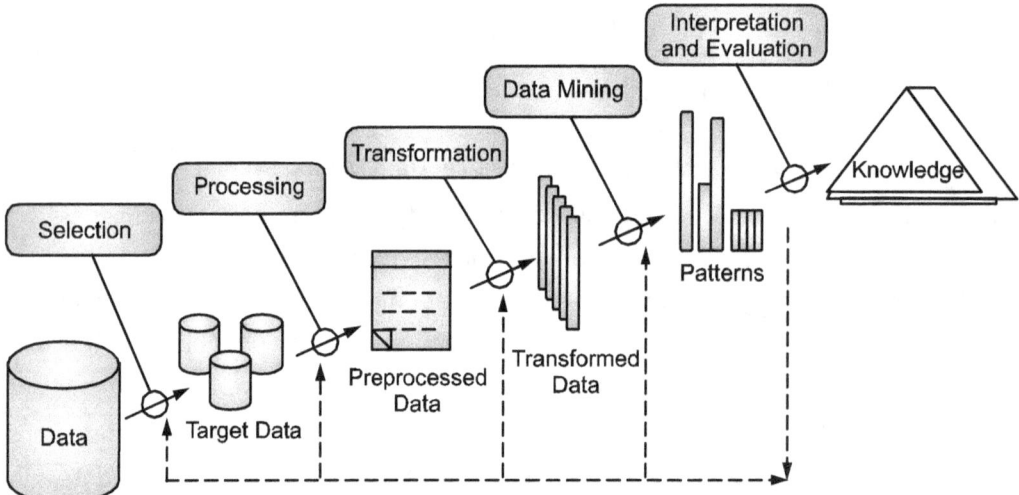

Fig. 3.16: Stages identified in Data Mining

4. **Data mining:** This stage is concerned with the extraction of patterns from the data. A pattern can be defined as given a set of facts (data) F, a language L, and some measure of certainty C. a pattern is a statement S in L that describes relationships among; a subset F_S of F with a certainly C such that S is simpler in some: sense than the enumeration of all the facts in F.

5. **Interpretation and evaluation:** The patterns identified by the system are interpreted into knowledge which can then be used to support human decision-making e.g., prediction and classification tasks, summarizing the contents of a database or explaining observed phenomena.

Example of Data Mining

A classical example of data mining is its use in retail sales departments. If a store tracks the purchases of a customer and notices that a customer buys a lot of silk ties, the data mining system will make a correlation between that customer and silk ties. The sales department will look at that information and may begin direct mail marketing of silk ties to that customer, or it may alternatively attempt to get the customer to buy a wider range of products. In this case, the data mining system used by the retail store discovered new information about the customer that was previously unknown to the company.

Uses of Data Mining

Data mining is cost effective in a wide variety of situation. It has been used successfully, for example, in the following situations.

1. Finding relationships among the items purchased by people in a simple visit to a store. Here, the reasoning goes, if people often buy A and B in the same visit, placing them in proximity might increase the sales of one or the other.

2. Finding relationships among items purchased by people in successive shopping trips. For example, people who purchase a barbeque grill may be candidates for charcoal or fire extinguishers. A store that knows this can offer coupons or discounts on those items. This is not as profitable as selling them at full price, but it's more profitable than having a competitor sell them.

3. Fraud detection in credit card used. How do the spending patterns of card thieves tend to differ from those of legitimate users?

4. Risk analysis for insurance policies. What combination of policy holder characteristics increase or decrease, the likelihood of future claims or fraud?

5. Medical diagnosis. What symptoms, which may not have a known common cause tend to be found with each other and with what underlying medical conditions?

6. Identifying customers who are likely to switch to another supplier. This function allows a vendor to make these customers special offers to induce them to remain, within the legal limits for preferential treatment of one customer over another.

Advantages of Data Mining   [Oct. 16]

The various advantages of data mining are discussed as follows

1. **Marketing/Retailing:** Data mining can aid direct marketers by providing them with useful and accurate trends about their customers purchasing behavior. Based on these trends, marketers can direct their marketing attentions to their customers with more precision.

    Retail stores can also benefit from data mining in similar ways. For example, through the trends provide by data mining, the store managers can arrange shelves, stock certain items, or provide a certain discount that will attract their customers.

2. **Banking/Crediting:** Data mining can assist financial institutions in areas such as credit reporting and loan information. For example, by examining previous customers with similar attributes, a bank can estimated the level of risk associated with each given loan.

    In addition, data mining can also assist credit card issuers in detecting potentially fraudulent credit card transaction.

3. **Law Enforcement:** Data mining can aid law enforcers in identifying criminal suspects as well as apprehending these criminals by examining trends in location, crime type, habit, and other patterns of behaviors.

4. **Researchers:** Data mining can assist researchers by speeding up their data analyzing process: thus, allowing those more time to work on other projects.

Disadvantages of Data Mining   **[Oct. 16]**

The various disadvantages of data mining are as follows:

1. **Privacy Issues:** Personal privacy has always been a major concern in this country. In recent years, with the widespread use of Internet, the concerns about privacy have increase tremendously. Because of the privacy issues, some people do not shop on Internet. They are afraid that somebody may have access to their personal information and then use that information in an unethical way; thus causing they harm.

2. **Security Issues:** Although companies have a lot of personal information about us available online, they do not have sufficient security systems in place to protect that information.

   For example, recently the Ford Motor credit company had to inform 13,000 of the consumers that their personal information including Social Security number, address, account number and payment history were accessed by hackers who broke into a database belonging to the Experian credit reporting agency. This incidence illustrated that companies are willing to disclose and share your personal information, but they are not taking care of the information properly. With so much personal information available, identity theft could become a real problem.

3. **Misuse of Information/Inaccurate Information:** Trends obtain through data mining intended to be used for marketing purpose or for some other ethical purposes, may be misused. Unethical businesses or people may used the information obtained through data mining to take advantage of vulnerable people or discriminated against a certain group of people. In addition, data mining technique is not a 100 percent accurate; thus mistakes do happen which can have serious consequence.

3.8 Functionalities

Data Mining Functionalities

While large-scale information technology has been evolving separate transaction and analytical systems, data mining provides a link between the two. Data mining software analyzes relationships and patterns in stored transaction data based on open-ended user queries. Several types of analytical software are available: statistical, machine learning, and neural networks. Generally, the following types of relationships are sought:

Prediction Methods: Use some variables to predict unknown or future values of other variables.

Sr. No.	Relationship	Method
1.	Classification	Predictive
2.	Clustering	Descriptive
3.	Association Rule Discovery	Descriptive
4.	Sequential Pattern Discovery	Descriptive
5.	Regression	Predictive
6.	Time Series Analysis	Predictive
7.	Prediction	Predictive
8.	Summarization	Descriptive

Description Methods: Find human-interpretable patterns that describe the data. In other words, a descriptive model identifies patterns of relationships in data.

The various types of relationships are discussed in the following paragraphs:

1. **Classification:** Classification maps the data into predefined groups or classes. Stored data is used to find data in predetermined groups. It is often referred to as supervised learning because the classes are determined before examining the data.

   For example, a restaurant chain could mine, customer purchase data to determine when customers visit and what they typically order. This Information could be used to increase traffic by having daily specials.

2. **Clustering:** Clustering is similar to classification except that the groups are not predefined, but rather defined by the data alone. Clustering is alternatively referred to as unsupervised learning or segmentation. It can be thought of as partitioning or segmenting the data into groups that might or might not be disjointed. The clustering is usually accomplished by determining the similarity among the data on predefined attributes. The most similar data are grouped Into clusters. Data items are grouped according to logical relationships or consumer preferences. For example, data can be mined to identify market segments or consumer affinities.

3. **Association Rules:** It is a model that identifies specific types of data associations. These associations are often used in the retail sales community to identify items that are frequently purchased together. Data can be mined to identify associations.

4. **Sequence Pattern Discovery:** Sequential analysis or sequence discovery is used to determine sequential patterns in data. In other words we can say that data is milled to anticipate behavior patterns and trends. These patterns are based on a time sequence of actions. These patterns are similar to associations in that data (or events) are found to be related, but the relationship is based on time.

   For example, an outdoor equipment retailer could predict the likelihood of a backpack being purchased based on a consumes purchase of sleeping bags and hiking shoes.

5. **Regression:** Regression is used to map a data item to a real valued prediction variable. In actuality, regression involves the learning of the function that does this mapping. Regression assumes that the target data fit into some known type of function (e.g., linear, logistic etc.,) and then determines the best function of this type that models the given data. Some type of error analysis is used to determine which function' is "best".

6. **Time Series Analysis:** With time series analysis, the value of an attribute is examined as it varies over time. The values usually are obtained as evenly spaced time points (daily, weekly, hourly, etc.)

7. **Prediction:** Many real-world data mining applications can be seen as predicting future data states based on past and current data. Prediction can be viewed as a type of classification. (Note: This is a data mining task that is different from the prediction model, although the prediction task is a type of prediction model.) The difference is that prediction is predicting a future state rather than a current state. Prediction applications include flooding, speech recognition, machine learning, and pattern recognition.

8. **Summarization:** Summarization maps data into subsets with associated simple descriptions. Summarization is also called characterisation or generalisation. It extracts or derives representative information about the database. This may be accomplished by actually retrieving portions of the data. Alternatively, summary type information can be derived from the data. The summarization briefly characterizes the contents of the database.

3.9 Data Cleaning   [April 16]

Noisy data is meaningless or corrupt data. In other words, any data that has been received, stored, or changed in such a manner that it cannot be read or used by the program that originally created it can be described as noisy.

Data could be noisy by following reasons:
- Incorrect attribute values
- Faulty data collection instruments
- Data entry problems
- Data transmission problems
- Technology limitation
- Inconsistency in naming convention

Noisy data unnecessarily increases the amount of storage space required and can also adversely affect the results of any data mining analysis.

We will deal with this noise in 4 ways.

1. Cross validation that helps one choose parameters, and also shows the influence of noise.
2. Identify and maybe remove outliers.

3. Directly considering uncertainty in data, and modeling its effect on the output.
4. Develop robust estimators to make the prediction inflexible to a moderate amount of noise.

Data cleaning, also called data cleansing or scrubbing, is a process used to determine inaccurate, incomplete, or unreasonable data. This improves the quality through correction of detected errors and omissions. Data quality problems are present in single data collections, such as files and databases.

Since a data warehouse is used for decision making, it is important that the data in the warehouse be correct. However, since large volumes of data from multiple sources are involved, there is a high probability of errors and exceptions in the data.. Therefore, tools that help to detect data exceptions and correct them can have a high payoff.

Some examples where data cleaning becomes necessary are: inconsistent field lengths, inconsistent descriptions, inconsistent value assignments, missing entries and violation of integrity constraints. Not surprisingly, optional fields in data entry forms are significant sources of inconsistent data.

There are three related, but somewhat different, classes of data cleaning tools:

1. **Data Migration Tools** allow simple transformation rules to be specified; e.g., "replace the string gender by sex". Warehouse Manager from Prism is an example of a popular tool of this kind.
2. **Data Scrubbing Tools** use domain-specific knowledge (e.g., postal addresses) to do the scrubbing of data. They often exploit parsing and fuzzy matching techniques to accomplish cleaning from multiple sources. Some tools make it possible to specify the "relative cleanliness" of sources. Tools such as Integrity and Trillum fall in this category.
3. **Data Auditing Tools** make it possible to discover rules and relationships (or to signal violation of stated rules) by scanning data. Thus, such tools may be considered variants of data mining tools. For example, such a tool may discover a suspicious pattern (based on statistical analysis) that a certain car dealer has never received any complaints.
4. The general framework for data cleaning is:
   - Define and determine error types.
   - Search and identify error instances.
   - Correct the errors.
   - Document error instances and error type.
   - Modify data entry procedures to reduce future errors.

Data Cleansing Process

Data cleansing is not an easy process. Not only is it time-consuming and requires a considerable amount of work, but also the expense of it is significant. This may be the reason why some organizations underestimate the importance of data cleansing, which can lead to numerous business failures as well as adverse effects caused by inaccurate or inconsistent data.

The data cleansing process includes a few stages:

- **Data Analysis:** In order to detect which kinds of errors and inconsistencies are to be removed, a detailed data analysis is required. In addition to a manual inspection of the data or data samples, analysis programs should be used to gain metadata about the data properties and detect data quality problems.

- **Definition of Transformation Workflow and Mapping Rules:** Depending on the number of data sources, their degree of heterogeneity and the "dirtyness" of the data, a large number of data transformation and cleaning steps may have to be executed. Sometime, a schema translation is used to map sources to a common data model; for data warehouses, typically a relational representation is used. Early data cleaning steps can correct single-source instance problems and prepare the data for integration. Later steps deal with schema/data integration and cleaning multi-source instance problems, e.g., duplicates. For data warehousing, the control and data flow for these transformation and cleaning steps should be specified within a workflow that defines the ETL (Extract, Transform, Load) process.

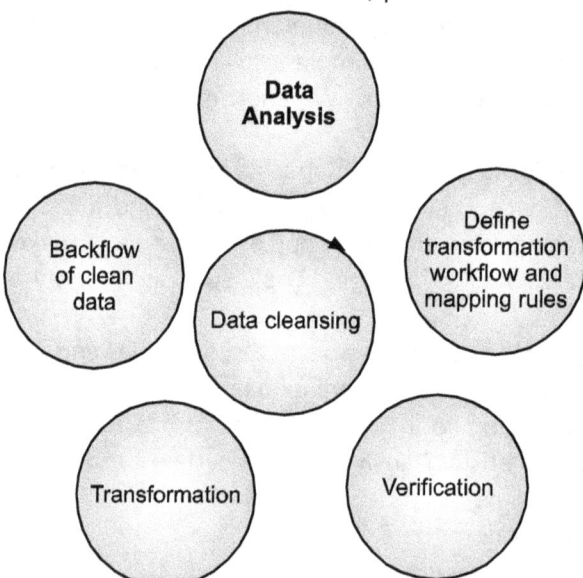

Fig. 3.17: Data Cleansing Stages

- **Verification:** The correctness and effectiveness of a transformation workflow and the transformation definitions should be tested and evaluated, e.g., on a sample or copy of the source data to improve the definitions if necessary. Multiple iterations of the analysis, design and verification steps may be needed e.g., since some errors only become apparent after applying some transformations.

- **Transformation:** Execution of the transformation steps is performed either by running the ETL workflow for loading and refreshing a data warehouse or during answering queries on multiple sources.

- **Backflow of cleaned data:** After (single-source) errors are removed, the cleaned data should also replace the dirty data in the original sources in order to give legacy applications and to avoid redoing the cleaning work for future data extractions. For data warehousing, the cleaned data is available from the data staging area.

Data cleansing is especially of great importance when a large amount of data is stored. The goal of corrective action on the dirty data then is to make any errors as insignificant as possible. Unless data cleansing is undertaken regularly, mistakes can accumulate and lead to decreasing the efficiency of work.

Data Cleaning Approaches:

- **Ajax** is an extensible and flexible framework attempting to separate the logical and physical level of data cleaning.
- **FraQL** is a declarative language supporting the specification of a data cleansing process.
- **Potter's Wheel** is an interactive data cleansing system that integrates data transformation and error detection using spread sheet like interface.

Benefits of Data Cleansing:

- Reduced duplicates
- Improved data quality and accuracy
- Improved operational efficiency & reduced hurdles
- Reduced risks, costs and turnaround
- Enables trend analysis and benchmarking
- Improved data security and accessibility

3.10 Data Integration   [April 16, Oct. 16]

Data integration technique combines data from multiple sources into a coherent store or a dataset. In other words, data integration is the integration of multiple databases, data cubes, or files. Data integration is the process of combining data residing at different sources and providing the user with a unified view of these data. It involves integrating multiple databases or files. Typical issues that need to be resolved are checking attribute names in different databases. Also, same records in multiple databases can have different values. Attributes can be in different units (height in feet or in meters). Some attributes may he redundant and thus not add any additional information.

One popular approach is Data warehousing. Here data from several sources are extracted, transformed, and loaded into source and can be queried with a single schema. This can be perceived architecturally as a tightly coupled approach because the data reside together in a single repository at query time. Problems with tight coupling can arise with the "freshness" of data, for example when an original data source is updated, but the warehouse still contains the older data and the ETL process needs to be executed again. It is also difficult to construct data warehouses when you only have a query interface to the data sources and no access to the full data. This problem frequently arises when integrating several commercial query services like travel or classified advertisement web applications.

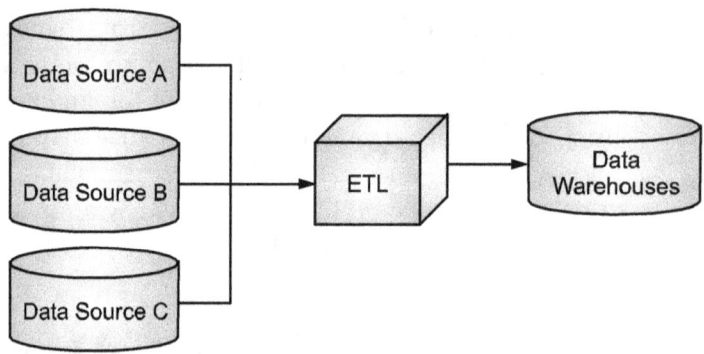

Fig. 3.18: Simple schematic for a data warehouse.

In above Fig. 3.18 the information from the source databases is extracted, transformed then loaded into the data warehouse.

Data integration systems are formally defined as a triple (G, S, M) where G is the global (or mediated) schema, S is the heterogeneous set of source schemes, and M is the mapping that maps queries between the source and the global schemas. Both G and S are expressed in languages over alphabets comprised of symbols for each of their respective relations. The mapping M consists of assertions between queries over G and queries over S. When users pose queries over the data integration system, they pose queries over G and the mapping then asserts connections between the elements in the global schema and the source schemes.

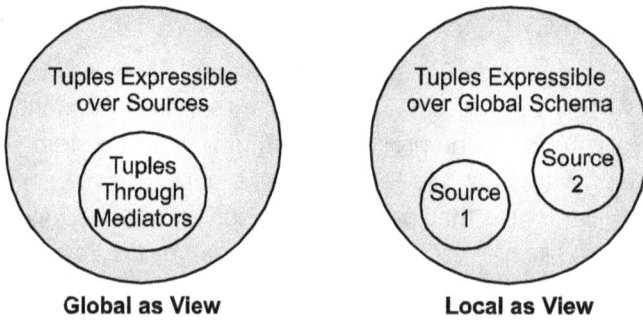

Fig. 3.19: Illustration of tuple space of the GAV and LAV mappings

A database over a schema is defined to be a set of sets, one for each relation (in a relational database). The database corresponding to the source schema S would be the set of sots of tuples for each of the heterogeneous data sources and is called the source database. Note that this single source database may actually be a collection of disconnected databases. The database corresponding to the virtual mediated schema G is called the

Issues to be considered in Data Integration:

There are a number of issues to consider during data integration.

1. Schema Integration:

Schema integration organization of a data is referred to as a *schema*. When multiple sources of data must be combined to retrieve information that is not contained entirely in either one, typically they do not have the same schemas. For example, database A's schema may store information about roads as "roads" and database B's schema may use "streets" for roads. In order for information from database A and database B to be integrated, they must resolve the fact that the same information is stored in different schemas.

2. Redundancy Detection:

Redundant data occur often when integration of multiple databases is done. An attribute (such as annual revenue, for instance) is redundant if it can be derived from another attribute or a group of other attributes. Redundancy can also occur when the same attribute may have different names in different databases. Correlation Analysis can be used to detect redundancies.

Given two attributes, such analysis can measure how strongly one attribute implies the other, based on the available data.

3. Detection and Resolution of Data Value Conflicts:

A third important issue in data integration is the detection and resolution of data value conflicts. For example, for the same real-world entity, attribute values from different sources may differ. This may be due to differences in representation, scaling or encoding. For instance, a weight attribute may be stored in metric units in one system and British imperial units in another. For a hotel chain, the price of rooms in different cities may involve not only different currencies but also different services (such as free breakfast) and taxes. An attribute in one system may be recorded at a lower level of abstraction than the "same" attribute in another.

When matching attributes from one database to another during integration, special attention must be paid to the structure of the data. This is to ensure that any attribute functional dependencies and referential constraints in the source system match those in the target system. For example, in one system, a discount may be applied to the order, whereas in another system it is applied to each individual line item within the order. If this is not caught before integration, items in the target system may be improperly discounted.

Data Integration Techniques

There are several organizational levels on which the integration can be performed. As we go down the level of automated integration increases.

- **Manual Integration or Common User Interface:** Users operate with all the relevant information accessing all the source systems or web page interface. No unified view of the data exists.

- **Application Based Integration:** Requires the particular applications to implement all the integration efforts. This approach is manageable only in case of very limited number of applications.

- **Middleware Data Integration:** Transfers the integration logic from particular applications to a new middleware layer. Although the integration logic is not implemented in the applications anymore, there is still a need for the applications to partially participate in the data integration.

- **Uniform Data Access or Virtual Integration:** Leaves data in the source systems and defines a set of views to provide and access the unified view to the customer across whole enterprise. For example, when a user accesses the customer information, the particular details of the customer are transparently acquired from the respective system. The main benefits of the virtual integration are nearly zero. Latency of the data updates propagation from the source system to the consolidated view, no need for separate store for the consolidated data. However, the drawbacks include limited possibility of data's history and version management, limitation to apply the method only to 'similar' data sources (e.g. same type of database) and the fact that the access to the user data generates extra load on the source systems which may not have been designed to accommodate.

- **Common Data Storage or Physical Data Integration:** Usually means creating a new system which keeps a copy of the data from the source systems to store and manage it independently of the original system. The most well known example of this approach is called Data Warehouse (DW). The benefits comprise data version management, combining data from very different sources (mainframes, databases, flat files, etc.). The physical integration, however, requires a separate system to handle the vast volumes of data.

- **Extract, Load, Transform (ELT) is a data integration process for transferring** raw data from a source server to a data warehouse on a target server and then preparing the information for downstream uses. ELT is a variation of the Extract, Transform, Load (ETL), a data integration process in which transformation takes place on an intermediate server before it is loaded into the target. In contrast, ELT allows raw data to be loaded directly into the target and transformed there. This capability is most useful for processing the large data sets required for business intelligence (BI) and big data analytics.

3.11 Data Transformation   [Oct. 16]

Data is normalized, aggregated and generalized in data transformation.

From an architectural perspective, you can transform your data in two ways:

- Multistage Data Transformation
- Pipelined Data Transformation
- Staging Area

Multistage Data Transformation: The data transformation logic for most data warehouses consists of multiple steps. For example, in transforming new records to be inserted into a sales table, there may be separate logical transformation steps to validate each dimension key.

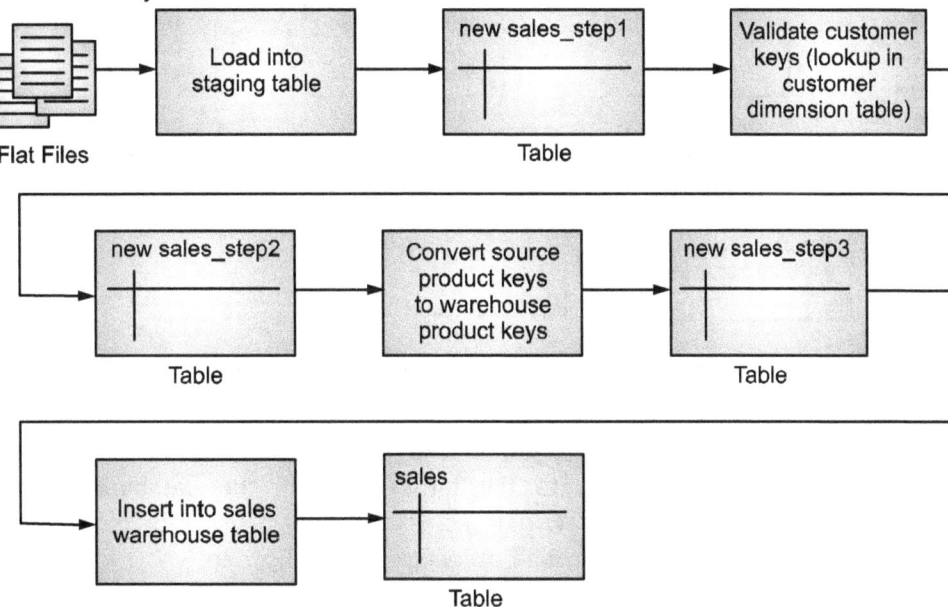

Fig. 3.20: Multistage Data Transformation

When using Oracle Database as a transformation engine, a common strategy is to implement each transformation as a separate SQL operation and to create a separate, temporary staging table (such as the tables new_sales_step1 and new_sales_step2 in Fig. 3.19 to store the incremental results for each step. This load-then-transform strategy also provides a natural checkpointing scheme to the entire transformation process, which enables the process to be more easily monitored and restarted. However, a disadvantage to multistaging is that the space and time requirements increase.

Pipelined Data Transformation

The ETL process flow can be changed dramatically and the database becomes an integral part of the ETL solution.

The new functionality renders some of the former necessary process steps obsolete while some others can be remodeled to enhance the data flow and the data transformation to become more scalable and non-interruptive. The task shifts from serial transform-then-load process (with most of the tasks done outside the database) or load-then-transform process, to an enhanced transform-while-loading.

Oracle offers a wide variety of new capabilities to address all the issues and tasks relevant in an ETL scenario. It is important to understand that the database offers toolkit functionality rather than trying to address a one-size-fits-all solution. The underlying database has to enable the most appropriate ETL process flow for a specific customer need, and not dictate or constrain it from a technical perspective.

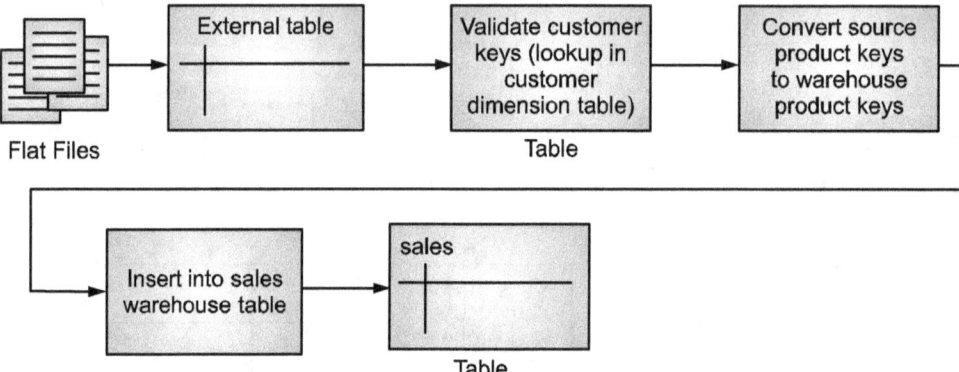

Fig. 3.21: Pipelined Data Transformation

Staging Area:

The overall speed of your load is determined by how quickly the raw data can be read from the staging area and written to the target table in the database. It is highly recommended that you stage your raw data across as many physical disks as possible to ensure the reading of the raw data is not a bottleneck during the load.

3.12 Data Reduction

A data warehouse may store terabytes of data. Complex data analysis/mining may take a very long time to run on the complete data set. Data reduction techniques can be applied to obtain a reduced representation of the data set that is much smaller in volume, but yet the same (or almost the same) analytical results i.e. it closely maintains the integrity of the original data. Data reduction technique obtain reduced representation in veins but produces the same or similar analytical results. That is, mining on the reduced data set should be more efficient yet produce the same (or almost the same) analytical results.

Strategies for data reduction include the following:

1. **Data cube aggregation**, where aggregation operations are applied to the data in the construction of a data cube.
2. **Attribute subset selection**, where irrelevant, weakly relevant or redundant attributes or dimension may be detected and removed.
3. **Dimension reduction**, where encoding mechanism are used to reduce the data set size.
4. **Numerosity reduction**, where the data replaced or estimated by alternative, smaller date representations such as parametric models (which need only the model parameters instead of the actual data) or nonparametric methods such as clustering, sampling and the use of histograms.

5. **Descretization and concept hierarchy,** where raw date values for attributes are replaced by ranges or higher conceptual levels. Data discretization is a form of numersoity reduction that is very useful for the automatic generation of concept hierarchies. Discretization and concept hierarchy generation are powerful tools for data mining, in that they allow the mining of data at multiple levels of abstraction.

3.13 Data Warehouse Vs Operational Database

We can divide IT systems into transactional (OLTP) and analytical (OLAP). In general we can assume that OLTP systems provide source data to data warehouses, whereas OLAP systems help to analyze it.

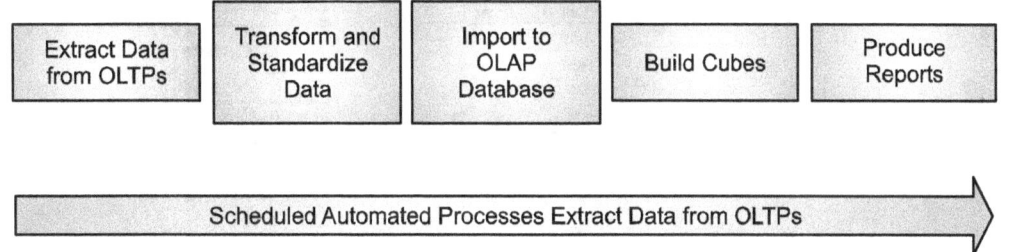

Fig. 3.22: Steps in the OLAP Creation Process

OLAP :

OLAP (Online Analytical Processing) allows business users to slice and dice data at will. Normally data in an organization is distributed in multiple data sources and are incompatible with each other.

A retail example: Point-of-sales data and sales made via call-centre or the Web are stored in different location and formats. It would a time consuming process for an executive to obtain OLAP reports such as - What are the most popular products purchased by customers between the ages 16 to 35?

Part of the OLAP implementation process involves:

• Extracting data from the various data repositories and making them compatible.

• Making data compatible involves ensuring that the meaning of the data in one repository matches all other repositories.

An example of incompatible data: Customer ages can be stored as birth date for purchases made over the web and stored as age categories (i.e. between 15 and 30) for in store sales.

OLTP: **[Oct. 16]**

It is not always necessary to create a data warehouse for OLAP analysis. Data stored by operational systems, such as point-of-sales, are in types of databases called OLTPs. OLTP (Online Transaction Process), databases do not have any difference from a structural perspective from any other databases. The main difference is the way in which data is stored.

Now a days major database vendor have started to incorporate OLAP modules within their database offering - Microsoft SQL Server 2000 with Analysis Services, Oracle with Express and Darwin, and IBM with DB2.

Examples of OLTPs can include ERP, CRM, SCM, Point-of-Sale applications, Call Center.

OLTPs are designed for optimal transaction speed. When a consumer makes a purchase online, they expect the transactions to occur instantaneously. With a database design, call data modeling, optimized for transactions the record 'Consumer name, Address, Telephone, Order Number, Order Name, Price, Payment Method' is created quickly on the database and the results can be recalled by managers equally quickly if needed.

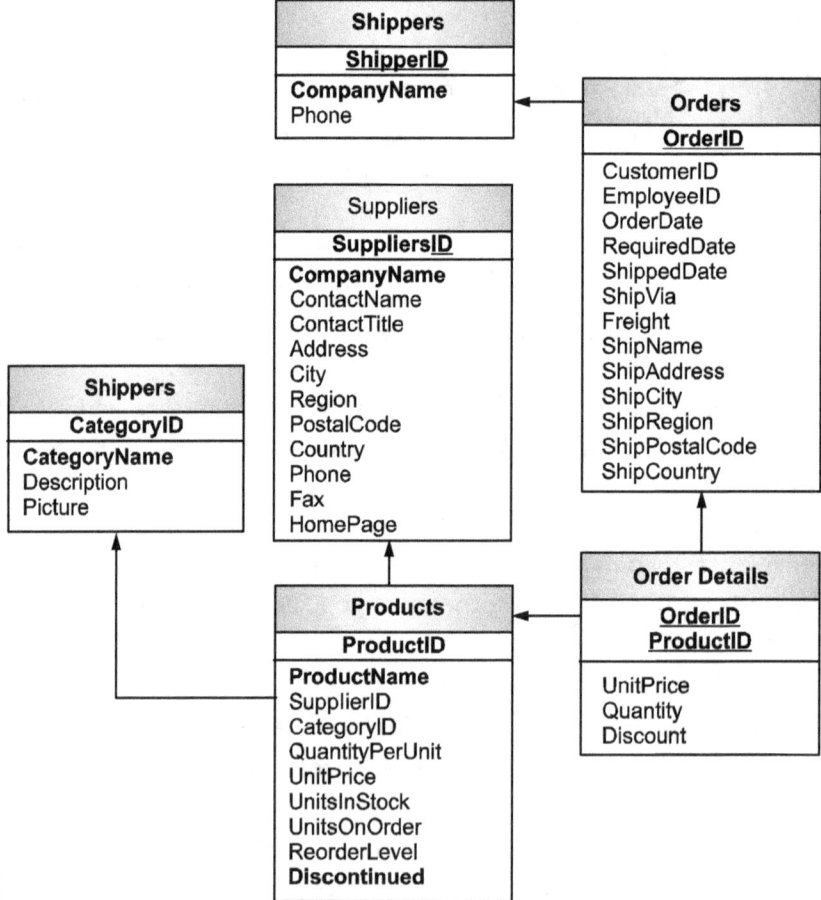

Fig. 3.23: Data Model for OLTP

Data are not typically stored for an extended period on OLTPs for storage cost and transaction speed reasons.

OLAPs have a different command from OLTPs. OLAPs are designed to give an overview analysis of what happened. Hence the data storage (i.e. data modeling) has to be set up differently. The most common method is called the star design.

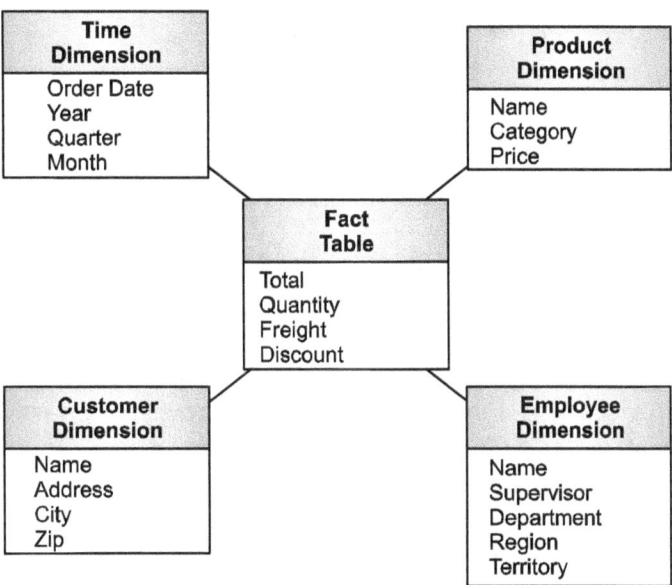

Fig. 3.24: Star Data Model for OLAP

The central table in an OLAP start data model is called the fact table. The surrounding tables are called the dimensions. Using the above data model, it is possible to build reports that answer questions such as:

- The supervisor that gave the most discounts.
- The quantity shipped on a particular date, month, year or quarter.
- In which zip code did product A sell the most.

To obtain answers, such as the ones above, from a data model OLAP *cubes* are created. OLAP cubes are not strictly cuboids - it is the name given to the process of linking data from the different dimensions. The cubes can be developed along business units such as sales or marketing. Or a giant cube can be formed with all the dimensions.

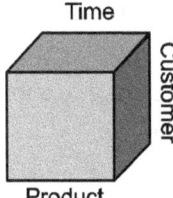

Fig. 3.25: OLAP Cube with Time, Customer and Product Dimensions

OLAP can be a valuable and rewarding business tool. Aside from producing reports, OLAP analysis can aid an organization evaluate balanced scorecard targets.

Sr. No.	OLAP System Online Analytical Processing (Data Warehouse)	OLTP System Online Transaction Processing (Operational Database)
1.	It involves historical processing of information.	It involves day-to-day processing.

contd. ...

2.	OLAP systems are used by knowledge workers such as executives, managers and analysts.	OLTP systems are used by clerks, DBAs, or database professionals.
3.	It is used to analyze the business.	It is used to run the business.
4.	It focuses on information out.	It focuses on Data in.
5.	It is based on Star Schema, Snowflake Schema and Fact Constellation Schema.	It is based on Entity Relationship Model.
6.	It focuses on information out.	It is application oriented.
7.	It contains historical data.	It contains current data.
8.	It provides summarized and consolidated data.	It provides primitive and highly detailed data.
9.	It provide summarized and multi-dimensional view of data.	It provides detailed and flat relational view of data.
10.	The number of users is in hundreds.	The number of users is in thousands.
11.	The number of records accessed in the millions.	The number of records accessed in tens.
12.	The database size is from 100 GB to 100 TB.	The database size is from 100 MB to 100 GB.
13.	These are highly flexible.	It provides high performance.

Practice Questions

1. Write a short note on Data Warehouse.
2. What is Multidimensional Data Model in Data Warehouse?
3. Define the terms
   (a) Fact Table in Multidimensional Data Model
   (b) Dimension Table in Multidimensional Data Model
   (c) OLAP Server architecture in Data Warehouse
   (d) Data Cleaning in Data Warehouse
4. Explain Architecture of Data Warehouse.
5. State the Implementation of Data Warehouse.
6. Explain: "Need of Foundation of Data Mining".
7. What is Data Mining? Describe its architecture.
8. Describe the process of Data Mining.
9. Describe the functionalities of Data Mining.
10. Write a short note on Data Integration and Transformation in Data warehouse.
11. Explain Data Reduction in Data Warehouse.

■■■

Chapter 4...

Network Security

Contents ...

4.1 Network Security   [Oct. 16]

Computer data often travels from one computer to another, leaving the safety of its protected physical surroundings. Once the data is out of hand, people with bad intention could modify or forge your data, either for enjoyment or for their own benefit.

Cryptography can reformat and transform our data, making it safer on its trip between computers. The technology is based on the essentials of secret codes, improved by modern mathematics that protects our data in powerful ways.

- **Computer Security:** This is a generic name for the collection of tools designed to protect data and to prevent hackers.

- **Internet Security:** These are measures to protect data during their transmission over a collection of interconnected networks.

- **Network Security:** These are measures to protect data during their transmission.

Network security is a specialized field in computer networking that involves securing a computer network infrastructure. Network security is typically handled by a network administrator or system administrator who implements the security policy, network software and hardware needed to protect a network and the resources accessed through the network from unauthorized access and also ensure that employees have adequate access to the network and resources to work.

Many network security threats today are spread over the Internet. The most common include:

- Viruses, worms, and Trojan horses
- Spyware and adware
- Zero-day attacks, also called zero-hour attacks
- Hacker attacks
- Denial of service attacks
- Data interception and theft
- Identity theft

How Does Network Security Work?

There is no single solution protects user from a variety of threats. You need multiple layers of security. If one fails, others still stand.

Network security is accomplished through hardware and software. The software must be constantly updated and managed to protect you from emerging threats.

A network security system usually consists of many components. All thesel components work together, which minimizes maintenance and improves security.

Network security components often include:

- Anti-virus and anti-spyware
- Firewall, to block unauthorized access to your network
- Intrusion prevention systems (IPS), to identify fast-spreading threats, such as zero-day or zero-hour attacks
- Virtual Private Networks (VPNs), to provide secure remote access

4.2 Cryptography   [April 16, Oct. 16]

Cryptography is the science of coding and decoding messages so as to keep these messages secure. Coding takes place using a key that ideally is known only by the sender and intended recipient of the message.

Cryptology (coming from the Greek words kryptos meaning "hidden" and logia denoting "study of", and hence is the study of hidden writings or secret writing) is a very broad subject. In its broadest sense, it is split into two sections: Cryptography (where graphein means "wriring") and Steganography (where (steganos) means "covered" or "protected").:

Historically, four groups of people have used and contributed to the art of cryptography: the military, the diplomatic corps, diarists, and lovers. Of these, the military has had the most important role and has shaped the field over the centuries. Within military organizations, the messages to be encrypted have traditionally been given to poorly-paid, low-level code clerks for encryption and transmission.

As the Internet and other forms of electronic communication become more common, electronic security is becoming increasingly important. Cryptography is used to protect e-mail messages, credit card information, and business data.

Cryptography systems can be broadly classified into symmetric-key systems that use a single key that both the sender and recipient have, and public-key systems that use two keys, a public key known to everyone and a private key that only the recipient of messages uses.

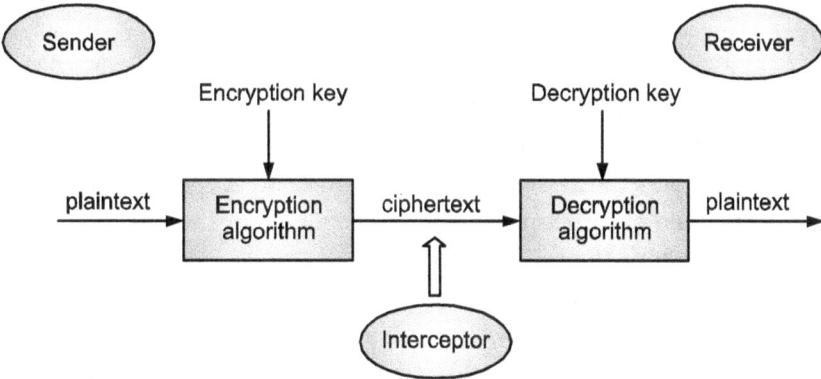

Fig. 4.1: Basic Model of Cryptography

Basic model of a cryptosystem

Above Fig. 4.1 shows a sender who wishes to transfer some data to a receiver in such a way that any party intercepting the transmitted data cannot determine the content. The various components of the model are as follows:

- **Plaintext** is the raw data to be protected during transmission from sender to receiver. Raw data of this type is sometimes referred to as being in the clear. This is also often (ambiguously) referred to as the message. The intention is that at the end of the process only the sender and the receiver will know the plaintext. In particular, an interceptor cannot determine the plaintext.

- **Cipher Text:** The art of protecting information by transforming /encrypting it into an unreadable format, called cipher text. Only those who possess a secret key can decipher (or decrypt) the message into plain text.

  Encrypted messages can sometimes be broken by cryptanalysis, also called code-breaking, although modern cryptography techniques are virtually unbreakable.That means, the ciphertext is not a secret and can be obtained by anyone who has access to the communication channel.

- **Encryption Algorithm** is the set of rules that determines, for any given plaintext and encryption key, a ciphertext. Using our terminology more appropriately, it is a cryptographic algorithm that takes as input a plaintext and an encryption key, and outputs a ciphertext. The choice of encryption algorithm must be agreed between sender and receiver.
- **Decryption Algorithm** is the set of rules that determines, for any given ciphertext and decryption key, a unique plaintext. In other words, it is a cryptographic algorithm that takes as input a ciphertext and a decryption key, and outputs a plaintext. The decryption algorithm essentially 'reverses' the encryption algorithm and is thus closely related to it.
- **Encryption Key** is a value that is known to the sender. The sender inputs the encryption key into the encryption algorithm along with the plaintext in order to compute the ciphertext. The receiver normally also knows the encryption key. It may or may not be known by an interceptor.
- **Decryption Key** is a value that is known to the receiver. The decryption key is related to the encryption key, but is not always identical to it. The receiver inputs the decryption key into the decryption algorithm along with the ciphertext in order to compute the plaintext. The interceptor must not know the decryption key. It may or may not be known by the sender.
- **Interceptor** is an entity other than the sender or receiver who attempts to determine the plaintext. The interceptor will be able to see the ciphertext. The one piece of information that the interceptor must never know is the decryption key.

Cryptanalysis

The art and science of breaking the cipher text is known as Cryptanalysis. Cryptanalysis is the sister branch of cryptography and they both co-exist. The strategy used by the cryptanalysis depends on the nature of the encryption scheme and the information available to the cryptanalyst.

There are various types of cryptanalytic attacks based on the amount of information known to the cryptanalyst.

- **Cipher Text Only:** A copy of cipher text alone is known to the cryptanalyst.
- **Known Plaintext:** The cryptanalyst has a copy of the cipher text and the corresponding plaintext.
- **Chosen Plaintext:** The cryptanalysts gains temporary access to the encryption machine. They cannot open it to find the key, however; they can encrypt a large number of suitably chosen plaintexts and try to use the resulting cipher texts to deduce the key.
- **Chosen Cipher Text:** The cryptanalyst obtains temporary access to the decryption machine, uses it to decrypt several string of symbols, and tries to use the results to deduce the key.

Steganography   [Oct. 16]

Steganography is similar but adds another dimension to Cryptography. In this method, people not only want to protect the secrecy of an information by concealing it, but they also want to make sure any unauthorized person gets no evidence that the information even exists.

A plaintext message may be hidden in any one of the two ways. The methods of steganography hides the existence of the message, whereas the methods of cryptography render the message jumbled to outsiders by various transformations of the text.

For example:

(i)   the sequence of first letters of each word of the overall message spells out the real (Hidden) message.

(ii) Subset of the words of the overall message is used to convey the hidden message. Various other techniques have been used historically, some of them are

- **Character Marking:** Selected letters of printed or typewritten text are overwritten in pencil. The marks are ordinarily not visible unless the paper is held to an angle to bright light.

- **Invisible Ink:** A number of substances can be used for writing but leave no visible trace until heat or some chemical is applied to the paper.

- **Pin Punctures:** Small pin punctures on selected letters are ordinarily not visible unless the paper is held in front of the light.

- **Typewritten Correction Ribbon:** Used between the lines typed with a black ribbon, the results of typing with the correction tape are visible only under a strong light.

Drawbacks of steganography:

- Requires a lot of overhead to hide a relatively few bits of information.
- Once the system is discovered, it becomes virtually worthless.

Cryptographic Attacks

In the present era, not only business but almost all the aspects of human life are driven by information. Hence, it has become critical to protect useful information from malicious activities such as attacks. Let us consider the types of attacks to which information is typically subjected to. Cryptography provides many tools and techniques for implementing cryptosystems capable of preventing most of the attacks.

Attacks are typically categorized based on the action performed by the attacker. An attack thus can be passive or active.

Passive Attacks

The main goal of a passive attack is to obtain unauthorized access to the information. For example, actions such as intercepting the communication channel can be regarded as passive attack.

These actions are passive in nature, as they neither affect information nor disrupt the communication channel. A passive attack is often seen as stealing information. The only difference in stealing physical goods and stealing information is that theft of data still leaves the owner in possession of that data. So Passive information attack is more dangerous than stealing of goods, as information theft may go unnoticed by the owner.

Active Attacks

An active attack involves changing the information in some way by conducting some process on the information. For example,

- Modifying the information in an unauthorized manner.
- Initiating unintended or unauthorized transmission of information.
- Alteration of authentication data such as originator name or timestamp associated with information.
- Unauthorized deletion of data.
- Denial of access to information for legitimate users (denial of service).

Basic Principles of Cryptography

1. **Encryption:** In a simplest form, encryption is to convert the data in some unreadable form. This helps in protecting the privacy while sending the data from sender to receiver. On the receiver side, the data can be decrypted and can be brought back to its original form. The reverse of encryption is called as decryption. The concept of encryption and decryption requires some extra information for encrypting and decrypting the data. This information is known as key. There may be cases when same key can be used for both encryption and decryption while in certain cases, encryption and decryption may require different keys.

2. **Authentication:** This is another important principle of cryptography. Authentication ensures that the message was originated from the originator claimed in the message.

3. **Integrity:** Now, one problem that a communication system can face is the loss of integrity of messages being sent from sender to receiver. This means that cryptography should ensure that the messages that are received by the receiver are not altered anywhere on the communication path. This can be achieved by using the concept of cryptographic hash.

Types of Cryptography

There are three types of cryptography techniques:

- Symmetric key or Secret key Cryptography
- Asymmetric key or Public key cryptography
- Hash Functions

1. Symmetric Key or Secret Key Cryptography

This type of cryptography technique uses just a single key. The sender applies a key to encrypt a message while the receiver applies the same key to decrypt the message. Since only single key is used so we say that this is a symmetric encryption.

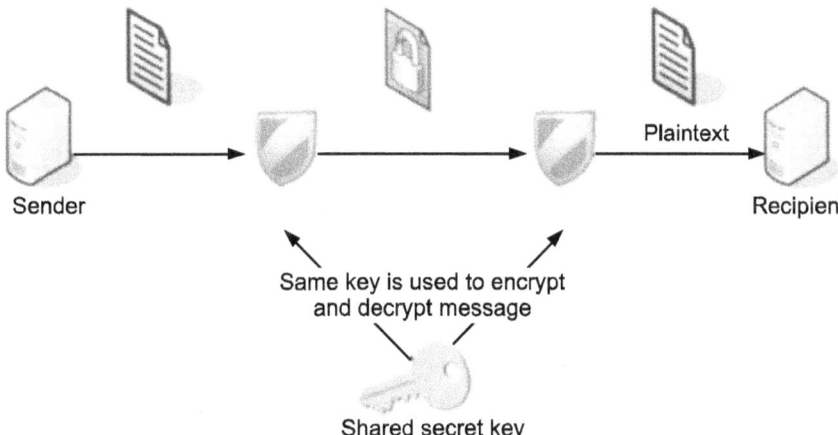

Fig. 4.2: Symmetric Key Cryptography

Types of symmetric algorithm(symmetric key algorithm): Symmetric cryptosystems are also sometimes referred to as secret key cryptosystems.

A few well-known examples of symmetric key encryption methods are – Digital Encryption Standard (DES), Triple-DES (3DES), IDEA, and BLOWFISH.

Symmetric algorithms can be divided into two types - block ciphers and stream ciphers.

- **Block Ciphers:** In this scheme, the plain binary text is processed in blocks of bits at a time; that means a block of plaintext bits is selected, a series of operations is performed on this block to generate a block of cipher text bits. The number of bits in a block is fixed. i.e. block ciphers take a number of bits (typically 64 bits in modern ciphers) and encrypt them as a single unit.

  For example, the schemes DES and AES have block sizes of 64 and 128, respectively.

- **Stream Ciphers:** In this scheme, the plaintext is processed one bit at a time i.e. one bit of plaintext is taken and a series of operations are performed on it to generate one bit of cipher text. Stream ciphers are block ciphers with a block size of one bit.

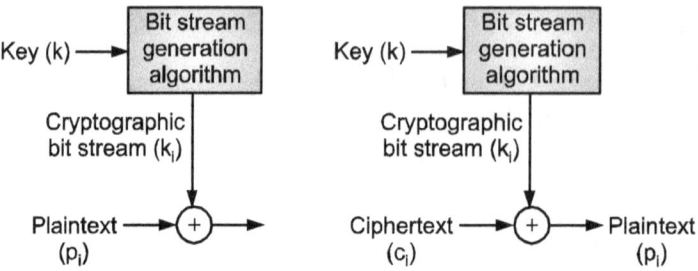

(a) Stream Cipher using algorithmic bit stream generator

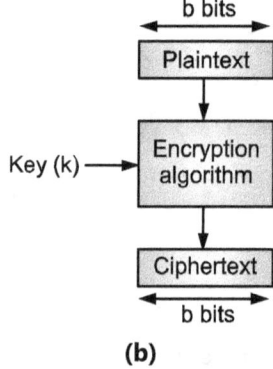

(b)

Fig. 4.3: Block vs Steam Ciphers

The salient features of Cryptography System based on symmetric key encryption are:

- Persons using symmetric key encryption must share a common key prior to exchange of information.
- Keys are recommended to be changed regularly to prevent any attack on the system.
- A robust mechanism needs to exist to exchange the key between the communicating parties. As keys are required to be changed regularly, this mechanism becomes expensive and cumbersome.
- In a group of n people, to enable two-party communication between any two persons, the number of keys required for group is $n \times (n - 1)/2$.
- Length of Key (number of bits) in this encryption is smaller and hence, process of encryption-decryption is faster than asymmetric key encryption.
- Processing power of computer system required to run symmetric algorithm is less.

2. Asymmetric key or Public Key Cryptography

This type of cryptography technique involves two key cryptosystem in which a secure communication can take place between receiver and sender over insecure communication channel. Since a pair of keys are applied here so this technique is also known as Asymmetric Encryption.

In this method, each party has a private key and a public key. The private is secret and is not revealed while the public key is shared with all those whom you want to communicate with. If person A wants to send a message to person B, then person A will encrypt it with person B's public key and B can decrypt the message with its private key.

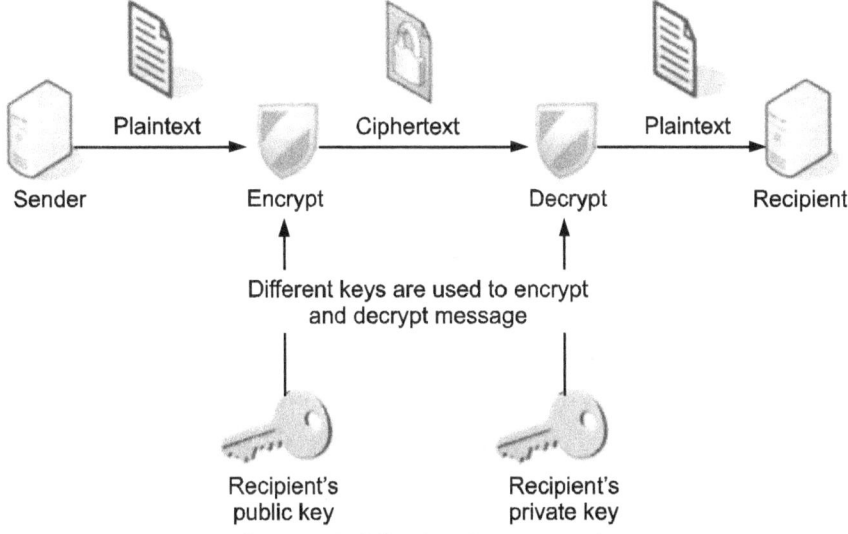

Fig. 4.4: Public Key Cryptography

This is what we use when we setup public key authentication in opens to login from one server to another server in the backend without having to enter the password.

Asymmetric algorithms:

The idea of asymmetric algorithms was first published 1976 by Diffie and Hellmann.

Asymmetric algorithms use pairs of keys. One is used for encryption and the other one for decryption. The decryption key is typically kept secretly, therefore called ``private key'' or ``secret key'', while the encryption key is spread to all who might want to send encrypted messages, therefore called ``public key''. Everybody having the public key is able to send encrypted messages to the owner of the secret key. The secret key can't be reconstructed from the public key.

Asymmetric algorithms seem to be ideally suited for real-world use, As the secret key does not have to be shared, the risk of getting known is much smaller. Every user only needs to keep one secret key in secrecy and a collection of public keys, that only need to be protected against being changed. With symmetric keys, every pair of users would need to have an own shared secret key. Well-known asymmetric algorithms are RSA, DSA.

There are a number of other secret-key cryptography algorithms that are also in use today like CAST-128 (Block Cipher), RC2 (Block Cipher) RC4 (Stream Cipher), RC5 (Block Cipher), Blowfish (Block Cipher), Two fish (Block Cipher). In 1997, NIST initiated a process to develop a new secure cryptosystem for U.S. government applications. The result, the Advanced Encryption Standard (AES), became the official successor to DES in December 2001.

Difference between algorithms:

Symmetric algorithms (Symmetric-key algorithm) use the same key for Encryption and Decryption. Symmetric algorithms require that both the sender and the receiver agree on a key before they can exchange messages securely. Symmetric-key algorithms can be divided into stream algorithms (Stream ciphers) and Block algorithms (Block ciphers). Asymmetric algorithms use a different key for encryption and decryption, and the decryption key cannot be derived from the encryption key.

Symmetric-key algorithms are generally much less computationally intensive than asymmetric key algorithms. In practice, this means that a quality asymmetric key algorithm is hundreds or thousands of times slower than a quality symmetric key algorithm.

New symmetric key algorithm

Encryption algorithm

Step 1: Generate the ASCII value of the letter

Step 2: Generate the corresponding binary value of it. [Binary value should be 8 digits e.g. for decimal 32 binary number should be 00100000

Step 3: Reverse the 8 digit's binary number

Step 4: Take a 4 digits divisor (>=1000) as the Key

Step 5: Divide the reversed number with the divisor

Step 6: Store the remainder in first 3 digits and quotient in next 5 digits (remainder and quotient wouldn't be more than 3 digits and 5 digits long respectively. If any of these are less then 3 and 5 digits respectively we need to add required number of 0's (zeros) in the left hand side.

So, this would be the cipher text i.e. encrypted text. Now store the remainder in first 3 digits and quotient in next 5 digits.

Example Let, the character is "T". Now according to the steps we will get the following:

Step 1: ASCII of "T" is 84 in decimal.

Step 2: The Binary value of 84 is 1010100. Since it is not an 8 bit binary number we need to make it 8 bit number as per the encryption algorithm. So it would be 01010100 0 1 0 1 0 1 0 0

Step 3: Reverse of this binary number would be 00101010 0 0 1 0 1 0 1 0

Step 4: Let 1000 as divisor i.e. Key

Step 5: Divide 00101010 (dividend) by 1000(divisor)

Step 6: The remainder would be 10 and the quotient would be 101. So as per the algorithm the ciphertext would be 01000101 which is ASCII 69 in decimal i.e. "E" 0 1 0 0 0 1 0 1

Decryption algorithm

Step 1: Multiply last 5 digits of the ciphertext by the Key

Step 2: Add first 3 digits of the ciphertext with the result produced in the previous step

Step 3: If the result produced in the previous step i.e. step 2 is not an 8-bit number we need to make it an 8- bit number

Step 4: Reverse the number to get the original text i.e. the plain text

3. Hash Functions

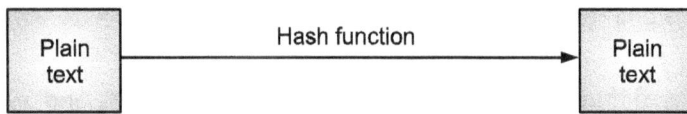

Fig. 4.5: Hash Function

Rather it uses a fixed length hash value that is computed on the basis of the plain text message.

A *cryptographic hash function* technique does not involve any key. This takes any amount of data and applies an algorithm that transforms it into a fixed-size output value. For a cryptographic hash function to be useful, it has to be extremely difficult or impossible to reconstruct the original data from the hash value and it must be extremely unlikely that the same output value could result from any other input data. Hash functions are used to check the integrity of the message to ensure that the message has not be altered, compromised or affected by virus.

The most common hash function you will use is SHA-1, an algorithm developed and published by the U.S. Government. There are also a number of more exotic algorithms such as SHA-2, elliptic-curve-based algorithms, and so on.

So we see that how different types of cryptography techniques (described above) are used to implement the basic principles that we discussed earlier. In the future article of this series, we'll cover more advanced topics on Cryptography.

4.3 Substitution Ciphers   [April 16, Oct. 16]

Substitution Ciphers are probably the most common form of cipher. They work by replacing each letter of the plaintext (and sometimes puntuation marks and spaces) with another letter (or possibly even a random symbol).

A monoalphabetic substitution cipher, also known as a simple substitution cipher, relies on a fixed replacement structure. That is, the substitution is fixed for each letter of the alphabet. Thus, if "a" is encrypted to "R", then every time we see the letter "a" in the plaintext, we replace it with the letter "R" in the ciphertext.

A simple example is where each letter is encrypted as the next letter in the alphabet: "a simple message" becomes "B TJNQMF NFTTBHF".

In general, when performing a simple substitution manually, it is easiest to generate the ciphertext alphabet first, and encrypt by comparing this to the plaintext alphabet. The table below shows how one might choose to, and we will, lay them out for this example.

Plaintext Alphabet	a	b	c	d	e	f	g	h	i	j	k	l	m	n	o	p	q	r	s	t	u	v	w	x	y	z
Ciphertext Alphabet	B	C	D	E	F	G	H	I	J	K	L	M	N	O	P	Q	R	S	T	U	V	W	X	Y	Z	A

The ciphertext alphabet for the cipher where you replace each letter by the next letter in the alphabet.

There are many different monoalphabetic substitution ciphers and each letter can be encrypted to any symbol.

4.4 Transposition Ciphers

Transposition Ciphers are a bit different to Substitution Ciphers. Whereas Substitution ciphers replace each letter with a different letter or symbol to produce the ciphertext, in a Transposition cipher the letters are just moved around. The letters or words of the plaintext are reordered in some way, fixed by a given rule (the key).

One example of a transposition cipher, is to reverse the order of the letters in a plaintext. So "a simple example" becomes "ELPMAXE ELPMIS A". Another, similar, way to encrypt a message would be to reverse the letters of each word, but not the order in which the words are written. In this case "a simple example" becomes "A ELPMIS ELPMAXE". Both of these are available in the activity at the bottom of the page.

Polyalphabetic Cipher: The first known polyalphabetic cipher was the Alberti Cipher invented by Leon Battista Alberti in around 1467. He used a mixed alphabet to encrypt the plaintext, but at random points he would change to a different mixed alphabet, indicating the change with an uppercase letter in the ciphertext. In order to utilise this cipher, Alberti used a cipher disc to show how plaintext letters are related to ciphertext letters.

Fig. 4.6: An example of a simple cipher disc for the English alphabet

For example, when the disc on the left is set as shown, we see that the plaintext letter "e" (on the outside ring) is encrypted to "Z" (on the inside ring).

Alberti would use this setting for a few letters of the message, and then rotate the inner disc to a different setting for the next few letters and so on.

For example we shall encrypt the plaintext "leon battista alberti". To keep with the convention of writing ciphertext in uppercase, we shall invert Alberti's own rule, and use lowercase letters to signify the change.

We start by referencing the starting position of the cipher disc, which in this case is "a" is encrypted as "V", so we start the ciphertext with a lowercase "v". We then encrypt the first few letters as a Caesar Shift, using the ciphertext alphabet given below.

Plaintext Alphabet	a	b	c	d	e	f	g	h	i	j	k	l	m	n	o	p	q	r	s	t	u	v	w	x	y	z
Ciphertext Alphabet	V	W	X	Y	Z	A	B	C	D	E	F	G	H	I	J	K	L	M	N	O	P	Q	R	S	T	U

The first shift used, as shown in the disc above.

Plaintext: leonbat...

Ciphertext: vGZJIWVOg...

The uppercase letters above encrypt the plaintext letters given. The "v" indicates the starting position of the disc, and the "g" indicates that we need to change the position so that "G" is beneath "a". We then get the new ciphertext alphabet as shown below.

Plaintext Alphabet	a	b	c	d	e	f	g	h	i	j	k	l	m	n	o	p	q	r	s	t	u	v	w	x	y	z
Ciphertext Alphabet	G	H	I	J	K	L	M	N	O	P	Q	R	S	T	U	V	W	X	Y	Z	A	B	C	D	E	F

The second shift used, when "a" is encrypted to "G".

4.5 One Time Pads   [April 16]

It is an unbreakable cryptosystem. It represents the message as a sequence of 0s and 1s. This can be accomplished by writing all numbers in binary, for example, or by using ASCII. The key is a random sequence of 0"s and 1"s of same length as the message. Once a key is used, it is discarded and never used again.

The system can be expressed as Follows:

Ci = Pi +Ki Ci - ith binary digit of cipher text

Pi - ith binary digit of plaintext

Ki - ith binary digit of key

Exclusive OR operation.

Thus the cipher text is generated by performing the bitwise XOR of the plaintext and the key. Decryption uses the same key. Because of the properties of XOR, decryption simply involves the same bitwise operation: Pi = Ci Ki

Example,   plaintext = 0 0 1 0 1 0 0 1 Key = 1 0 1 0 1 1 0 0

------------------- ciphertext = 1 0 0 0 0 1 0 1

Advantage:

- Encryption method is completely unbreakable for a cipher text only attack.

Disadvantages:

- It requires a very long key which is expensive to produce and expensive to transmit. Once a key is used, it is dangerous to reuse it for a second message; any knowledge on the first message would give knowledge of the second.

Uses of One-Time Pad:

In the modern-age, any digital storage device (USB stick, iPod, iPhone, Android phone, CD/DVD, portable hard drive, etc) can be used to store and/or transport one-time pad information. Although the one-time pad system has a number of physical security barriers to effective use, it continues to have practical interest in scenarios where a computation by hand is useful for a given situation in intelligence circles. In these cases, pads can be delivered by hand via a "handler" or centralized point of contact to agents in the field, or via secure phone or computer connection.

The cipher technique has also proved useful in cases where two people work in a secure environment and one must travel to a less secure location for work. In this case, the person traveling can take the one-time pad with them on the road and minimize the risk of interception of the pad by an adversary. Other uses of the pad include: super-encryption, quantum key distribution, and in educational contexts.

Historical Uses of One-Time Pad:

Since the early 1900s, one-time pads have been used by diplomatic services throughout the world. In the early 1920s, the Weimar Republic Diplomatic Service commenced using the method. In this same timeframe, the Soviet Union suffered several embarrassing cases of encrypted messages being made public and adopted the use of the pads in the 1930s. The Soviet KGB continued to use the method throughout the early Cold War with several cases of agents such as Colonel Rudolf Abel and the Krogers being arrested in the 1950s and 1960s with one-time pads in their possession.

During World War II, the British Special Operations Executive leveraged one-time-pads to encode message traffic sent between the agency's offices. Agent use of the system was introduced later in the war along with one-time tape cipher machines (Noreen and Rockex). One-time tape systems 5-UCO and SIGTOT were introduced by the United States NSA for use in sending and receiving intelligence traffic. The KW-26 electronic cipher was introduced in 1957 for use by the United States intelligence agencies.

The UK Army uses the BATCO tactical communications code that is based on a one-time pad system using pencil and paper. Key material is provided on paper sheets that are kept in a plastic wallet that uses a sliding indicator to show the last key used in the pad. When deployed in the field, new sheets for the codebook are provided daily, and used on voice nets. When transmitted via voice, ciphertext is verbally read over the net.

4.6 Two Fundamental Cryptographic Principles

1. Redundancy:

The first cryptographic principle is that all encrypted messages must contain some redundancy i.e. information not needed to understand the message.

All encrypted messages decrypt to something. Redundancy lets receiver recognize a valid message. But redundancy helps attackers break the design.

2. Freshness:

- The second cryptographic principle is that some measures must be taken to ensure that each message received can be recent message.

- Some method is needed to foil replay attacks. Without a way to check if messages are fresh then old messages can be copied and resent. For example, add a date stamp to messages.

- The receiver can then just keep messages around for 10 seconds, to compare newly arrived messages to previous ones to filter out duplicates. Messages older than 10 seconds can be thrown out, since any replays sent more than 10 seconds later will be rejected as too old.

4.7 Symmetric Key Algorithm

As shown in Fig. 4.7, a Symmetric Key Algorithm is an algorithm used for cryptography using the same cryptographic key to encrypt and decrypt the message.

Symmetric Key Algorithm:

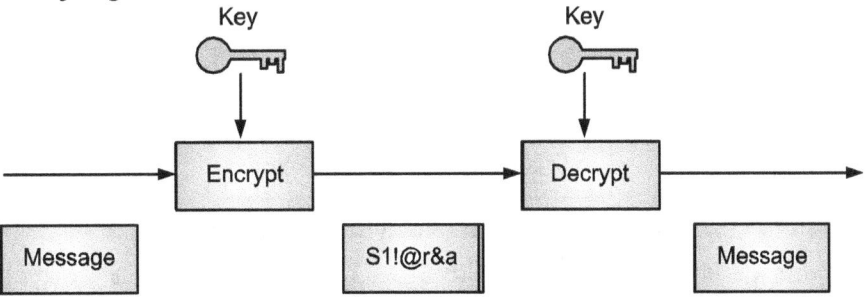

Fig. 4.7: Symmetric Key Algorithm

The sender and the receiver must therefore share the same secret key before they can communicate securely. The security of a symmetric algorithm rests in the secrecy of the key. Anybody who has the key can encrypt and decrypt messages.

There are two different techniques in symmetric encryption cryptography: stream ciphers and block ciphers. Stream ciphers encrypt the bits of the messages one at a time and block ciphers take a number of bits and encrypt them as a single unit. Blocks of 64 bits are a commonly used. The Advanced Encryption Standard (AES), which is discussed in more detail in subsequent sections, uses block sizes with a multiple of 32 bits.

4.8 DES-The Data Encryption Standard   [Oct. 16]

The Data Encryption Standard (DES) has been the worldwide encryption standard for a long time. IMB developed DES in 1975, and it has held up remarkably well against years of cryptanalysis. DES is a symmetric encryption algorithm with a fixed key length of 56 hits. The algorithm is still good, but because of the short key length, it is susceptible to brute-force attacks that have sufficient resources.

DES usually operates in block mode, whereby it encrypts data in 6A-bit blocks. The same algorithm and key are used for both encryption and decryption.

Because DES is based on simple mathematical function, it can be easily implemented and accelerated in hardware.

Triple Data Encryption Standard

With advances in computer processing power, the original 56-bit DES key became too short to face an attacker with even a limited budget. One way of increasing the effective key length of DES without changing the well-analyzed algorithm itself is to use the same algorithm with different keys several times in a row.

The technique of applying DES three times in a row to a plain text block is called Triple DES (3DES). The 3DES technique is shown in Fig. 4.8. Brute-force attacks on 3DES are considered unfeasible today. Because the basic algorithm has been tested in the field for more than 25 years, it is considered to be highly trustworthy.

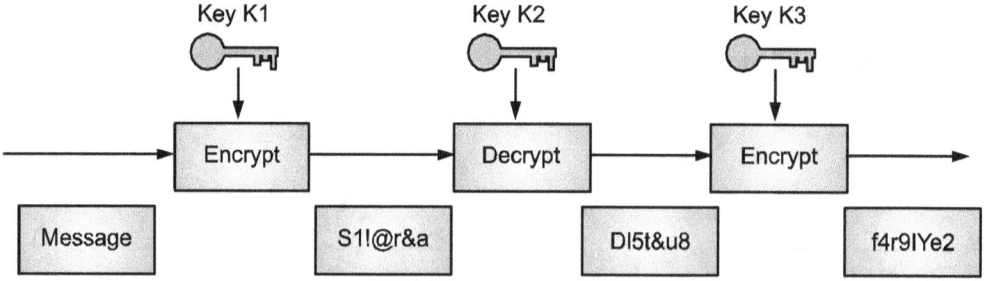

Fig. 4.8: Triple Data Encryption Standard

When a message is to be encrypted with 3DFS, a method called EDE (Encrypt-Decrypt-Encrypt) is used.

The EDE method is described in the following list:

Step 1: The message is encrypted with the first 56-bit key, K1.

Step 2: The data is decrypted with a second 56-bit key, K2.

Step 3: The data is again encrypted with the third 56-bit key, K3.

The EDE procedure provides encryption with an effective key length of 168 bits. If keys K1 and K3 are equal (as in some implementations), a less secure encryption of 112 (56 + 56) bits is achieved.

To decrypt the message, you must use the following procedure, which is the opposite of the EDE method:

Step 1: Decrypt the ciphertext with key K3.

Step 2: Encrypt the data with key K2.

Step 3: Finally, decrypt the data with key K1.

Encrypting the data three tittles with three different keys does not significantly increase security. The EDE method has to be used. Encrypting three times in a row with different 56-bit keys equals an effective 58-bit key length and not the full 128-bit, as expected.

Key Length:

Key Length in DES:

- In the DES specification, the key length is 64-bit.
- 8 bytes; in each byte, the 8th bit is a parity-check bit.

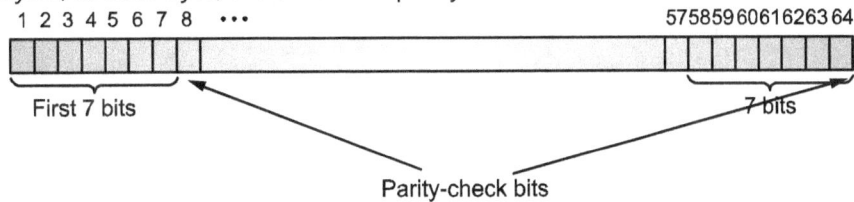

Fig. 4.9: Key Length in DES

Algorithm:

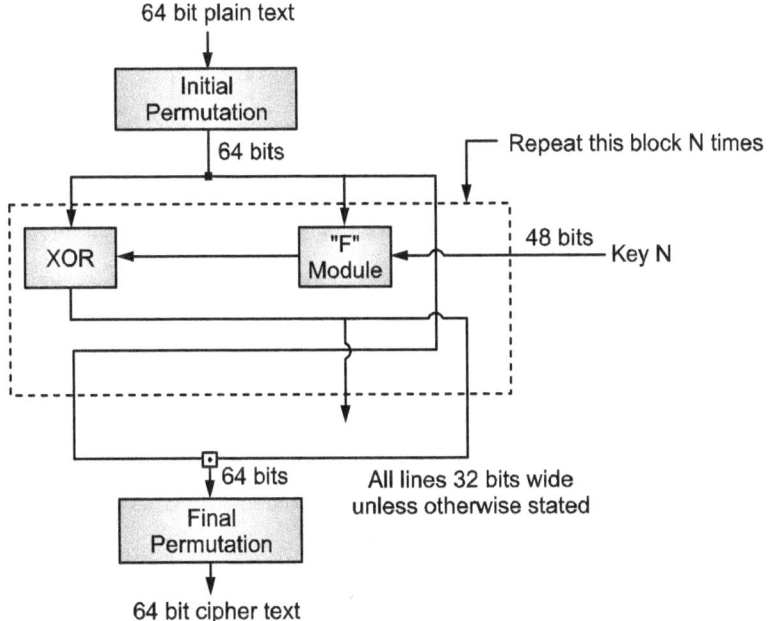

Fig. 4.10: DES Block Diagram

Fundamentally DES performs only two operations on its input bit shifting, and bit substitution. The key controls exactly how this process works. By doing these operations repeatedly and in a non-linear manner you end up with a result which can not be used to retrieve without the key. Those who familiar with chaos theory should see a great deal of similarity to what DES does. By applying relatively simple operations repeatedly a system can achieve a state of near total randomness.

DES works on 64 bits of data at a time. Each 64 bits of data is iterated on from 1 to 16 times (16 is the DES standard). For each iteration a 48 bit subset of the 56 bit key is fed into the encryption block represented by the dashed rectangle above.

Decryption is the inverse of the encryption process. The "F" module shown in the diagram is the heart of DES. It actually consists of several different transforms and non-linear substitutions.

DES General Structure:

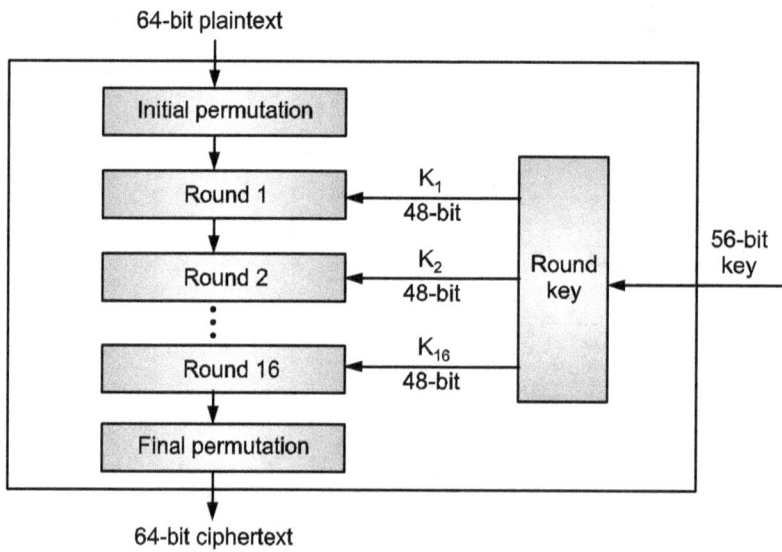

Fig. 4.11: General Structure of DES

Inner workings of DES

DES (and most of the other major symmetric ciphers) is based on a cipher known as the Feistel Block Cipher. It consists of a number of rounds where each round contains bit-shuffling, non-linear substitutions (S-boxes) and exclusive OR operations. Most symmetric encryption schemes today are based on this structure.

DES expects two inputs - the plaintext to be encrypted and the secret key. The manner in which the plaintext is accepted, and the key arrangement used for encryption and decryption, both determine the type of cipher it is.

DES is therefore a symmetric, 64 bit block cipher as it uses the same key for both encryption and decryption and only operates on 64 bit blocks of data at a time 5 (be they plaintext or cipher text). The key size used is 56 bits, however a 64 bit (or eight-byte) key is actually input. The least significant bit of each byte is either used for parity (odd for DES) or set arbitrarily and does not increase the security in any way. All blocks are numbered from left to right which makes the eight bit of each byte the parity bit. Once a plain-text message is received to be encrypted, it is arranged into 64 bit blocks required for input. If the number of bits in the message is not evenly divisible by 64, then the last block will be padded. Multiple permutations and substitutions are incorporated throughout in order to increase the difficulty of performing a cryptanalysis on the cipher. However, it is generally accepted that the initial and final permutations offer little or no contribution to the security of DES and in fact some software implementations omit them (although strictly speaking these are not DES as they do not adhere to the standard).

Modes of operation

The DES algorithm is a basic building block for providing data security. To apply DES in a variety of applications, five modes of operation have been defined which cover virtually all variation of use of the algorithm and these are shown in below table.

Table: DES Modes of Operation

Mode	Description	Typical Application
1. Electronic Codebook (ECB)	Each block of 64 plaintext bits is encoded independently using the same key.	• Secure transmission of single values (e.g., an encryption key).
2. Cipher Block Chaining (CBC)	The input to the encryption algorithm is the XOR of the next 64 bits of plaintext and the preceding 64 bits of ciphertext.	• General purpose block-oriented transmission. • Authentication.
3. Cipher Feedback (CFB)	Input is processed J bits at a time. Preceding ciphertext is used as input to the encryption algorithm to produce pseudorandom output, which is XORed with plaintext to produce next unit of ciphertext.	• General purpose stream-oriented transmission. • Authentication.
4. Output Feedback (OFB)	Similar to CFB, except that the input to the encryption algorithm is the preceding DES output.	• Stream-oriented transmission over noisy channel (e.g. satellite communication)
5. Counter (CTR)	Each block of plaintext is XORed with an encrypted counter. The counter is incremented for each subsequent block.	• General purpose block-oriented transmission. • Useful for high-speed requirements.

4.9 The Advanced Encryption Standard (AES)

The Advanced Encryption Standard (AES) is a symmetric-key block cipher algorithm. It is U.S. government standard for secure and classified data encryption and decryption. The Advanced Encryption Standard (AES) is one of the most frequently used and most secure encryption algorithms available today. Its story of success started 1997, when the National Institute of Standards and Technology NIST announced the search for a successor to the aging encryption standard DES. An algorithm named "Rijndael", developed by the Belgian cryptographists Daemen and Rijmen, excelled in security as well as in performance and flexibility. It came out on top of several competitors, and was officially announced as the new encryption standard AES in 2001.

Advanced Encryption Standard Rules for AES proposals

1. The algorithm must be a symmetric block cipher.
2. The full design must be public.
3. Key lengths of 128, 192, and 256 bits supported.
4. Both software and hardware implementations required
5. The algorithm must be public or licensed on non-discriminatory terms.

The algorithm is based on several substitutions, permutations and linear transformations, each executed on data blocks of 16 byte (blockcipher). Those operations are repeated several times, called "rounds". During each round, a unique roundkey is calculated out of the encryption key, and incorporated in the calculations.

Based on this block structure of AES, the change of a single bit either in the key, or in the plaintext block results in a completely different ciphertext block.

The difference between AES-128, AES-192 and AES-256 finally is the length of the key: 128, 192 or 256 bit – all drastic improvements compared to the 56 bit key of DES. By way of illustration: Cracking a 128 bit AES key with a state-of-the-art supercomputer would take longer than the presumed age of the universe. As of today, no practicable attack against AES exists. Therefore, AES remains the preferred encryption standard for governments, banks and high security systems around the world.

Advanced Encryption Standard (AES)

The AES design is based on a substitution-permutation network (SPN) .

The AES replaced the DES with new and updated features:

- Block encryption implementation
- 128-bit group encryption with 128, 192 and 256-bit key lengths
- Symmetric algorithm requiring only one encryption and decryption key
- Data security for 20-30 years
- Worldwide access
- No royalties
- Easy overall implementation

An Overview of the AES Algorithm

The AES algorithm is currently the standard block-cipher algorithm that has replaced the Data Encryption Standard (DES). Back in 1997 the National Institute of Standards and Technology (NIST) made a public call for new cipher algorithms that could replace the DES. A rough summary of the requirements made by NIST for the new AES were the following:

- Symmetric-key cipher
- Block cipher
- Support for 128-bit block sizes
- Support for 128-, 192-, and 256-bit key lengths

Finally in October 2000, the Rijndael algorithm was chosen as the basis for the new standard encryption algorithm (Hironobu 2001). The original Rijndael algorithm also supported both fixed-size and variable-size bit cipher blocks. However, currently the Federal Information Processing Standards specification for the AES algorithm supports only the fixed-size, 128-bit blocks.

The operation of the AES algorithm is shown in below Figure. The encryption step uses a key that converts the data into an unreadable ciphertext, and then the decryption step uses the same key to convert the ciphertext back into the original data. This type of key is a *symmetric key*; other algorithms require a different key for encryption and decryption.

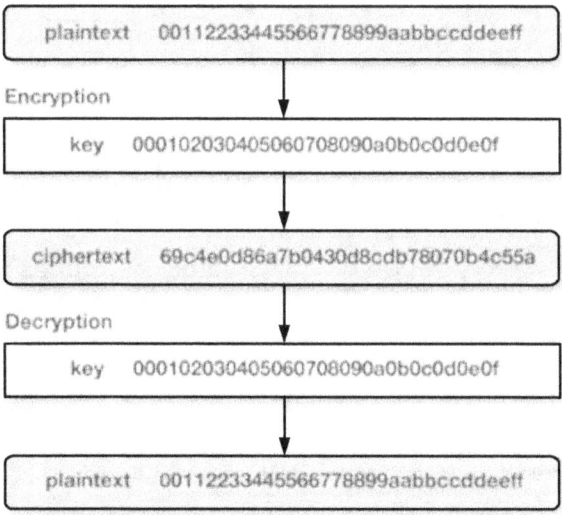

Fig. 4.12: AES Cipher Operation

The precise steps involved in the algorithm can be seen in Fig. 4.13. The process is relatively simple, but some brief cryptographic explanations are necessary to understand what is going on. In cryptography, algorithms such as AES are called *product ciphers*. For this class of ciphers, encryption is done in *rounds*, where each round's processing is accomplished using the same logic. Moreover, many of these product ciphers, including AES, change the cipher key at each round. Each of these round keys is determined by a *key schedule*, which is generated from the cipher key given by the user.

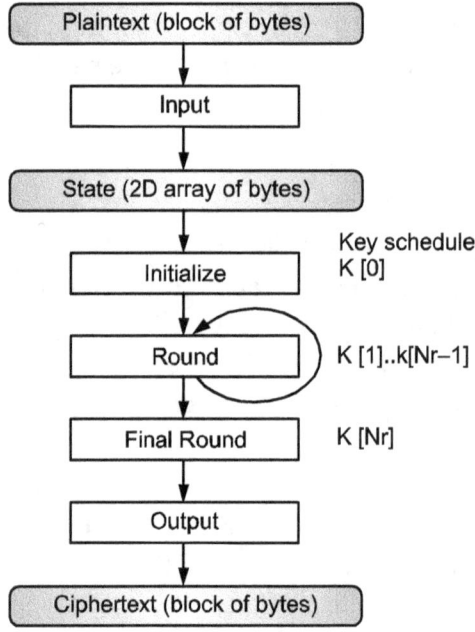

Fig. 4.13: Steps in Algorithm

An Illustration of the AES Algorithm

Generally speaking, the strength of an encryption by product ciphers can be heightened by increasing the number of rounds used to process the data. The AES standard specifies that the number of rounds is determined by the length of the cipher key, as shown in below:

Key length	Number of Rounds
128	10
192	12
256	14

The above table shows Key Length and the Number of Rounds

Comparison of DES and AES

The characteristics of DES and AES are compared in Table below.

When Rijndael's predecessor, DES, was adopted, two questions arose quickly:

1. How strong is it, and in particular are there any backdoors?

2. How long would it be until the encrypted code could be routinely cracked?

With over 20 years of use, doubts of weakness (intentional or not) and backdoors have pretty much been quashed. Not only have analysts its failed to find any significant flaws, but in fact research has shown that seemingly insignificant changes weaken the strength of the algorithm—that is, the algorithm is the best it can he. The second question, about how long DES would last, went unanswered for a long time but then was answered cry quickly by two experiments in which DES was cracked in days. Thus, after 20 years, the power of individual specialized processors and of massive parallel searches has overtaken the fixed DES key size.

Table: Comparison of DES and AES

	DES	AES
Date	1976	1999
Block size	64-bits	128 bits
Key length	56 bits (effective length)	128, 192, 256 (and possibly more) bits
Encryption primitives	Substitution, permutation	Substitution, shift, bit mixing
Cryptographic primitives	Confusion, diffusion	Confusion, diffusion
Design	Open	Open
Design rationale	Closed	Open
Selection process	Secret	Secret, but accepted open public comment
Source	IBM, enhanced by NSA	Independent Dutch cryptographers

We must ask the same questions about AES: Does it have flaws and for how long

will it remain sound? We cannot address the question of flaws yet, other than to say that teams of cryptanalysts pored over the design of Rijndael during the two-year review period without finding any problems. But the longevity question is more difficult to answer for AES than for DES. The AES algorithm as defined can use 128-, 192- or 256-hit keys. This characteristic means that AES starts with a key more than double the size of a DES key and can extend to double it yet again. (Remember that doubling the key length squares the number of possible keys that need to be tested in attempts to break the encryption.) But because there is an evident underlying structure. it is also possible to use the same general approach on a slightly different underlying problem and accommodate keys of even larger size. (Even a key size of 256 is prodigious, however.) Thus, unlike DES, AES can move to a longer key length any time technology seems to allow an analyst to overtake the current key size.

Moreover, the number of cycles can be extended in it natural way. With DES the algorithm was defined for precisely 16 cycles; to extend that number would require substantial redefinition of the algorithm. The internal structure of AES has no a prior limitation on the number of cycles. If a cryptanalyst ever concluded that 9 or 11 or 13 rounds were too low, the only change needed to improve the algorithm would be to change the limit on a repeat loop.

Moreover, the number of cycles can be extended in a natural way. With DES the algorithm was defined for precisely 16 cycles: to extend that number would require substantial redefinition of the algorithm. The internal structure of AES has no prior limitation on the number of cycles. Cryptanalyst ever concluded that 9 or 11 or 13 rounds were too low, the only change needed to improve the algorithm would be to change the limit on a repeat loop.

It is impossible to predict now what limitations cryptanalysts might identify in the future. At present, AES seems to the a significant improvement over DES and it can be improved in a natural way if necessary.

4.10 Public Key Algorithms

Public Key Cryptography (PKC)   [Oct. 16]

Public key cryptography (PKC) is an encryption technique that uses a paired public and private key (or asymmetric key) algorithm for secure data communication. A message sender uses a recipient's public key to encrypt a message. To decrypt the sender's message, only the recipient's private key may be used.

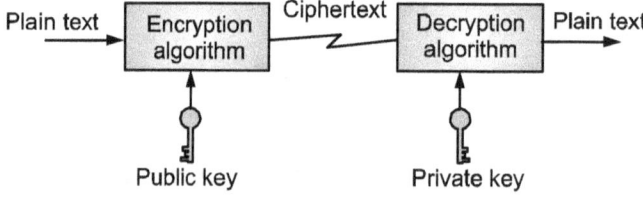

Fig. 4.14: Public Key Cryptography

Public Key (Asymmetric) Algorithms

Public-key algorithms are asymmetric, that is to say the key that is used to encrypt the message is different from the key used to decrypt the message. The encryption key, known as the public key is used to encrypt a message, but the message can only be decoded by the person that has the decryption key, known as the private key.

This type of algorithm has a number of advantages over traditional symmetric ciphers. It means that the recipient can make their public key widely available - anyone wanting to send them a message uses the algorithm and the recipient's public key to do so. An eavesdropper may have both the algorithm and the public key, but will still not be able to decrypt the message. Only the recipient, with their private key can decrypt the message.

The disadvantage of public-key algorithms is that they are more computationally intensive than symmetric algorithms and therefore encryption and decryption take longer. This may not be significant for a short text message, but certainly is for long messages or audio/video.

The Public-Key Cryptography Standards (PKCS) are specifications produced by RSA Laboratories in cooperation with secure systems developers worldwide for the purpose of accelerating the deployment of public-key cryptography. First published in 1991 as a result of meetings with a small group of early adopters of public-key technology, the PKCS documents have become widely referenced and implemented. Contributions from the PKCS series have become part of many formal and de facto standards, including ANSI X9 documents, PKIX, SET, S/MIME and SSL.

PKC is also known as public key encryption, asymmetric encryption, and asymmetric key encryption.

- PKC is a cryptographic algorithm and cryptosystem component implemented by a variety of Internet standards, including Transport Layer Security (TLS), Pretty Good Privacy (PGP), GNU Privacy Guard (GPG), Secure Socket Layer (SSL) and Hypertext Transfer Protocol (HTTP) websites.

  PKC facilitates secure communication through an insecure channel, which allows a message to be read by the intended recipient only. For example, A uses B's public key to encrypt a message to B, which can be decrypted using B's unique private key.

  PKC maintains email privacy and ensures communication security while messages are in transit or stored on mail servers. PKC is also a DSA component used to authenticate a private key verifiable by anyone with authorized public key access, which validates message origin and sender. Thus, PKC facilitates confidentiality, data integrity, authentication and non-repudiation, which form key Information Assurance (IA) parameters.

  PKC is slower than secret key cryptography (or symmetric cryptography) methods, due to high computational requirements. Unlike symmetric cryptography, PKC uses a fixed buffer size, depending on particular and small data amounts, which may only be encrypted and not chained in streams. Because a broad range of possible encryption keys are used, PKC is more robust and less susceptible to third party security breach attempts.

- Asymmetric cryptography or public-key cryptography is cryptography in which a pair of keys is used to encrypt and decrypt a message so that it arrives securely. Initially, a network user receives a public and private key pair from a certificate authority. Any other user who wants to send an encrypted message can get the intended recipient's public key from a public directory. They use this key to encrypt the message, and they send it to the recipient. When the recipient gets the message, they decrypt it with their private key, which no one else should have access to.

Types of Public Key Algorithm

RSA

The algorithm proposed by Ron Rivest, Adi Shamir and Len Adleman in 1978, known as RSA is one of the earliest and most versatile of the public-key algorithms. It is suitable for for signing/verification (and, therefore, for data integrity), and for key establishment (specifically key transfer). It can be used as the basis for a secure pseudorandom number generator as well as for the security in some electronic current games. Its security is based on the difficulty of factoring very large integers.

DSA

The Digital Signature Algorithm (DSA) is a Federal Information Processing Standard (FIPS) publication of the National Institute of Standards and Technology (NIST) of the U.S. Department of Commerce. It is a variant of the ElGamal signature mechanism. The DSA was designed exclusively for signing/verification (and, therefore, also for data integrity), but, other algorithms in the ElGamal family can be used for encryption/ decryption (and, therefore, key transfer if what is being encrypted and decrypted is a symmetric key). The security of these algorithms is based on the difficulty of computing logarithms in a finite field.

DH

The algorithm that Whitfield Diffie and Martin Hellman proposed, known as DH, is a wonderful example of elegance and simplicity. The earliest public-key algorithm, it is exclusively a key establishment (specifically key agreement) protocol; each of two entities uses its own private key and the other entity's public key to create a symmetric key that no third entity call compute. It derives its security from the difficulty of computing logarithms in a finite field.

ECDSA and ECDH

The DSA and DFI algorithms can also be computed over the group of points defined by the solution to an equation for an elliptic curve over a finite field (Kob87, Mil86]. The resulting elliptic curve DSA (ECDSA) and elliptic curve DH (FCDH) algorithms have identical uses to their finite field counterparts earlier, but the security now rests on the difficulty of computing logarithms over the group of EC points. This different foundation leads to more complicated implementation and processing, but has the benefit of significantly smaller key sizes for a similar level of security.

SHA-1

The Secure Hash Algorithm SHA-1 (a slight revision of the original Secure Hash Algorithm SHA) is described in a NIST FIPS publication. This hash algorithm was designed specifically for use with the DSA but can be used with RSA or other public-key signature algorithms as well, its design principles are similar to those used in the MD2, MD4 and (especially) MD5 hash functions. Hash functions are not public-key algorithms but arc included here because digital signature algorithms are always used in conjunction with hash algorithms to provide the services of signing/verification and data integrity. Thus, they are an essential component of the digital signature and integrity security services.

4.11 RSA   [Oct. 16]

RSA is a cryptosystem for public-key encryption, and is widely used for securing sensitive data, particularly when being sent over an insecure network such as the Internet.

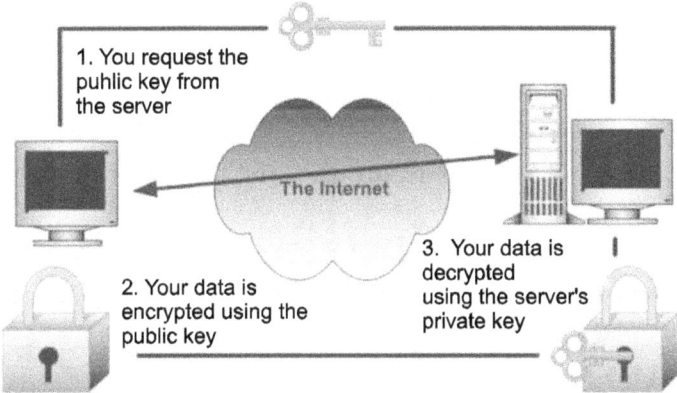

1. You request the puhlic key from the server

The Internet

2. Your data is encrypted using the public key

3. Your data is decrypted using the server's private key

Fig. 4.15: Working of RSA Encryption

Public-key cryptography, also known as asymmetric cryptography, uses two different but mathematically linked keys, one public and one private. The public key can be shared with everyone, whereas the private key must be kept secret. In RSA cryptography, both the public and the private keys can encrypt a message; the opposite key from the one used to encrypt a message is used to decrypt it. This attribute is one reason why RSA has become the most widely used asymmetric algorithm: It provides a method of assuring the confidentiality, integrity, authenticity and non-reputability of electronic communications and data storage.

Many protocols like SSH, OpenPGP, S/MIME, and SSL/TLS rely on RSA for encryption and digital signature functions. It is also used in software programs - browsers are an obvious example, which need to establish a secure connection over an insecure network like the Internet or validate a digital signature. RSA signature verification is one of the most commonly performed operations in IT.

RSA's Popularity

RSA derives its security from the difficulty of factoring large integers that are the product of two large prime numbers. Multiplying these two numbers is easy, but determining the original prime numbers from the total -- factoring -- is considered infeasible due to the time it would take even using today's super computers.

The public and the private key-generation algorithm is the most complex part of RSA cryptography. Two large prime numbers, p and q, are generated using the Rabin-Miller primality test algorithm. A modulus n is calculated by multiplying p and q. This number is used by both the public and private keys and provides the link between them. Its length, usually expressed in bits, is called the key length. The public key consists of the modulusn, and a public exponent, e, which is normally set at 65537, as it's a prime number that is not too large. The e figure doesn't have to be a secretly selected prime number as the public key is shared with everyone. The private key consists of the modulus n and the private exponent d, which is calculated using the Extended Euclidean algorithm to find the multiplicative inverse with respect to the totient of n.

Example of RSA

Sudha generates her RSA keys by selecting two primes: p=11 and q=13. The modulus n = p × q = 143. The totient of n $\phi(n)$ = (p − 1) × (q − 1) = 120. She chooses 7 for her RSA public key and calculates her RSA private key using the Extended Euclidean Algorithm which gives her 103.

Rahul wants to send Sudha an encrypted message M so he obtains her RSA public key (n, e) which in this example is (143, 7). His plaintext message is just the number 9 and is encrypted into ciphertext C as follows:

$$M^e \bmod n = 9^7 \bmod 143 = 48 = C$$

When Sudha receives Rahul's message she decrypts it by using her RSA private key (d, n) as follows:

$$C^d \bmod n = 48^{103} \bmod 143 = 9 = M$$

To use RSA keys to digitally sign a message, Sudha would create a hash or message digest of her message to Rahul, encrypt the hash value with her RSA private key and add it to the message. Rahul can then verify that the message has been sent by Sudha and has not been altered by decrypting the hash value with her public key. If this value matches the hash of the original message, then only Sudha could have sent it (authentication and non-repudiation) and the message is exactly as she wrote it (integrity). Sudha could, of course, encrypt her message with Rahul's RSA public key (confidentiality) before sending it to Rahul. A digital certificate contains information that identifies the certificate's owner and also contains the owner's public key. Certificates are signed by the certificate authority that issues them, and can simplify the process of obtaining public keys and verifying the owner.

The first PKC implementation, named for the three MIT mathematicians who developed it — Ronald Rivest, Adi Shamir, and Leonard Adleman. RSA today is used in hundreds of software products and can be used for key exchange, digital signatures, or encryption of small blocks of data. RSA uses a variable size encryption block and a variable size key. The key-pair is derived from a very large number, n, that is the product of two prime numbers chosen according to special rules.

Security of RSA

The security of RSA relies on the computational difficulty of factoring large integers. As computing power increases and more efficient algorithms are discovered, the ability to factor larger and larger numbers also increases. Encryption strength is directly tied to key size, and doubling key length delivers an exponential increase in strength, although it does impair performance. RSA keys are typically 1024- or 2048-bits long, but experts believe that 1024-bit keys could be broken in the near future, which is why government and industry are moving to a minimum key length of 2048-bits. Barring an unexpected breakthrough in quantum computing, it should be many years before longer keys are required, but elliptic curve cryptography is gaining favor with many security experts as an alternative to RSA for implementing public-key cryptography. It can create faster, smaller and more efficient cryptographic keys. Much of today's hardware and software is ECC-ready and its popularity is likely to grow as it can deliver equivalent security with lower computing power and battery resource usage, making it more suitable for mobile apps than RSA. Finally, a team of researchers which included Adi Shamir, a co-inventor of RSA, has successfully determined a 4096-bit RSA key using acoustic cryptanalysis, however any encryption algorithm is vulnerable to this type of attack.

4.12 Other Public Key Algorithms

The following list summarizes the public key systems in common use today:

1. **Diffie-Hellman key exchange:** After the RSA algorithm was published, Diffie and Hellman came up with their own algorithm. D-H is used for secret-key key exchange only, and not for authentication or digital signatures.

   A Diffie-Hellman system for exchanging cryptographic keys between active parties. Diffie-Hellman is not actually a method of encryption and decryption, but a method of developing and exchanging a shared private key over a public communications channel. In effect, the two parties agree to some common numerical values, and then each party creates a key. Mathematical transformations of the keys are exchanged. Each party can then calculate a third session key that cannot easily be derived by an attacker who knows both exchanged values.

2. **Digital Signature Algorithm (DSA):** The Digital Signature Standard (DSS) was developed by the U.S. National Security Agency and adopted as a Federal Information Processing Standard (FIPS) by the National Institute for Standards and Technology. DSS is based on the Digital Signature Algorithm (DSA). Although DSA allows keys of any length, only keys between 512 and 1,024 bits are permitted under the DSS FIPS. As specified, DSS can be used only for digital signatures, although it is possible to use some DSA implementations for encryption as well.

3. **ElGamal:** Designed by Taher Elgamal, a PKC system similar to Diffie-Hellman and used for key exchange.

4. **Elliptic Curve Cryptography (ECC):** Public key systems have traditionally been based on factoring (RSA), discrete logarithms (Diffie-Helman), and the knapsack problem. Elliptic curve cryptosystems are public key encryption systems that are based on an elliptic curve rather than on a traditional logarithmic function; that is, they are based on solutions to the equation $y^2 = x^3 + ax + b$.

   The advantage to using elliptic curve systems stems from the fact that there are no known sub exponential algorithms for computing discrete logarithms of elliptic curves. Thus, short keys in elliptic curve cryptosystems can offer a high degree of privacy and security, while remaining easily calculatable. Elliptic curves can be computed very efficiently in hardware. Certicom has attempted to commercialize implementations of elliptic curve cryptosystems for use in mobile computing.

5. **Public-Key Cryptography Standards (PKCS):** The Public-Key Cryptography Standards (PKCS) are a set of intervendor standard protocols for making possible secure information exchange on the Internet using a public key infrastructure (PKI). The standards include RSA encryption, password-based encryption, extended certificate syntax, and cryptographic message syntax for S/MIME, RSA's proposed standard for secure e-mail. The standards were developed by RSA Laboratories in cooperation with a consortium that included Apple, Microsoft, DEC, Lotus, Sun, and MIT.

6. **Cramer-Shoup:** A public-key cryptosystem proposed by R. Cramer and V. Shoup of IBM in 1998.

7. **Key Exchange Algorithm (KEA):** A variation on Diffie-Hellman; proposed as the key exchange method for Capstone.

8. **LUC:** A public-key cryptosystem designed by P.J. Smith and based on Lucas sequences. Can be used for encryption and signatures, using integer factoring.

4.13 Digital Signature

A digital signature is a technique to validate the authority of a digital message or a document. A valid digital signature provides the surety to the recipient that the message was generated by a known sender, such that the sender cannot deny having sent the message. Digital signatures are mostly used for software distribution, financial transactions, and in other cases where there is a risk of forgery.

Electronic Signature

An electronic signature or e-signature, indicates either that a person who demands to have created a message is the one who created it.

A signature can be defined as a schematic script related with a person. A signature on a document is a sign that the person accepts the purposes recorded in the document. In many engineering companies digital seals are also required for another layer of authentication and security. Digital seals and signatures are same as handwritten signatures and stamped seals.

Digital Signature to Electronic Signature

How digital signatures work

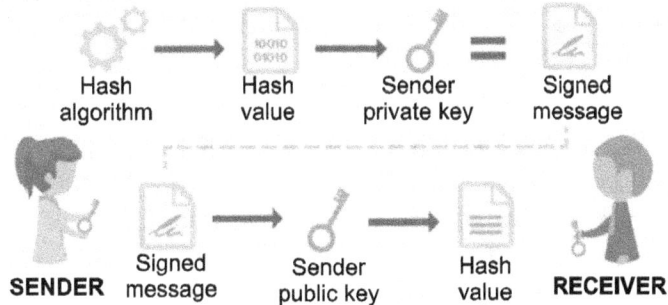

Fig. 4.16: Working of Digital Signature

Digital signatures are based on public key cryptography, also known as asymmetric cryptography. Using a public key algorithm such as RSA, one can generate two keys that are mathematically linked: one private and one public. To create a digital signature, signing software (such as an email program) creates a one-way hash of the electronic data to be signed. The private key is then used to encrypt the hash. The encrypted hash -- along with other information, such as the hashing algorithm -- is the digital signature. The reason for encrypting the hash instead of the entire message or document is that a hash function can convert an arbitrary input into a fixed length value, which is usually much shorter. This saves time since hashing is much faster than signing.

The value of the hash is unique to the hashed data. Any change in the data, even changing or deleting a single character, results in a different value. This attribute enables others to validate the integrity of the data by using the signer's public key to decrypt the hash. If the decrypted hash matches a second computed hash of the same data, it proves that the data hasn't changed since it was signed. If the two hashes don't match, the data has either been tampered with in some way (integrity) or the signature was created with a private key that doesn't correspond to the public key presented by the signer (authentication).

A digital signature can be used with any kind of message -- whether it is encrypted or not -- simply so the receiver can be sure of the sender's identity and that the message arrived intact. Digital signatures make it difficult for the signer to deny having signed something (non-repudiation) -- assuming their private key has not been compromised -- as the digital signature is unique to both the document and the signer, and it binds them together. A digital certificate, an electronic document that contains the digital signature of the certificate-issuing authority, binds together a public key with an identity and can be used to verify a public key belongs to a particular person or entity.

The holder of a digital certificate can also use it to digitally sign other digital documents, for example, purchase orders, grant applications, financial reports or student transcripts. A digital signature is an attachment to a document that contains an encrypted version of the document created using the signer's private key.

Most modern email programs support the use of digital signatures and digital certificates, making it easy to sign any outgoing emails and validate digitally signed incoming messages. Digital signatures are also used extensively to provide proof of authenticity, data integrity and non-repudiation of communications and transactions or conducted over the Internet.

Digital Certificates   [Oct. 16]

Digital Certificates are part of a technology called Public Key Infrastructure or PKI. Digital certificates have been described as virtual ID cards. This is a useful similarity. There are many ways that digital certificates and ID cards really are the same. Both ID cards and client digital certificates contain information about you, such as your name, and information about the organization that issued the certificate or card to you.

In creating digital certificates a unique cryptographic key pair is generated. One of these keys is referred to as a public key and the other as a private key.

In PKI (public key infrastructure) terms, the public key for an individual is put into a digital document, along with information about that individual, and then the digital document is signed by the organization's certification authority. This signed document can be transmitted to anyone and used to identify the subject of the certificate. However, the private key of the original key pair must be securely managed and never given to anyone else.

An added value of digital certificates is that they provide a higher level of security than what we currently have with PIN and password combinations.

4.14 Symmetric-Key Signatures   [April 16]

Digital signature can be accomplished using Symmetric key signature, Upon receiving digital signature, one should be able to prove, in a court of law, that the document is indeed signed by the person indicated by his/her signature.

Symmetric-Key Signature needs a central authority (The Big Brother). In Big brother method, it is assumed that all parties faith on one entity that is Big brother. He knows encryption keys of all parties but never shares keys with others.

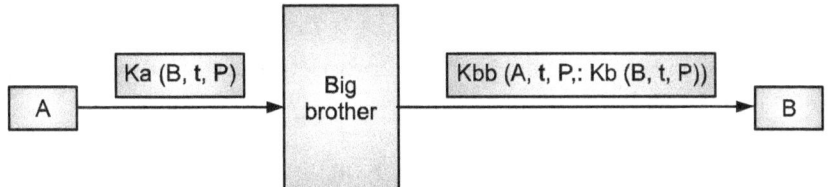

Fig. 4.17: Symmetric Key Signature

In this method, sender (say A) sends Message P along with timestamp t, (the time at which it was sent by A). The message is sent to Big brother not to B in fact. The Big brother kept a receipt of it along with the timestamp t then sends this message to B. Big brother also sends a receipt Kb (B,t,P) to B along with the message. In case some controversy arises later on, sender may show the receipt issued by the Big brother, receipt issued by the big brother is treated as authenticated.

4.15 Public-key Signature   [April 16]

A public key infrastructure (PKI) supports the distribution and identification of public encryption keys, enabling users and computers to both securely exchange data over networks such as the Internet and verify the identity of the other party.

The problems of key distribution are solved by public key cryptography, the concept of which was introduced by Whitfield Diffie and Martin Hellman in 1975.

Public key cryptography is an asymmetric scheme that uses a pair of keys for encryption: a public key, which encrypts data, and a corresponding private, or secret key for decryption. You publish your public key to the world while keeping your private key secret. Anyone with a copy of your public key can then encrypt information that only you can read. Even people you have never met.

It is computationally infeasible to deduce the private key from the public key. Anyone who has a public key can encrypt information but cannot decrypt it. Only the person who has the corresponding private key can decrypt the information.

The primary benefit of public key cryptography is that it allows people who have no preexisting security arrangement to exchange messages securely. The need for sender and receiver to share secret keys via some secure channel is eliminated; all communications involve only public keys, and no private key is ever transmitted or shared. Some examples of public-key cryptosystems are Elgamal (named for its inventor, Taher Elgamal), RSA (named for its inventors, Ron Rivest, Adi Shamir, and Leonard Adleman), Diffie-Hellman (named, you guessed it, for its inventors), and DSA, the Digital Signature Algorithm (invented by David Kravitz).

In public-key signature/verification, the private key is used to sign a document. Anyone can use the public key in order to verify that the proported signature was indeed generated by someone possessing the (secret) private key. The picture is

$$\text{Original message} \rightarrow \left\{ \begin{array}{l} \text{Original mesasge} \\ \text{Private key} \end{array} \right\} \xrightarrow{\text{Signing}} \underbrace{\text{Signature}}_{\text{transmitted}}$$

$$\text{Signature} \rightarrow \left\{ \begin{array}{l} \text{Signature} \\ \text{Public key} \\ \text{Original message} \end{array} \right\} \xrightarrow{\text{Verification}} \left\{ \begin{array}{l} \text{Yes/No, this was/wasn't} \\ \text{the valid signature} \end{array} \right\}$$

Note that in this model, in order to perform the verification, the verifying party needs a copy of the original message, as well. This isn't always the case - some signature/verification algorithms allow message recovery of (very) short messages.

As before, one of the key problems is the question of how the verifying party gains assurance that it is verifying with the correct public key.

4.16 Message Digest   [April 16]

A message digest is a cryptographic hash function containing a string of digits created by a one-way hashing formula.

Message digests are designed to protect the integrity of a piece of data or media to detect changes and alterations to any part of a message. They are a type of cryptography utilizing hash values that can warn the copyright owner of any modifications applied to their work.

It takes a variable length input - often an entire disk file - and reduces it to a small value (typically 128 to 512 bits). Give it the same input, and it always produces the same output. And, because the output is very much smaller than the potential input, for at least one of the output values there must be more than one input value that can produce it.

We would expect that to be true for all possible output values for a good message digest algorithm.

Properties of good message digest algorithms:

The first is that the algorithm cannot be predicted or reversed. That is, given a particular output value, we cannot come up with an input to the algorithm that will produce that output, either by trying to find an inverse to the algorithm, or by somehow predicting the nature of the input required. With at least 128 bits of output, a brute force attack is pretty much out of the question, as there will be 1.7×1038 possible input values of the same length to try, on average, before finding one that generates the correct output.

The second useful property of message digest algorithms is that a small change in the input results in a significant change in the output. Change a single input bit, and roughly half of the output bits should change. This is actually a consequence of the first property, because we don't want the output to be predictable based on the input. However, this aspect is a valuable property of the message digest all by itself.

Message digests are also called one-way hash functions because they produce values that are difficult to invert, resistant to attack, effectively unique, and widely distributed.

Many message digest functions have been proposed and are now in use. Here are a few:

MD2   :   Message Digest #2, developed by Ronald Rivest. This message digest is probably the most secure of Rivest's message digest functions, but takes the longest to compute. As a result, MD2 is rarely used. MD2 produces a 128-bit digest.

MD4   :   Message Digest #4, also developed by Ronald Rivest. This message digest algorithm was developed as a fast alternative to MD2. Subsequently, MD4 was shown to have a possible weakness. It may be possible to find a second file that produces the same MD4 as a given file without requiring a brute force search (which would be infeasible for the same reason that it is infeasible to search a 128-bit keyspace). MD4 produces a 128-bit digest.

MD5   :   Message Digest #5, also developed by Ronald Rivest. MD5 is a modification of MD4 that includes techniques designed to make it more secure. Although MD5 is widely used, in the summer of 1996 a few flaws were discovered in MD5 that allowed some kinds of collisions in a weakened form of the algorithm to be calculated. As a result, MD5 is slowly falling out of favor. MD5 and SHA-1 are both used in SSL and in Microsoft's Authenticode technology. MD5 produces a 128-bit digest.

SHA   :   The Secure Hash Algorithm, related to MD4 and designed for use with the U.S. National Institute for Standards and Technology's Digital Signature Standard (NIST's DSS). Shortly after the publication of the SHA, NIST announced that it was not suitable for use without a small change. SHA produces a 160-bit digest.

SHA-1 :   The revised Secure Hash Algorithm incorporates minor changes from SHA. It is not publicly known if these changes make SHA-1 more secure than SHA, although many people believe that they do. SHA-1 produces a 160-bit digest.

SHA-256, SHA-384, SHA-512

These are, respectively, 256-, 384-, and 512-bit hash functions designed to be used with 128-, 192-, and 256-bit encryption algorithms. These functions were proposed by NIST in 2001 for use with the Advanced Encryption Standard.

Besides these functions, it is also possible to use traditional symmetric block encryption systems such as the DES as message digest functions. To use an encryption function as a message digest function, simply run the encryption function in cipher feedback mode. For a key, use a key that is randomly chosen and specific to the application. Encrypt the entire input file. The last block of encrypted data is the message digest. Symmetric encryption algorithms produce excellent hashes, but they are significantly slower than the message digest functions described previously.

Practice Questions

1. What is Cryptography?
2. Explain different types of Cipher text in Cryptography?
3. Which are fundamental Cryptographic Principles?
4. What is a concept of Symmetric - Key Algorithm in Cryptography?
5. Which are types of Encryption Standards in Cryptography? Explain it with example.
6. Explain terms - Public Key Algorithm, RSA.
7. Explain Symmetric Key Signature and Public Key Signature.
8. What is a Message Digest in Cryptography?
9. Which are properties of a good Message Digest?
10. Explain following terms: (a) Network Security (b) Ciphertext (c) Digital Signature.

■■■

Chapter 5...

Computing and Informatics

Contents ...

5.1 Introduction of Computing and Informatics

1. Computing

Computing is any goal-oriented activity requiring benefit from processes or creating algorithmic processes. For example, through Computers. Computing includes designing, developing and building hardware and software systems; processing, structuring, and managing various kinds of information. Doing scientific research on and with computers; making computer systems behave intelligently.

Computing has changed the world more than any other invention of the past hundred years, and has come to complete nearly all human aims. Yet, we are just at the beginning of the computing revolution; today's computing offers just a glimpse of the potential impact of computing.

There are two reasons why everyone should study computing:

- Nearly all of the most exciting and important technologies, arts, and sciences of today and tomorrow are driven by computing.
- Understanding computing illuminates deep insights and questions into the nature of our minds, our culture, and our universe.

Anyone who has submitted a query to Google, watched a movie, had LASIK eye surgery, used a smart phone, seen a TV show, shopped with a credit card. None of these would be possible without the tremendous advances in computing over the past half century.

Processes, Procedures, and Computers

Computing changes how we think about problems and how we understand the world.

2. Informatics:

Informatics is the study of the structure, behaviour interactions, representation, processing, and communication of information in natural and engineered systems. It has computational, cognitive and social aspects. The central notion is the transformation of information - whether by computation or communication, whether by organisms or artifacts.

Informatics is developing its own fundamental concepts of communication, knowledge, data, interaction and information, and relating them to such phenomena as computation, thought, and language.

Informatics has many aspects, and encompasses a number of existing academic disciplines - Artificial Intelligence, Cognitive Science and Computer Science. Each takes part of Informatics as its natural domain: in broad terms, Cognitive Science concerns the study of natural systems; Computer Science concerns the analysis of computation, and design of computing systems; Artificial Intelligence plays a connecting role, designing systems which emulate those found in nature. Informatics also informs and is informed by other disciplines, such as Mathematics, Electronics, Biology, Linguistics and Psychology. Thus Informatics provides a link between disciplines with their own methodologies and perspectives, bringing together a common scientific paradigm, common engineering methods and a major boost from technological development and practical application.

Expert system

Artificial intelligence based system that converts the knowledge of an expert in a specific subject into a software code. This code can be merged with other such codes (based on the knowledge of other experts) and used for answering questions (queries) submitted through a computer.

Expert systems typically consist of three parts:

1. A knowledge base which contains the information acquired by interviewing experts, and logic rules that govern how that information is applied;
2. An Inference engine that interprets the submitted problem against the rules and logic of information stored in the knowledge base; and
3. An Interface that allows the user to express the problem in a human language such as English.

Despite its earlier high hopes, expert systems technology has found application only in areas where information can be reduced to a set of computational rules, such as insurance underwriting or some aspects of securities trading. Also called rule based system.

Expert systems have played a large role in many industries including in financial services, telecommunications, healthcare, customer service, transportation, video games, manufacturing, aviation and written communication.

Characteristics of Expert Systems:

- **High performance:** They should perform at the level of a human expert.
- **Adequate response time:** They should have the ability to respond in a reasonable amount of time. Time is crucial especially for real time systems.

- **Reliability:** They must be reliable and should not crash.
- **Understandable:** They should not be a black box instead it should be able explain the steps of the reasoning process. It should justify its conclusions in the same way a human expert explains why he arrived at particular conclusion.

Advantages of Expert Systems:
- **Availability:** Expert systems are available easily due to mass production software.
- **Cheaper:** The cost of providing expertise is not expensive.
- Reduced danger: They can be used in any risky environments where humans cannot work with.
- **Permanence:** The knowledge will last long indefinitely.
- **Multiple expertise:** It can be designed to have knowledge of many experts.
- **Explanation:** They are capable of explaining in detail the reasoning that led to a conclusion.
- **Fast response:** They can respond at great speed due to the inherent advantages of computers over humans.
- **Unemotional and response at all times:** Unlike humans, they do not get tense, fatigue or panic and work steadily during emergency situations.

5.2 Types of Computing

Computing Environment is a collection of computers which are used to process and exchange the information to solve various types of computing problems. Some are as follows:

5.2.1 Cloud Computing

Cloud computing is the delivery of computing services over the Internet. Cloud services allow individuals and businesses to use software and hardware that are managed by third parties at remote locations.

The cloud computing model allows access to information and computer resources from anywhere that a network connection is available. It provides a shared pool of resources, including data storage space, networks, computer processing power, and specialized corporate and user applications.

Cloud computing means that instead of all the computer hardware and software you're using sitting on your desktop, or somewhere inside your company's network, it's provided for you as a service by another company and accessed over the Internet, usually in a completely seamless way. Exactly where the hardware and software is located and how it all works doesn't matter to you, the user—it's just somewhere up in the nebulous "cloud" that the Internet represents.

Examples of cloud services include online file storage, social networking sites, web mail, and online business applications. Cloud computing is a buzzword that means different things to different people. For some, it's just another way of describing IT (information technology) "outsourcing"; others use it to mean any computing service provided over the Internet or a similar network and some define it as any bought-in computer service you use that sits outside your firewall.

Concept of cloud computing evolved in 1950 (IBM) called RJE (Remote Job Entry Process). In 2006 Amazon provided first public cloud AWS (Amazon Web Service)

Characteristics of Cloud Computing:

1. **On-Demand Self:** Service means that customers (usually organizations) can request and manage their own computing resources.
2. **Broad Network Access:** It allows services to be offered over the Internet or private networks.
3. **Resource Pooling:** Pooled resources means that customers draw from a pool of computing resources, usually in remote data centres.
4. **Services:** It can be scaled larger or smaller; and use of a service is measured and customers are billed accordingly.
5. **Agility:** Without slowing up with unnecessary processes customer can focus on core business and improve "Time to market" of ideas thus enhancing business agility.
6. **Cost:** Customers save considerable cost associated with building, maintenance, operating technology etc. Additionally, can redirect traditional capital investment (CapEx) to operating expenditures (OpEx) to grow and increase productivity.
7. **Device Independence:** Customer can use cloud computing using any web browser (like Internet explorer, Google chrome, apple safari, opera, etc) and on any device (like desktop, tablets, smart phones, etc) without installing any additional software on the client device.
8. **Implementation:** For fraction of a cost and in record time as compared to on-premise solution, customer can get cloud computing off the ground as there is no need to purchase hardware, software, implementation services, etc.
9. **Innovation:** Innovation in Cloud computing happens faster as the vendor needs to keep up with the competition and these innovations are deployed faster with less cost to the customer.
10. **Location Independence:** Cloud computing can be accessed via your local network or public network giving a great deal of flexibility to meet customer computing needs from virtually anywhere customer have access to a computer device and internet access.
11. **Maintenance:** Maintenance responsibility of cloud computing is handled by the vendor.
12. **Performance:** Performance of the solution is going to be significantly higher and predictable because of extensive monitoring and efficient use of infrastructure.

Types of Cloud Computing

There are four separate types of clouds, They are:

1. **Public Cloud:** The whole cloud computing infrastructure is fully controlled by the third party providers like Google, Amazon and opens for the usage of the public based on pay-per-use model. But it offers poor security and hence the data is prone to malicious attacks.

2. **Private Cloud:** The purpose of private cloud is to meet the internal computational needs within an organization. This cloud offers more security as it is implemented within the internal firewall. Every aspect of cloud implementation is fully controlled by the organization and hence security will be enhanced.

3. **Hybrid Cloud:** The combination of private and public clouds forms the hybrid cloud. The organization uses the public cloud services along with its own cloud to perform resource intensive applications.

4. **Community Cloud:** The computing infrastructure created by a group of organizations having similar security interests. Member organizations or a third party provider can hold the responsibility of managing the cloud.

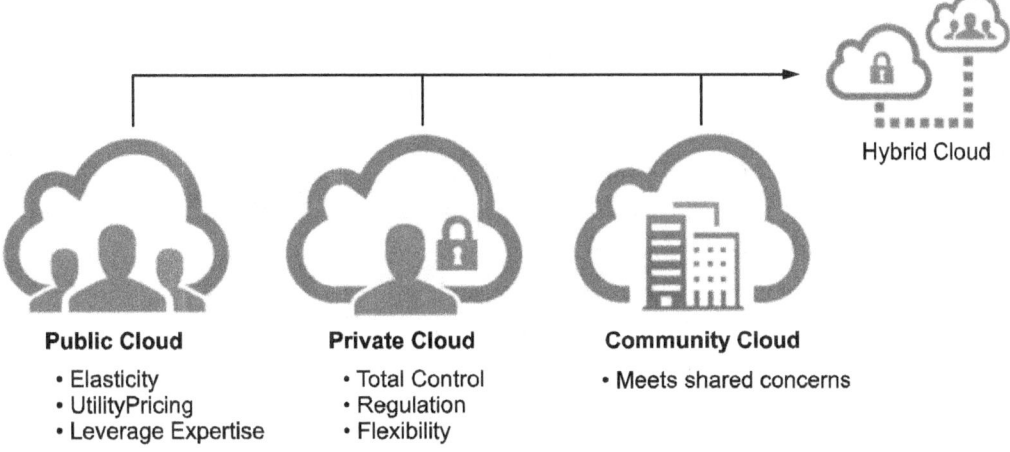

Hybrid Cloud

Public Cloud
- Elasticity
- UtilityPricing
- Leverage Expertise

Private Cloud
- Total Control
- Regulation
- Flexibility

Community Cloud
- Meets shared concerns

Fig. 5.1: Types of Cloud Computing

Some users may only be interested in cloud computing if they can create a private cloud – which if shared at all, is only between locations for a company or corporation. Some groups feel the idea of cloud computing is just too insecure. In particular, financial institutions and large corporations do not want to handover control to the cloud, because they don't believe there are enough safeguards to protect information.

Private clouds don't share the elasticity and often there is multiple site redundancy found in the public cloud. As an adjunct to a hybrid cloud, they allow privacy and security of information, while still saving on infrastructure with the utilization of the public cloud, but information moved between the two could still be compromised.

Cloud Architecture

The systems architecture of the software systems involved in the delivery of cloud computing, typically involves multiple cloud components communicating with each other over a loose coupling mechanism such as a messaging queue. Elastic provision implies intelligence in the use of tight or loose coupling as applied to mechanisms such as these and others.

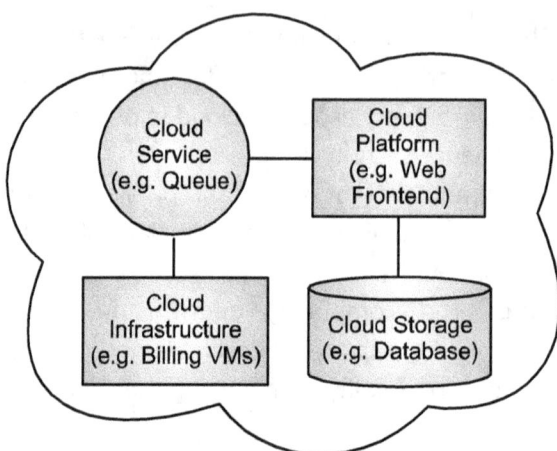

Fig. 5.2: Cloud Architecture

When talking about a cloud computing system, it's helpful to divide it into two sections: the front end and the back end.

They connect to each other through a network, usually the Internet. The front end is the side the computer user, or client, sees. The back end is the "cloud" section of the system. The front end includes the client's computer (or computer network) and the application required to access the cloud computing system. Not all cloud computing systems have the same user interface. On the back end of the system are the various computers, servers and data storage systems that create the "cloud" of computing services. In theory, a cloud computing system could include practically any computer program you can imagine, from data processing to video games. Usually, each application will have its own dedicated server.

A central server administers the system, monitoring traffic and client demands to ensure everything runs smoothly. It follows a set of rules called protocols and uses a special kind of software called middleware. Middleware allows networked computers to communicate with each other. Most of the time, servers don't run at full capacity. That means there's unused processing power going to waste.

If a cloud computing company has a lot of clients, there's likely to be a high demand for a lot of storage space. Some companies require hundreds of digital storage devices. Cloud computing systems need at least twice the number of storage devices it requires to keep all its clients' information stored. That's because these devices, like all computers, occasionally break down. A cloud computing system must make a copy of all its clients' information and store it on other devices. The copies enable the central server to access backup machines to retrieve data that otherwise would be unreachable. Making copies of data as a backup is called redundancy.

What are some of the applications of cloud computing? Keep reading to find out.

Service Models

The cloud computing service models are:

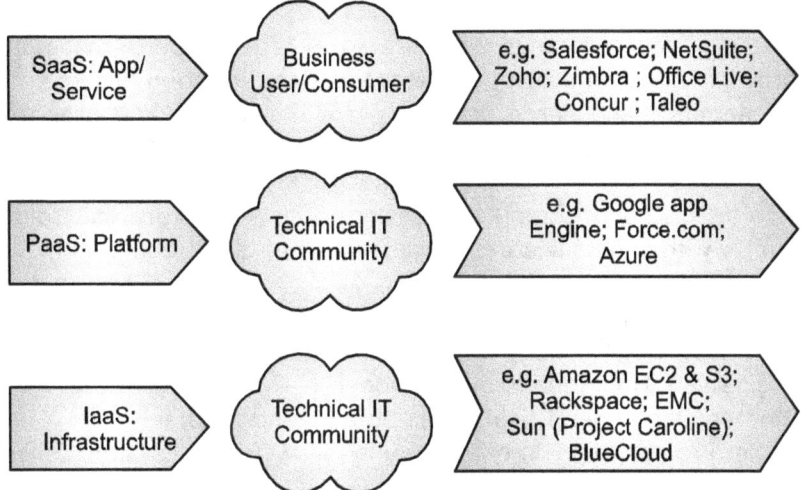

Fig. 5.3: Service Models

1. **Software as a Service (SaaS):** In a Software as a Service model, a pre-made application, along with any required software, operating system, hardware, and network are provided.SaaS applications are designed for end-users, delivered over the web.

2. **Platform as a Service (PaaS):** In PaaS, an operating system, hardware, and network are provided, and the customer installs or develops its own software and applications. It is the set of tools and services designed to make coding and deploying those applications quick and efficient

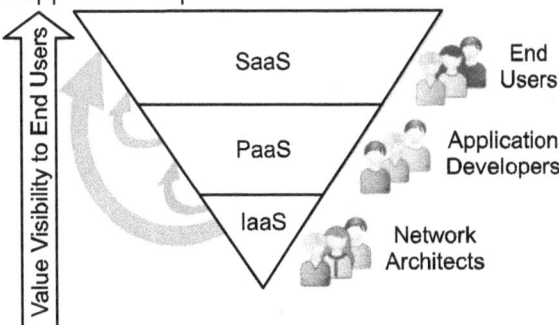

Fig. 5.4: Service Models Value Visibility

3. **Infrastructure as a Service (IaaS):** IaaS is the hardware and software that powers it all – servers, storage, networks, operating systems. The customer installs or develops its own operating systems, software and applications.

1. Software as a Service (SAAS)

Software as a Service (SaaS) is defined as software that is deployed over the internet with SaaS, a provider licenses an application to customers either as a service on demand, through a subscription, in a "pay-as-you-go" model, or (increasingly) at no charge when there is opportunity to generate revenue from streams other than the user, such as from advertisement or user list sales

SaaS is a rapidly growing market as indicated in recent reports that predict ongoing double digit growth. This rapid growth indicates that SaaS will soon become common place within every organization and hence it is important that buyers and users of technology understand what SaaS is and where it is suitable.

Characteristics of SaaS

Like other forms of Cloud Computing, it is important to ensure that solutions sold as SaaS in fact comply with generally accepted definitions of Cloud Computing. Some defining characteristics of SaaS include:

- Web access to commercial software.
- Software is managed from a central location.
- Software delivered in a "one to many" model.
- Users not required to handle software upgrades and patches.
- Application Programming Interfaces (APIs) allow for integration between different pieces of software.

Uses of SaaS

Cloud Computing generally and SaaS in particular, is a rapidly growing method of delivering technology. Organizations considering a move to the cloud will want to consider which applications they move to SaaS. There are particular solutions to consider prime candidate for an initial move to SaaS:

- "Vanilla" offerings where the solution is largely undifferentiated. A good example of a vanilla offering would include email where many times competitors use the same software precisely because this fundamental technology is a requirement for doing business, but does not itself confer an competitive advantage.
- Applications where there is significant interplay between the organization and the outside world. For example, email newsletter campaign software.
- Applications that have a significant need for web or mobile access. An example would be mobile sales management software.
- Software that is only to be used for a short term need. An example would be collaboration software for a specific project.
- Software where demand spikes significantly, for example tax or billing software used once a month.

SaaS is widely accepted to have been introduced to the business world by the Salesforce. Customer Relationship Management (CRM) product. As one of the earliest entrants it is not surprising that CRM is the most popular SaaS application area, however e-mail, financial management, customer service and expense management have also gotten good uptake via SaaS.

2. Platform as a Service(PAAS)

Platform as a Service (PaaS) brings the benefits that SaaS bought for applications, but over to the software development world. PaaS can be defined as a computing platform that allows the creation of web applications quickly and easily and without the complexity of buying and maintaining the software and infrastructure underneath it.

PaaS is analogous to SaaS except that, rather than being software delivered over the web, it is a platform for the creation of software, delivered over the web.

Characteristics of PaaS:

1. Services to develop, test, deploy, host and maintain applications in the same integrated development environment. All the varying services needed to fulfil the application development process.
2. Web based user interface creation tools help to create, modify, test and deploy different UI scenarios.
3. Multi-tenant architecture where multiple concurrent users utilize the same development application.
4. Built in scalability of deployed software including load balancing and failover.
5. Integration with web services and databases via common standards.
6. Support for development team collaboration – some PaaS solutions include project planning and communication tools.
7. Tools to handle billing and subscription management.

PaaS, which is similar in many ways to Infrastructure as a Service that will be discussed below, is differentiated from IaaS by the addition of value added services and comes in two distinct flavours.

1. A collaborative platform for software development, focused on workflow management regardless of the data source being used for the application. An example of this approach would be Heroku, a PaaS that utilizes the Ruby on Rails development language.
2. A platform that allows for the creation of software utilizing proprietary data from an application. This sort of PaaS can be seen as a method to create applications with a common data form or type. An example of this sort of platform would be the Force.com PaaS from Salesforce.com which is used almost exclusively to develop applications that work with the Salesforce.com CRM

Uses of PaaS

PaaS is especially useful in any situation where multiple developers will be working on a development project or where other external parties need to interact with the development process. It is proving invaluable for those who have an existing data source – for example sales information from a customer relationship management tool, and want to create applications which leverage that data. Finally PaaS is useful where developers wish to automate testing and deployment services.

The popularity of agile software development, a group of software development methodologies based on iterative and incremental development, will also increase the uptake of PaaS as it eases the difficulties around rapid development and iteration of software.

Some examples of PaaS include Google App Engine ,Microsoft Azure Services, and the Force.com platform.

3. Infrastructure as a Service:

Infrastructure as a Service (IaaS) is a way of delivering Cloud Computing infrastructure – servers, storage, network and operating systems – as an on-demand service. Rather than purchasing servers, software, datacenter space or network equipment, clients instead buy those resources as a fully outsourced service on demand.

Within IaaS, there are some sub-categories that are worth noting. Generally IaaS can be obtained as public or private infrastructure or a combination of the two. "Public cloud" is considered infrastructure that consists of shared resources, deployed on a self-service basis over the Internet.

By contrast, "private cloud" is infrastructure that emulates some of Cloud Computing features, like virtualization, but does so on a private network. Additionally, some hosting providers are beginning to offer a combination of traditional dedicated hosting alongside public and/ or private cloud networks. This combination approach is generally called "Hybrid Cloud".

Characteristics of IaaS

As with the two previous sections, SaaS and PaaS, IaaS is a rapidly developing field. That said there are some core characteristics which describe what IaaS is. IaaS is generally accepted to comply with the following;

1. Resources are distributed as a service.
2. Allows for dynamic scaling.
3. Has a variable cost, utility pricing model.
4. Generally includes multiple users on a single piece of hardware.

There are a many of IaaS providers out there from the largest Cloud players like Amazon Web Services and Rackspace to more boutique regional players.

As mentioned previously, the line between PaaS and IaaS is becoming more blurred as vendors introduce tools as part of IaaS that help with deployment including the ability to deploy multiple types of clouds.

Uses of IaaS

IaaS makes sense in a number of situations and these are closely related to the benefits that Cloud Computing bring. Situations that are particularly suitable for Cloud infrastructure include:

- Where demand is very volatile – any time there are significant spikes and canals in terms of demand on the infrastructure.
- For new organizations without the capital to invest in hardware.
- Where the organization is growing rapidly and scaling hardware would be problematic.
- Where there is pressure on the organization to limit capital expenditure and to move to operating expenditure.
- For specific line of business, trial or temporary infrastructural needs.

Advantages:

1. Lower upfront costs and reduced infrastructure costs.
2. Easy to grow your applications.
3. Scale up or down at short notice.
4. Only pay for what you use.

5. Everything managed under SLAs.
6. Overall environmental benefit (lower carbon emissions) of many users efficiently sharing large systems.

Disadvantages:
1. Higher ongoing operating costs.
2. Greater dependency on service providers.
3. Risk of being locked into proprietary or vendor-recommended systems. You cannot easily migrate to another system or service provider if you need to.
4. Uncertainty of product/system support from the cloud supplier.
5. Potential privacy and security risks of putting valuable data on someone else's system which is at unknown location.
6. Dependency on a Reliable Internet Connection.

Examples of Cloud Computing:
- Most of us use cloud computing all day long without realizing it. When you sit at your PC and type a query into Google, the computer on your desk isn't playing much part in finding the answers you need: it's no more than a messenger. The words you type are swiftly shuttled over the Net to one of Google's hundreds of thousands of clustered PCs, which dig out your results and send them promptly back to you. When you do a Google search, the real work in finding your answers might be done by a computer sitting in California, Dublin, Tokyo, or Beijing; you don't know.
- The same applies to Web-based email. Once upon a time, email was something you could only send and receive using a program running on your PC (sometimes called a mail client). But then Web-based services such as Hotmail came along and carried email off into the cloud. Now we're all used to the idea that emails can be stored and processed through a server in some remote part of the world, easily accessible from a Web browser, wherever we happen to be. Pushing email off into the cloud makes it supremely convenient for busy people, constantly on the move.
- Preparing documents over the Net is a newer example of cloud computing. Simply log on to a web-based service such as Google Documents and you can create a document, spreadsheet, presentation, or whatever you like using Web-based software. Instead of typing your words into a program like Microsoft Word or OpenOffice, running on your computer, you're using similar software running on a PC at one of Google's world-wide data centers. Like an email drafted on Hotmail, the document you produce is stored remotely, on a Web server, so you can access it from any Internet-connected computer, anywhere in the world, any time you like. Using a Web-based service like this means you're "contracting out" or "outsourcing" some of your computing needs to a company such as Google: they pay the cost of developing the software and keeping it up-to-date and they earn back the money to do this through advertising and other paid-for services.

Future Trends in Cloud Computing:
Cloud computing is a dynamic technology and the following are some **of the trends** that experts and analysts have identified.
1. **Cloud computing is scaling investment value**: Cloud computing streamlines how software, business processes, and services are accessed. More than ever before, this is

helping businesses scale operations and optimize their investments. This is not only through lower costs, efficient business models, or greater agility in operations. It has a lot to do with how businesses use it to optimize their investments. In the same breadth, businesses are scaling into more innovation with their IT capacity. This will certainly help them make more investments and draw corporate income.

2. **The emergence hybrid cloud computing**: Hybrid cloud computing combines local and cloud computing. Businesses are using cloud computing (both private and public) to supplement their internal infrastructure and applications. Experts predict that these services will optimize business process performance. The adoption of cloud services is a new development in business functions. Under these circumstances, scaling down on the strengths of both worlds will become a common feature, if it's not already happening as it is.

3. **Growing popularity for cloud-centric design**: More than ever before, organizational design is incorporating cloud computing migration elements. This simply means the need for optimal cloud experiences is on top of the list of the companies that are adopting this technology. This is a trend that is expected to grow more as cloud computing expands into different industries.

4. **Cloud services optimized for mobile**: The future is firmly mobile, one way or another. The exceptional rise in the number of mobile devices— tablet computers, iPhones, and smartphones—comes into play here. Many of these devices are used to scale business processes, communications, and other functions. To make cloud computing useful to business owners and employees, the cloud is taking a 'mobile' approach. More cloud computing platforms and APIs will become accessible on mobile.

5. **Security:** Cloud computing security is one of the most documented cloud computing issues. People are worried about the security of the data they store in the cloud. Because of this, you should expect to see more secure security applications and techniques coming up. The number of new encryption techniques, security protocols, and so much more will grow in the future.

Case Study

Cloud Computing Security Case Studies and Research
Chimere Barron, Huiming Yu and Justin Zhan

Abstract: Cloud computing is an emerging technological paradigm that provides a flexible and scalable information technology infrastructure to enable business agility. There are different vulnerabilities in cloud computing and various threats to cloud computing. We have investigated several real-world cases where companies' cloud was infiltrated by attacks. In this paper several types of attacks are discussed, real-world cases are studied, and the solutions that providers developed are presented. Our current research will also be discussed.

Index Terms: Cloud computing security, real-world cases, security case studies, algorithms.

I. Introduction:

Cloud computing has become the newest rave in the computing industry. Its ability to save business's cost by eliminating the need to purchase huge amounts of software and/or software licenses for every employee, reducing the need for advanced hardware, eliminating the need for companies to rent physical space to store servers and databases, and shifting the workload from local computers that has appealed to cloud computing providers such as Amazon, Google, IBM, Yahoo, Microsoft, etc.

There is no fixed definition for cloud computing, but it is the general term used for computing that involves delivering hosted services over the internet. Cloud services offer three distinct amenities - it is sold on demand (typically by the minute or hour), it is elastic (a user can have as much or as little of a service as needed at any given time), and the service is fully managed by the provider. These services are categorized as Infrastructure as a Service (IaaS), Platform as a Service (PaaS), and Software as a Service (SaaS). Infrastructure as a Service provides low-level services which can be booted with a user-defined hard disk image such as Amazon EC2. In Platform as a Service, the cloud provider offers an API which can be used by an application developer to create applications on the provider's platform. Examples of PaaS include Force.com, GoogleApps, etc. With Software as a Service, the vendor supplies the software product and interacts with users through a front-end portal; web-based office applications like Google Docs or Calendar are examples of SaaS.

Cloud computing offers numerous advantages, therefore hackers are also interested in it. Various attacks such as social engineering attack, XML signature wrapping attack, malware injection, data manipulation, account hijacking, traffic flooding, and wireless local area network attack pose a great risk to cloud computing systems. There have been many instances where companies have fallen victims to cloud computing being hacked.

We have examined cloud computing providers that were compromised, how the attack was completed, and solutions the company developed to make sure the incident can never be repeated in the future. In section II, the guest and provider sides of cloud computing will be discussed. The details of these real-world cases will be presented in section III. In section IV our current research will be discussed. The conclusion and future work will be given in section V.

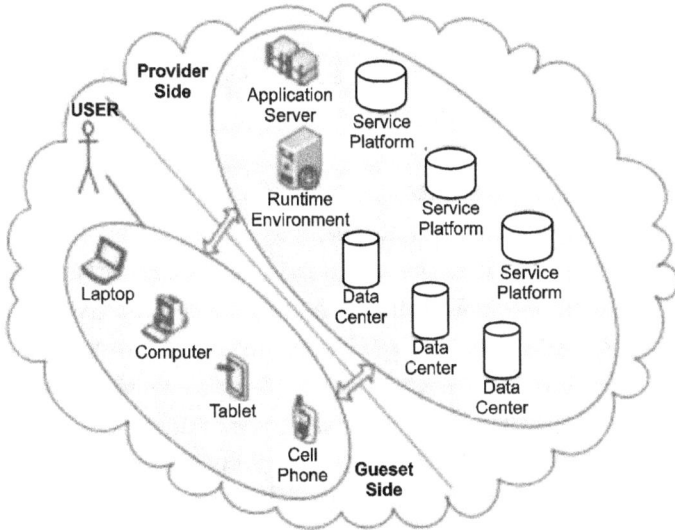

Fig. 5.5: Cloud Computing Users and Providers

Cloud computing providers must keep users' privacy and assure the information stored on the cloud is always secure. The Service-Level Agreement (SLA) between cloud providers and customers specifies details of the service. A typical cloud SLA specifies service objectives such as 99.9% uptime, compensation to the user. The Cloud Security Alliance (CSA) offer certification to cloud providers that meet the criteria. The CSA's Trusted Cloud Initiative program was created to help cloud service providers develop industry recommended, secure interoperable identity, access and compliance management configuration and practices

II. Guest and Provider Sides of Cloud Computing:

When companies, governments or organizations decide to make the shift to cloud computing security is a main consideration. Cloud computing consists of guest and provider sides. The guest side is the end users who use the cloud. It provides the end users with the ability to choose cloud services and environment. It is the interface that clients see after they enter credentials and have the ability to use the services provided by the cloud. The guest side may consist of different users, laptops, tablets, cell phones, various computers and enterprise centers. The provider side of cloud computing is the service providers which consists of application servers, service platforms, runtime environment, and datacenters etc. An application server can be WebSphere Application Server that is a Java EE, EJB supported technology-based application platform. Service platforms provide capabilities to users to build, deploy and manage robust, agile and reusable SOA business applications and services. A datacenter can provide huge capacity to store users' data and keep them secure. Figure 1 is an example that shows the basic layout of the guest side and provider side of cloud computing. The guest side is the enterprise portion and the provider side is the service provider portion.

III. Security Case Studies:

Multiple real-world cases where cloud computing were compromised and the ways the company mitigated the incident will be discussed. For each case the attack type will be briefly described, the details of the case will be presented and the prevention methods will be discussed.

(A) XML Signature Wrapping Attack: Wrapping attacks aim at injecting a faked element into the message structure so that a valid signature covers the unmodified element while the faked one is processed by the application logic. As a result, an attacker can perform an arbitrary Web Service request while authenticating as a legitimate user.

In 2011, researchers lead by Dr. Jorg Schwenk from Ruhr-University Bochum found a cryptographic hole in Amazon's EC2 and S3 services. The flaw was located in the web services security protocol and enabled attackers to trick servers into authorizing digitally signed SOAP messages that have been altered. The attackers hijacked control interfaces used to manage cloud computing resources, which would allow attackers to create, modify, and delete machine images, and change administrative passwords and settings.

A proposed solution is to use the SOAP message during message passing from the web server to the web browser. A redundant bit (STAMP bit) will be added onto the signature value when it is appended in the SOAP header. This bit will be transmitted when the message is interfered with by a third party during the transfer. When the message reaches its destination the STAMP bit is checked. If the STAMP BIT has been changed, then a new signature value is generated by the browser and the new value is sent back to the server as recorded to modify the authenticity checking.

(B) Malware Injection: In a malware-injection attack an adversary attempts to inject malicious code into a system. This attack can appear in the form of code, scripts, active content, and/or other software. When an instance of a legitimate user is ready to run in the cloud server, the respective service accepts the instance for computation in the cloud. The only checking done is to determine if the instance matches a legitimate existing service. However, the integrity of the instance is not checked. By penetrating the instance and duplicating it as if it is a valid service, the malware activity succeeds in the cloud.

Case one occurred in May 2009. The United States Treasury Department moved four public websites offline for the Bureau of Engraving and Printing after discovering malicious code was added to the parent side. The thirdparty cloud service provider hosting the company's website was victim to an intrusion attack. As a result numerous websites (BEP and non-BEP) were affected. Roger Thompson, chief research officer for Anti-Virus Guard (AVG) Technologies, discovered malicious code was injected into the affected pages. Hackers added a tiny snippet of a virtually undetectable iFrame HTML code that redirected visitors to a Ukrainian website. IFrame (Inline Frame) is an HTML document embedded inside another HTML document on a website. From there, a variety of web-based attacks were launched using an easy-to-purchase malicious toolkit called the Eleonore Exploit Pack

To prevent this type of attack server operators need to check for and exploit iFrame code. Firefox users should install NoScript and set "Plugins | Forbid iFrame" option. Window users should make sure they have installed all security updates and have an active anti-malware guard running.

Case two occurred in June 2011. The cyber criminals from Brazil who first launched their attacks as spam/phishing campaigns, where users were sent spoofed emails with links that took them to one of the malicious domains, created some major problems in Amazon Web Services [3]. The attackers installed a variety of malicious files on the victims' machines. One component acted as a rootkit (a type of malicious software that is activated each time a user's system boots up) and attempted to disable installed anti-malware applications. Additional components that were downloaded during the attack attempted to retrieve login information from a list of nine Brazilian banks and two other international banks, steal digital certificates from eTokens stored on the machine, and collect unique data about the PC itself that is used by some banks as part of an authentication routine

A proposed solution is to utilize the File Allocation Table (FAT) system architecture. The FAT table identifies the code or application that a customer is going to run. It checks with the previous instances that have already executed from the customer's machine to determine the validity and integrity of the new instance. A secure and unbreakable hypervisor would be needed on the provider's end. The hypervisor would be responsible for scheduling all instances, but not before checking the integrity of the instance from the FAT table of the customer's virtual machine.

(C) Social Engineering Attack: A social engineering attack is an intrusion that relies heavily on human interaction and often tricking other people to break normal security procedures [9]. It can happen in cloud computing.

In August 2012, hackers used a social engineering attack to completely destroy technical writer Mat Honan's digital life by remotely deleting the information from his iPad, MacBook, and iPod. The heart of the story revealed the dangerous blind spot between the identity verification systems used by Amazon and Apple. The hackers found the victim's @me.com address online which informed them that there was an associated AppleID account. The hacker called Amazon customer service wanting to add a credit card number to the victim's account. The representative asked the hacker for the name, billing address, and an associated email address (all information the hacker found on the internet) on the victim's account. Once the hacker answered these questions successfully the representative added the new credit card onto the account. Once ending the call, the hacker called Amazon customer service back and explained to the representative that he had lost access to his account. The Amazon representative asked the hacker for his billing address and a credit card associated with the account; the hacker used the new credit card information he provided from the previous phone call. Once the hacker gave the representative the information they added a new email address to the victim's account. Upon logging onto Amazon's website the hacker requested a password reset the email address he just created. The hacker now had access to the victim's Amazon account and credit card information on file. The hacker then called Apple technical support and requested a password reset on the victim's @me.com email account. The hacker could not answer any of the victim's account security questions, but Apple offered him another option. The Apple representative only needed a billing address and the last four digits of the victim's credit card and issued the hacker a temporary password. Once the hacker had access to the victim's Apple iCloud account all the information from the victim's iPad, MacBook, and iPod account was remotely erased.

Apple confirmed that it temporarily disabled its customers' ability to reset an AppleID password over the phone. Instead, customers have to use Apple's online "iForgot" system. In the process they will work on a much stronger authentication method that proves customers are who they say they are. Amazon customer service representatives will no longer change account settings like credit card or email addresses by phone.

(D) Account Hijacking: Account hijacking is usually carried out with stolen credentials. Using the stolen credentials, attackers can access sensitive information and compromise the confidentiality, integrity, and availability of the services offered. Examples of such attacks include: eavesdropping on transactions/sensitive activities, manipulation of data, returning falsified information, and redirection to illegitimate sites.

In July 2012, the hacker group, UGNazi, exploited a major flaw in Google's gmail password recovery process and AT&T's voicemail system which in turned allowed the group to access the CEO of CloudFare's personal gmail account. The hacker deceived AT&T'S system into redirecting the victim's cell phone to a fraudulent voicemail box. The hacker visited gmail and initiated the account recovery feature for the victim's personal email address. A voicemail message was recorded on the compromised voicemail box to sound like someone was answering the phone. A call was placed to the victim from Google, but the victim did not recognize the number and let the call go to voicemail. Google's system was tricked by the fraudulent voicemail and a temporary PIN was left (which allowed the password to be reset) in the voicemail. The hacker logged into the victim's gmail account and added his email address to the 'account recovery control' feature. The victim's linked Cloudfare account received an email informing him that the recent password was changed. The victim initiated the account recovery process and changed the password back. An email is sent to the hacker informing him that the victim changed passwords, but immediately the hacker changed the password. Both users continue going back and forth to get control over the account. Soon, the hacker is able to remove the victim's mobile phone and email addresses authorized for account recovery preventing the victim from resetting the gmail password. The team at CloudFare is called to investigate the situation.

A flaw in Google's account recovery system allowed two-factor authentication setup on the victim's Cloudfare account to be bypassed and the hacker now had access to the account. The victim's administrative privileges were used by the hacker to change passwords on other administrative accounts. Cloudfare's operations team suspended the victim's account, reset all CloudFare employee email passwords, and cleared all web mail sessions, which terminated the hacker's access to the email system.

Google fixed the flaw in the Google Enterprise Application account recovery process by no longer allowing a user to get around two-factor authentication. CloudFlare has stopped emailing blind copies of password resets and other transactional messages to administrative accounts.

Another case occurred in July 2012. Dropbox, the cloud storage service, confirmed that hackers used usernames and passwords stolen from third-party sites to access Dropbox users' accounts. It was altered after users complained about Spam they were receiving to email address used only for the Dropbox accounts. One stolen password was used to access an employee account that contains a file that included user email addressed. The company believed users who use the same password on multiple websites make it easier for hackers to access their accounts on other websites.

In order to prevent a repeat attack, Dropbox has implemented two-factor authentication into the company's security controls. Two-factor authentication (also called strong authentication) is defined as a user entering in two of the following three properties to prove his/her identity: something the user knows (e.g, password, PIN), something the user has (e.g., ATM card) and/or something the user is (e.g., biometric characteristic, such as a fingerprint). The company launched new automated mechanisms to identify suspicious activities and a new page to show all logins.

(E) Traffic Flooding: Traffic flooding attacks bring a network or service down by flooding it with large amounts of traffic. Traffic flooding attacks occur when a network or service becomes so weighed down with packets initiating incomplete connection requests it cannot process genuine connection requests. Eventually, the host's memory buffer becomes full and no further connections can be made, and the result is a Denial of Service.

In May 2011, LastPass, a cloud-based password storage and management company, announced a possible successful hack against its servers. There were no reports of any data leakage, but the company insisted that customer's take a few measures to ensure that their information is safe. Security experts discovered unusual behavior in the database servers that had more traffic going out compared to incoming data. The company presumed this was hacking activity related to siphoning stored login credentials and other sensitive user data. Master passwords (passwords that protect lists of passwords to access other websites and online services in the cloud) were immediately changed to protect customers from possible data leakage.

To prevent this problem from happening again Lastpass enhanced its encryption algorithms used in protecting customers' data and introduced additional measures to secure sensitive data on its servers.

(F) Wireless Local Area Network Attack: In a wireless local area network attack a hacker breaks into an authorized user's wireless local area network to perform attacks such as man-in-the-middle, accidental association, identify theft, denial of service, network injection attacks, etc.

In January 2011, German security researcher Thomas Roth used cloud computing to crack wireless networks that relied on pre-shared passphrases, such as those found in homes and small businesses. The results of the attack revealed that wireless computing that relies on the pre-shared key (WPA-PSK) system for protection is fundamentally insecure. Roth's program was run on Amazon's Elastic Cloud Computing (EC2) system. Using the massive power of Amazon's cloud the program was able to run through 400,000 possible passwords per second. It would typically cost tens of thousands of dollars to purchase the computers to run the program, but Roth claims that a typical password can be guessed by EC2 and his software in about six minutes. The type of EC2 computers used in the attack costs $.28 cents per minute, so $1.68 is all it took to hack into a wireless network.

WPA-PSK is believed to be secure because the computing power needed to run through all the possibilities of passphrases is huge. But cloud computing provides this kind computing power today, and is very inexpensive. It is suggested that up to 20 characters are enough to create a passphrase that cannot be cracked, but the more characters included, the stronger the passphrase will be. A good variety of symbols, letters, and numbers should be included in the passphrase and it should be changed regularly. Dictionary words and letter substitution (i.e "n1c3" instead of "nice") should be avoided.

IV. Our Current Research:

One of the severe types of attacks, that interrupt cloud computing normal functions, is a SYN flood attack which is simply a type of Denial of Service. An attacker sends a succession of SYN requests to a victim system in an attempt to consume system resources and make the system unresponsive to legitimate traffic. There are a number of existing countermeasures against SYN flood attacks such as Filtering, SYN Cache, SYN Cookies, Firewalls and Proxies, Reducing SYN-RECEIVED Time, etc

In cloud computing all servers work in a service specific manner with internal communication among them. When a server is overloaded or has reached the threshold, it transfers some of its jobs to similar service-specific server to offload tasks. If an adversary successfully attacks one server with SYN flood and causes the denial-of-service, the victim server will transfer upcoming tasks to other servers in order to offload jobs. Thus, the same thing will occur on other servers and the attacker is successful in engaging the whole cloud system by just interrupting the usual processing of one server, in essence flooding the cloud.

Based on the characteristics of cloud computing we are developing an approach to effectively detect and prevent SYN flood attacks. The first part of this approach is to design an algorithm to discover the malicious packets. The detecting algorithm will check some parameters of incoming IP packets to decide to filter an incoming packet out or not. The second part is to develop an algorithm to stop SYN flood to spread over cloud computing. Once a server is overloaded the preventing algorithm will check current situation, compare with normal cases, then decide it is SYN flood or normal overloaded work. If it is SYN flood it will keep the victim server from transferring upcoming jobs to other servers. These algorithms will run on the hypervisor of the provider side.

V. Conclusion and Future Work:

Cloud computing security involves different areas and issues. Many security mechanisms have been developed to prevent various attacks and protect cloud computing systems. Researchers continue to develop new technologies to improve the security of cloud computing. In this paper several realworld cases where companies' clouds were infiltrated by attacks are presented. Social engineering attack, XML signature wrapping attack, malware injection, data manipulation, account hijacking, SYN flood, and wireless local area network attack are discussed. The solutions that the companies developed to prevent similar attacks in the future are discussed. In order to protect cloud computing technologies of detection, prevention and responding various attacks must be developed. Our current research focuses on detecting and preventing SYN flood in cloud computing. We are developing one detecting algorithm and one preventing algorithm. We will implement and test these algorithms on cloud computing.

Acknowledgements

This work was partially supported by National Science Foundation under the award numbers 0909980, 0830686, 1247663, 1238767, and 1137443.

Case Study taken from: http://www.iaeng.org/publication/WCE2013/WCE2013_pp1287-1291.pdf

5.2.2 Green Computing   [April 16]

Faced with the absolute realities of global warming and rising energy costs, government agencies and private firms worldwide are examining ways to protect the environment. To address what is increasingly being perceived as a crisis, there is a growing global movement to implement more environmentally friendly computing "Green computing" is the name attached to this movement, which represents an environmentally responsible way to reduce power and environmental waste. Toward this goal, the U.S. Environmental Protection Agency's Energy Star program has developed compliance requirements for computer equipment. The U.S. House of Representatives Resolution 5646, passed in July 2006, calls for the EPA's Energy Star program to research:

- The amount of power consumed by corporate and federal data centers.
- Industry measures to develop energy-efficient servers.
- Possible incentives to convince businesses to use energy-saving technologies.

The first step toward the green computing movement was the initiation of the Energy Star program in 1992. This served as a voluntary label that was awarded to computer products that were successful in proving that they used minimum energy while maximizing efficiency. The rating was awarded to monitors, refrigerators, television sets, air conditioners and other household appliances.

The first result of green computing research resulted in the Sleep Mode function for computer monitors. This function allows the computer to enter Standby Mode after a pre-set period passes without any user activity.

After this, various concepts like energy cost accounting, thin client solutions, eWaste, and virtualization were developed.

Green IT

Green computing is commonly referred to as Green IT. The idea is to ensure the least human impact on the environment. Apart from this, it aims to achieve environmental sustainability.

In simple language, green computing is the scientific study of efficient and effective designing, manufacturing, using, disposing, and recycling of computers and computer related products like servers, network systems, communication systems, monitors, USBs, printers, etc. The study uses science to create technologies that help to preserve natural resources and reduce the harmful impact on the environment.

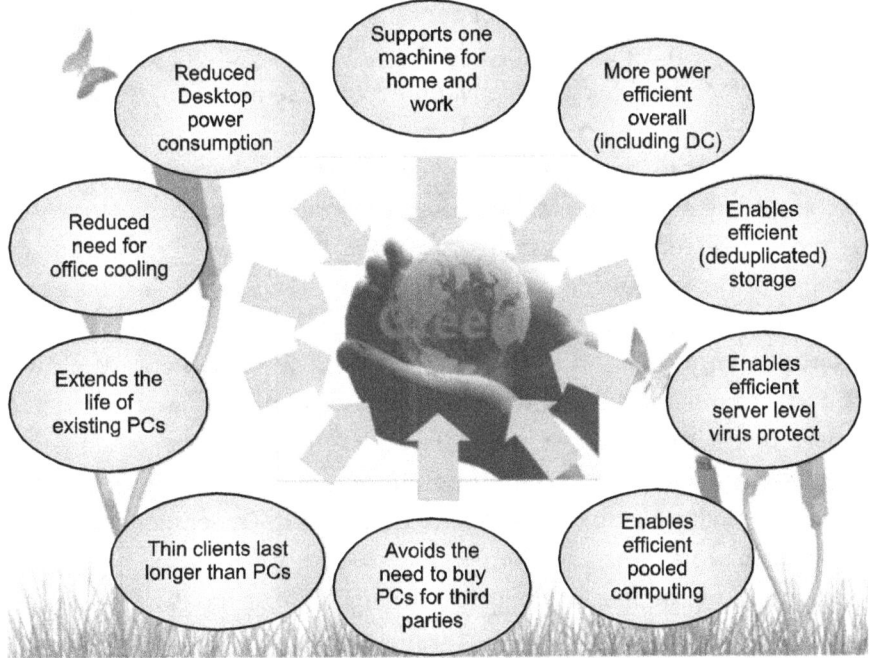

Fig. 5.6: Green Computing

Five steps to take towards Green Computing:

1. **Develop a sustainable green computing plan:** Discuss with your business leaders the elements that should be factored into such a plan, including organizational policies and checklists. Such a plan should include recycling policies, recommendations for disposal of used equipment, government guidelines and recommendations for purchasing green computer equipment.

Green computing best practices and policies should cover power usage, reduction of paper consumption, as well as recommendations for new equipment and recycling old machines. Organizational policies should include communication and implementation.

2. **Recycle:** Discard used or unwanted electronic equipment in a convenient and environmentally responsible manner. Computers have toxin metals and pollutants that can emit harmful emissions into the environment. Never discard computers in a landfill. Recycle them instead through manufacturer programs such as HP's Planet Partners recycling service or recycling facilities in your community. Or donate still-working computers to a non-profit agency.

3. Make environmentally sound purchase decisions: Purchase Electronic Product Environmental Assessment Tool registered products. EPEAT is a procurement tool promoted by the nonprofit Green Electronics Council to:

- Help institutional purchasers evaluate, compare and select desktop computers, notebooks and monitors based on environmental attributes.
- Provide a clear, consistent set of performance criteria for the design of products.
- Recognize manufacturer efforts to reduce the environmental impact of products by reducing or eliminating environmentally sensitive materials, designing for durability and reducing packaging materials.

4. Reduce Paper Consumption: There are many easy, obvious ways to reduce paper consumption: e-mail, electronic archiving, use the "track changes" feature in electronic documents, rather than redline corrections on paper. When you do print out documents, make sure to use both sides of the paper, recycle regularly, use smaller fonts and margins, and selectively print required pages.

5. Conserve energy: Turn off your computer when you know you won't use it for an extended period of time. Turn on power management features during shorter periods of inactivity. Power management allows monitors and computers to enter low-power states when sitting idle. By simply hitting the keyboard or moving the mouse, the computer or monitors awakens from its low power sleep mode in seconds. Power management tactics can save energy and help protect the environment.

Green computing represents a responsible way to address the issue of global warming. By adopting green computing practices, business leaders can contribute positively to environmental care and protect the environment while also reducing energy and paper costs.

Features of Green Computing

1. **Power Management:** This feature means conservation of power used by all electrical appliances. Many appliances now come with a power saving feature. Devices with this feature automatically turn off the power or switch the appliance to a low power state when not being used.

2. **Energy Efficient Computing:** Computers have a fan / heater-like component inside them. The energy waste of computers is increasing by the day. Energy waste is leading to a climatic change from burning coal and oil.

3. **Remediation of Environmental Pollutants:** This deals with reducing and removing pollution or contaminants from groundwater, soil, surface water or sediments.

4. **Server Virtualization:** This is popularly known as VPS and is commonly used to split the server. The idea is to use one server which connects to many individual computers. This development has been seen in software, technology, and other types of architecture virtualization.

5. **Sewage Treatment:** This wastewater treatment involves removing of contaminants from waste water and sewage. Various chemical and biological processes are used to remove chemicals and other contaminants.

6. **Efficient Disposal/Waste Management:** This is the collection, processing, recycling, and disposal of waste materials.

7. **Efficient Recycling:** Reusing products is much better than letting them stay in landfills.

8. **Regulatory Compliance:** A strategy must be designed by governments, which would offer rules to control waste management, reducing pollution and stringent penalties for non compliance.

9. **Recycling and Water Purification:** This is the process of removing all unneeded materials and contaminants from water.

10. **Green Metrics and Methodology:** It is important to quantify feasibility and environmental performance to help reach our goals.

11. **Renewable Resources:** Use of renewable sources of energy such as solar power and wind to serve purposes like heating, cooking etc.

12. **Eco-Labelling of IT Products:** More companies should design their products so they receive the eco-label. Consumers must check for the eco-label before investing their resources in a particular IT product.

13. **Thin Client Solutions:** Thin client is also known as a lean client solution, and requires computers to depend on another computer or server to function.

Going Green at Work

Organizations all over the world are beginning to understand their corporate social responsibility toward the environment. Most companies now believe in conserving energy and power and using environmentally friendly products that help in reducing their carbon footprint. Nowadays, it is necessary for all sized organizations to implement aspects of green computing in their daily workings.

Organizations must follow these simple steps for creating the green computing awareness in their workplaces:

1. Announcing green intentions to all employees.
2. Setting up a committee to form a green IT plan.
3. Centralization of all desktops.
4. Using efficient computer applications.
5. Power management tactics.
6. Business performance enhancement.

Common implementation of Green Computing in organizations:
- **Virtualization**: Virtualization is the combination of servers and systems to reduce power consumption and energy utilization. It leads to usage of more than one system on a single piece of physical hardware. This allows for minimum power consumption and maximum cooling.
- **Power Saving**: Industry standards like ACPI design and manufacture computer components in such a way that they result in power controlling and saving.
- **Telecommuting**: Employees working from home reduce the fuel emission created during commuting by vehicles. Moreover, there is reduction in overhead costs on utilities, etc. All of these initiatives result in increased power and energy savings.
- **VoIP:** VoIP stands for Voice over Internet Protocol and results in less telephone wiring and lower costs.

Case Study

Green Computing: A Case Study of Rajarshi Shahu Mahavidyalaya, Latur, INDIA

Abstract

College campuses and universities can use the concept of green computing very efficiently. The paper aims to assess awareness levels of IT users with regards to Green Computing; that is using IT in ways that are not harmful to the environment. A recommendation will be given on how Green Computing strategies can be implemented at RS College. Green computing is the study and practice of efficient and eco-friendly computing resources. Some common green computing practices include turning of the monitor when its not in use or using more energy efficient monitors like liquid crystal diode (LCD) instead of the traditional cathode ray tube (CRT) monitors. The objective of this paper is saving electricity consumption in computer science and information technology of RS College Latur In Case Of LCD and CRT monitors. This paper gives a description about laboratories of department of computer science and IT. Also, the paper explains the need of Green Computing at department of computer science and IT.The conclusion of the case study illustrates the saving in electricity by using some methods like payback period. Statistics were sought to establish the levels of awareness of negative impacts of IT and of environmental sustainability awareness or green computing.

Keywords:

RS College, Green Computing, electricity consumption

1. Introduction:

"Green Computing is the practice of using computer resources efficiently. Another definition is the one which defines green computing as the study and practice of efficient and eco-friendly computing resources. Green computing is no longer viewed as an issue of environmental organizations alone but other businesses such as commercial, universities, governments etc. have started paying attention to it as well. Green computing is:

- The environmentally responsible use of computers and related resources.
- The use of energy efficient technologies, techniques and devices aimed at helping the environment.
- Also referred to as Green IT The primary goals of green computing are:
  o To reduce the use of hazardous materials
  o To maximize the energy efficiency during the product's lifetime
  o To promote biodegradability or recycle ability of defunct products and factory waste.

Green computing is concerned with reducing the environmental impact of (Information Technology) IT before IT devices are purchased, during their lifetimes and after we have finished with them. Most manufacturers are improving their processes at the different levels of the product life to lessen harm as they are using the materials which are usually eco-friendly, renewable or might use less energy. Various Colleges and universities are implementing the following strategies to reduce environmental impact of computers during their use; when IT devices are not in use they are put in sleep mode, IT machines are switched off when not in use, sharing documents and files on the screen or use FTP servers and only print on demand and where necessary, using virtualization software instead of physical machines/servers, printing less etc. The product lives of product must be prolonged through upgrade options rather than finishing the lifespan of products. Old IT products can be donated to charities and refurbishing organizations which might increase the product life. The above are some of the strides made in ensuring green computing for sustainable environment. This paper is concerned with conducting a research on electricity consumption of department of computer science and IT in RS College.

2. Need of Green Computing at RSML:

Out of these areas, our CS and IT department of RS college is concentrated on electricity consumption. The focus of this paper is to reduce the electricity consumption in RS college. In this department what should be noted is that students and staff at department of CS and IT spend an average of nine hours a day on computers, either doing their assignments and doing practicals or doing their work everyday. What is evident is that the use of computers is growing at a phenomenal rate and naturally so is the consumption of electricity. A computer is made up of many components that consume power: the CPU, hard drives, graphic cards, monitors, speakers, printers, communication devices, scanners, etc. The average desktop computer consumes about 120 watts of electricity, on average, the monitor consumes 75 watts, and the CPU consumes 45 watts, laptops consumes between 15 and 45 watts. There are around 103 desktop computers at RS College and if they are all left on all the time they would consume a total of 1, 366megawatts-hours per year.

During their operations computers not only consume energy but also leave carbon foot prints. IT-related equivalent carbon dioxide (CO_2e) emissions alone have been estimated at two per cent of the world's total [3]. What prompted this research paper is the fact that, at face value, students and other computer users are oblivious to the negative impacts of computers. As stated earlier this research will attempt to establish how much RS College community has incorporated green policy strategies into their operations.

3. Research Problems:

Electricity Consumption Energy Conservation and Strategies and Practices Users must be encouraged to implement power management options on their machines.

- Reducing overall time the system as a whole and monitor is on.
- Ensuring the peripherals that are not in use are switched off as well as switching off air conditioners and lights that are not in use.

Improve electrical metering practices in order to enable the development of an energy consumption measurement program and energy indicators that break down energy consumption in a way that is easily communicable and relevant to the campus. Fig. 5.7 below shows comparative results of a study that was done to show the power consumption (in watts) of 20" Dell LCD monitors at different states . Note that from Fig. 5.7; when unplugged the monitor does not use any energy, but when it is off it can still use some bit of energy. In sleep mode it will use more energy than when it is off. Observe how, the study revealed elevated consumption of energy when the monitor is on. Fig. 5.7 below shows the desktop and laptop power consumption (in watts). Please note the differences in power consumptions for unplugged, off, sleep mode, ON, hibernate mode.

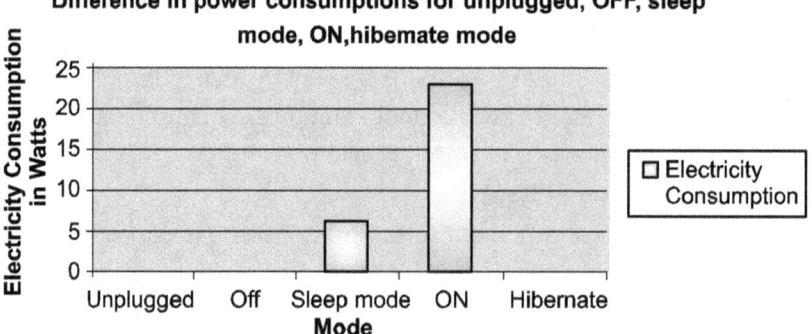

Fig. 5.7: Difference in Power Consumptions

Objectives of Case Study

Reduction Of electricity consumption is performed at department level as yet and it is desirable to perform at college level. The objectives are

1. To identify electricity consumption at department level based on data collection and analysis.
2. Preventive measures to reduce the electricity consumption
3. Uses of advance technologies to achieve the goal of reduction in consumption of electricity.

Methodology
Payback Analysis

It is the length of time required recovering the cost of an investment. If the cash inflows occur at a uniform rate, it is the ratio of the amount initial investment over expected annual cash inflows.

$$\text{Payback period} = \frac{\text{Initial Investment}}{\text{Annual Cash Inflows}}$$

For calculating payback period department information is required. Hence, department survey is carried out for gathering the information of laboratories, electrical consumption.

(a) Total number of laboratories in department
(b) Working and non-working hours of laboratories
(c) Total number of CRT and LCD monitors in laboratories = 103
(d) Last four years (from 2009 to 2012) price list of CRT and LCD monitor

Table 1 shows, the CS and IT department having total 4 laboratories, out of which only 3 laboratories (Lab-1, Lab-2 and Lab-6) currently contain LCD monitors. There are total 103 computers, out of which 27 are CRT and 76 are LCD monitors.

Table 5.1: Computer labs in CS and IT Department

A^p	Lab–1	Lab–2	Lab 4/5	Lab 6
B^q	54	48	48	54
C^r	1(a)	2(b)	2	1(c)
D^s	(X^2) 28	20	27	28
CRT	28	20	27	28
LCD	(Y^9) 28	20	0	28
$X^f + Y^g$	56	40	27	56

Total LCD = 28 + 20 + 28 = 76

[I]

p = Name of lab
q = Working hour per week
r = Non-working hours per week
s = Existing monitors for year 2009
a = Non-working hours of lab-1
b = Non-working hours of lab-2
c = Non-working hours of lab-6
a + b + c (Non-working hours of labs having LCD monitors) = 4
f = Total number of CRT monitors = 27
g = Total number of LCD monitors = 76

[II] Hours per week = Total hours per week, (Total 9 hours per day, Total 6 days per week. Therefore total 54 hours per week)

[III] Lab-1 = Laboratory 1, Lab-2=Laboratory 2, Laboratory 3= Laboratory 3.

As per the voltage is considered CRT monitor consumes 80 Watts and LCD monitors consume 40 Watts. Table 2 shows if one CRT monitor is ON for 54 hours per week (which are non-working hours of Lab-1, Lab-2 and Lab-6) it consumes 2 units/week which cost 6 ₹ per week and 216 per year in contrast. If one LCD monitor is ON for the same hours/week it consumes only 1 unit/week with cost 3 ₹/weeks and 108 ₹/year which is exactly half as compare to CRT monitor.

Table 5.2: Cost of electricity charges for single CRT and LCD monitor

Monitors	Quantity	Electricity Consumption (units/week)	Cost electricity (₹/Week)	Cost of electricity (₹ per year)
CRT	1	2	6	216
LCD	1	1	03	108

[I]   Cost of electricity charges is ₹ 3/unit (3 ₹) × 2 (units) = 6 ₹/week, unit = kwh.

[II] ₹ Indian Rupees.

[III] Total 9 hours per day, Total 6 days per week, Total 36 weeks per year (16 weeks per semester, for 2 semester (for one year) total 32 weeks and 4 weeks for exam) One semester = 6 months.

Table 5.3: Cost of electricity charges for 103 CRT and LCD monitor

Monitors	Quantity	Electricity Consumption (units/week)	Cost electricity (₹/Week)	Cost of electricity (₹ per year)
CRT	103	1236	7416	2,66,976
LCD	103	618	1854	66,744

Table 5.3 shows further calculations. If we utilize 103 CRT monitors for 54 hrs/week it costs 2,66,976 ₹/year and LCD monitor saves upto 2,00,232 ₹/year. So better option is to replace CRT with LCD monitors. Cost of LCD monitor is decreases year by year.

The market price of last four years (from 2009-2012) of LCD monitor is studied, the price found drastically decreasing as compared to previous year. If the same fact is considered it can be assumes that the rate will decrease in future also. This is shown in Table 5.4 and Fig. 5.8 given below:

Table 5.4

Years	Cost of 18.5" (inches) LCD monitors (₹)	Cost of 18.5" (inches) CRT monitors (₹)
2005	14,000	6,800
2006	13,000	6,500
2007	12,500	6,200
2008	10,500	5,500

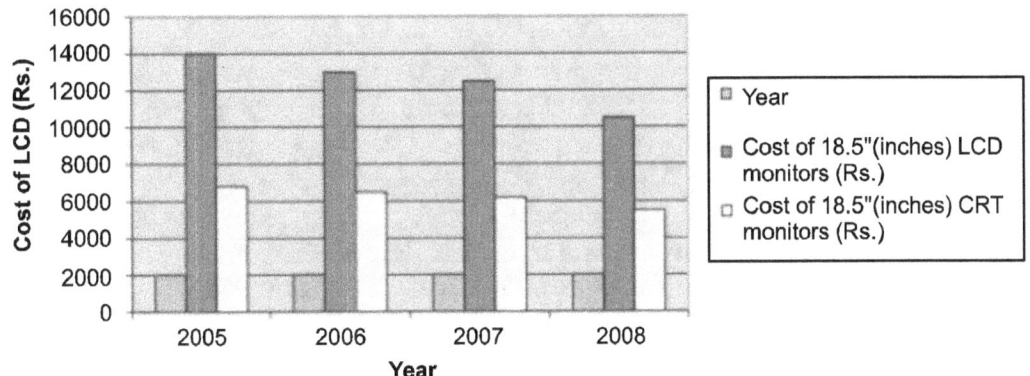

Fig. 5.8: Last 4 years (from 2005 to 2008) cost of LCD and CRT monitors

Table 5.5: Next 10 years (from 2009 to 2018) data for LCD monitor and its cost

Year	A	B	C	D	E	F	G	H
2008	1	0	0	7500	0	0	0	0
2009	1	56	56	7000	392000	336	12096	36288
2010	2	56	0	6500	0	336	12096	36288
2011	2	56	0	6500	0	336	12096	36288
2012	3	76	20	5500	110000	456	16416	49288
2013	3	86	10	5000	50000	516	18576	55728
2014	4	96	10	4500	45000	576	20736	62208
2015	4	106	10	4000	40000	636	22896	68688
2016	5	116	10	3500	35000	696	25056	75168
2017	5	126	10	3000	30000	756	27216	81648

where,

A – Electricity charges per unit (₹)

B – Existing LCD

C – New LCD

D – Cost per LCD monitor purchased

E – Total purchased cost (₹)

F – Electricity saved unit per week

G – Electricity saved unit per year

H – Cost of electricity saved ₹ per year

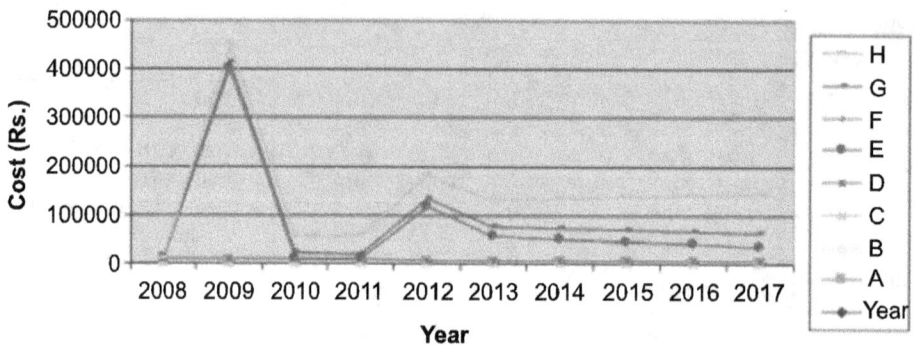

Fig. 5.9: Electricity Forecasting

Proposed Techniques:

1. Labs should be properly ventilated, not underground
2. Separate labs for low power computing requirement and high end computing.
3. Prevention from dust.

Conclusion:

This paper was motivated by the rising cost of electricity in RS College. The conclusion of the case study illustrates the saving in electricity in case of LCD and CRT monitors. But other equipments like fans, tables in our laboratories can save energy much more than one can think. We had kept fans, tables, personal computers in OFF mode when work is over. Right now this is limited to computer science and IT department. In future we will apply these techniques to all other departments of our college. The aim of this paper is to measure awareness levels of students and staff at RS College with regards to Green Computing. The research established that the awareness levels to electricity saving techniques for CS and IT department. By incorporating the green computing techniques discussed in this paper into RS College campus can have an immediate impact by reducing power consumption by computers and associated peripherals.

Note: Case study is taken from: http://research.ijcaonline.org/volume62/number2/pxc3884647.pdf

5.2.3 Soft Computing   [Oct. 16]

In real world, we have many problems which we have no way to solve logically, or problems which could be solved theoretically but actually impossible due to its requirement of huge resources and huge time required for computation. For these problems, methods motivated by nature sometimes work very efficiently and effectively these methods do not always equal to the mathematically strict solutions, a near optimal solution is sometimes enough in most practical purposes. These biologically inspired methods are called Soft Computing. Soft Computing is an umbrella term for a collection of computing techniques. The term was first coined by Professor Lotfi Zadeh , who developed the concept of fuzzy logic.

The idea behind soft computing is to model cognitive behavior of human mind.

Soft computing is an emerging collection of methodologies, which aim to achieve tolerance for defect, uncertainty, and partial truth to achieve robustness, tractability and total low cost.

Soft computing methodologies have been advantageous in many applications. In contrast to analytical methods. Soft computing methodologies mimic awareness in several important respects:

1. They can learn from experience.

2. Can universalize into domains where direct experience is absent.

3. Through parallel computer architectures that simulate biological processes, they can perform mapping from inputs to the outputs faster than inherently serial analytical representations.

4. The trade off, however, is a decrease in accuracy. If a tendency towards defects could be tolerated, then it should be possible to extend the scope of the applications even to those problems where the analytical and mathematical representations are readily available.

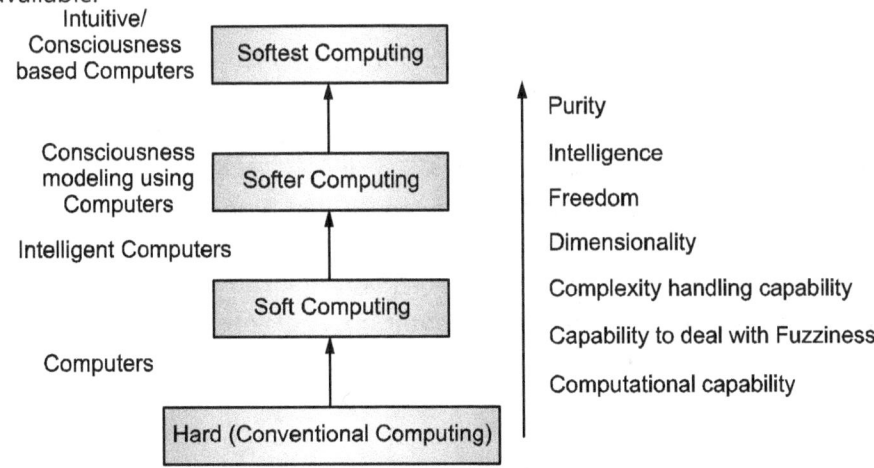

Fig. 5.10: Development of Soft Computing

Techniques in soft computing

The focus of soft computing is to publish quality research in application and convergence of the areas of Fuzzy Logic, Neural Networks, Evolutionary Computing, Rough Sets and other similar techniques to address real world complexities.

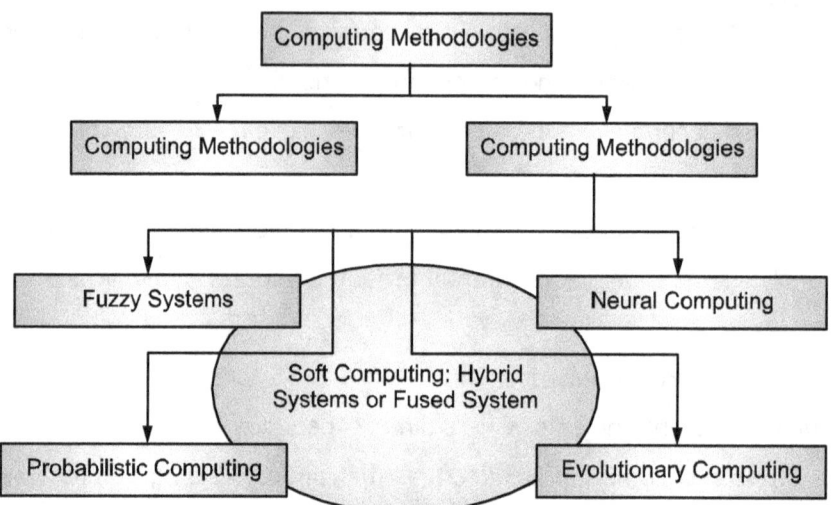

Fig. 5.11: Soft Computing Methodologies

Soft Computing Methodologies are as follows:

- **Neural Networks:** A neural net is an artificial representation of the human brain that tries to simulate its learning process. An artificial neural network (ANN) is often called a "Neutral Network" or simply Neural Net (NN). Artificial neural network is an interconnected group of artificial neurons that uses a mathematical model or computational model for information processing based on a connectionist approach to computation.

- **Fuzzy Logic (FL):** FL is a problem-solving control system methodology that lends itself to implementation in systems ranging from simple, small, embedded micro-controllers to large, networked, multichannel PC or workstation- based data acquisition and control systems. It can be implemented in hardware, software, or a combination of both. FL provides a simple way to arrive at a definite conclusion based upon vague, ambiguous, imprecise, noisy, or missing input information. FL's approach to control problems mimics how a person would make decisions, only much faster.

- **Genetic Algorithns in Evolutionary Computation:** A genetic or evolutionary algorithm applies the principles of evolution found in nature to the problem of finding an optimal solution to a Solver problem. in a "genetic algorithm." the problem is encoded in a series of bit strings that are manipulated by the algorithm: in an "evolutionary algorithm," the decision variables and problem functions are used directly. Most commercial Solver products are based on evolutionary algorithms.

- **Probabilistic Computing:** In the partnership of Fuzzy logic, Neuro computing, Probabilistic computing is mainly concerned with uncertainty and belief propagation.

- **Hard Vs Soft Computing Paradigms:** "Soft computing" is automating process of computation. "Hard computing" means you are doing computation process according to your needs only. For e.g., there are kind of problems[identifying vowels and counting them in any given sentence] which a human brain can compute very easily. This is an example of "Soft Computing". Our human brain scans vowels and counts them in seconds.

In "Hard computing" you make a program for this same above scenario and run it. That is part of "Hard Computing". You are telling the computer just a box to compute(or process) according to your needs. So that kind of computing is a part of "Hard computing". "Soft computing" is much faster than "Hard Computing".

Sr. No.	Hard Computing	Soft Computing
1.	Conventional computing requires a precisely stated analytical models.	Soft computing is tolerant of imprecision.
2.	Often requires a lot of computation time.	Can solve some real world problems in reasonably less time.
3.	Not suited for real world problems for which ideal model is not present.	Suitable for real world problems.
4.	It requires full truth.	Can work with partial truth.
5.	It is precise and accurate.	Imprecise.
6.	High cost for solution.	Low cost for solution.

Unique Features of Soft Computing:

Soft Computing is an approach for constructing systems which are computationally intelligent, possess human like expertise in particular domain, can adapt to the changing environment and can learn to do better can explain their decisions.

Applications of Soft Computing: **[Oct. 16]**

- Handwriting Recognition
- Image Processing and Data Compression
- Automotive Systems and Manufacturing
- Soft Computing to Architecture
- Decision-support Systems
- Soft Computing to Power Systems
- Neuro Fuzzy systems
- Fuzzy Logic Control
- Machine Learning Applications
- Speech and Vision Recognition Systems
- Process Control and so on

Future of Soft Computing:

Soft computing is likely to play an especially important role in science and engineering, but eventually its influence may extend much farther. Soft computing represents a significant paradigm shift in the aims of computing. A shift which reflects the fact that the human mind, unlike present day computers, possesses a remarkable ability to store and process information which is commonly imperfect and uncertain.

Case Study

Highway Entrance Ramp Monitoring And Control Using Soft Computing Techniques

Rahul Misra1 , Avani Patel2 , Rajender Singh3 1, 2, 3M.Tech Scholar (CSE), Bhagwant University,Ajmer

Abstract: Highway entrance ramp monitoring and control is used to regularize the flow of traffic entering through the highway entrance ramps. It detects the flow of traffic entering through the highway ramp monitoring system and controls the flow of traffic using ramp monitoring and control algorithm. This algorithm employs some soft computing techniques which is a suitable choice due to the imprecise information and the level of inaccuracy in the monitoring data available. The use of AI-based search algorithms to calibrate the parameters of a micro-simulation model or estimate the dynamic demand needed to run the model is an area that has received significant attention from researchers recently. Use of soft computing techniques improves the traffic flow as also increases the efficiency of the traffic system with enhanced control and safety.

Keywords: Soft Computing, Traffic Monitoring, Traffic Control, Agent-Based Algorithms, Transportation

1. Highway Ramp Monitoring

The objective is to find the optimal solution that minimizes the minimizes the cost for maintaining and operating the highway monitoring system employing some soft computing techniques which can be further extended in numbers and area of use. These techniques make them an appropriate choice for use in this kind of problems which is complex as well as showing a varying degree in predicting the behavior of the traffic on highway. As a ramp is the entrance and exit points on the highways those can be monitored and controlled using traffic signals.

2. Soft Computing

Soft Computing is term used in computer science to refer the problem in computer science whose solution is not predictable, uncertain and between 0 and 1. Soft Computing became a formal Computer Science area of study in early 1990s. [6] "Basically, soft computing is not a homogeneous body of concepts and techniques. Rather, it is a partnership of distinct methods that in one way or another conform to its guiding principle. At this juncture, the dominant aim of soft computing is to exploit the tolerance for imprecision and uncertainty to achieve tractability, robustness and low solutions cost. The principal constituents of soft computing are fuzzy logic, neurocomputing, and probabilistic reasoning, with the latter subsuming genetic algorithms, belief networks, chaotic systems, and parts of learning theory. In the partnership of fuzzy logic, neurocomputing, and probabilistic reasoning, fuzzy logic is mainly concerned with imprecision and approximate reasoning; neurocomputing with learning and curve-fitting; and probabilistic reasoning with uncertainty and belief propagation"

Agent-Based Algorithms Agents have behaviors, often described by simple rules, and rules to change their behavior. By modeling agents individually, the full effects of the diversity that exists among agents in their attributes and behaviors can be observed as it gives rise to the behavior of the system as a whole. By modeling systems from the ground up (agent by agent), self organization and system evolution can often be observed in such models.

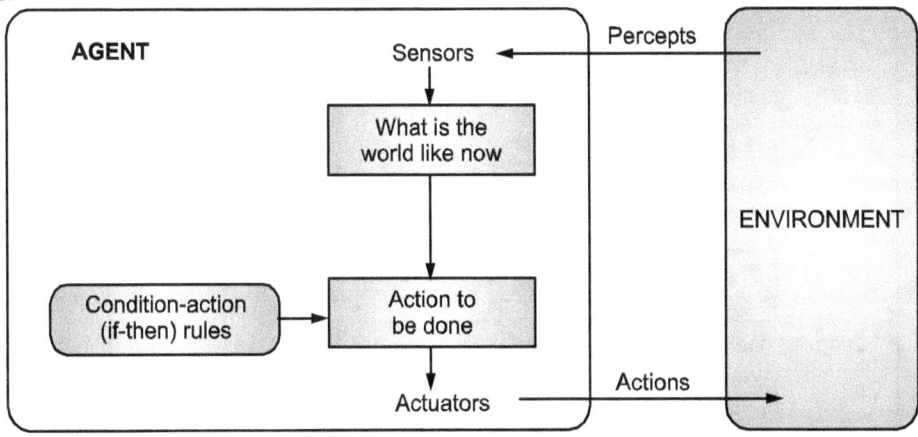

Fig. 5.12: A simple reflexive agent

Agent-based modeling and simulation (ABMS) is a new approach to modeling complex systems by dividing them into a set of interacting autonomous agents. ABMS techniques provide a rich framework for patterns, structures, and behaviors to emerge through the agent interactions. ABMS is arguably the only modeling technique that can simultaneously take into account the attributes and constraints imposed by geography of roadways, the impacts of continually evolving social networks, and the changes from individual decision making and learning in transportation modeling.

ABMS use in transportation reveals that existing efforts can be classified into two main areas of applications:

1. Using ABMS to model ill-structured decision-making processes that cannot otherwise be accurately modeled. For example, modeling the evolution of driver's route-choice behavior, or safety-critical and aggressive driving. This is an area where rule-based or artificial intelligence (AI) ABMS techniques are suitable.
2. Using ABMS to better optimize the performance of the transportation system when solving the problem otherwise could be NP complete or NP-hard. For example, optimizing a distributed control system. This is an area where cooperative agent techniques, such as game theory, are suitable.

The application of ABMS to transportation problems is an area that is still in its infancy in transportation area it will be expect to see many more applications of ABMS. As ABMS is the ideal tool to use to model complex systems, and given that the transportation system, where thousands of different types of agents interact on a continuous basis, is a very good example of a complex system. One of the most challenging technical aspects of ABMS is the identification of worthy aspects or problems for application of the technique—and not only applying the tools —because we Applying ABMS in existing optimization and simulation tools, translation of data and information or structure from one model to another will also poses a significant challenge with promising a enhanced possibilities.

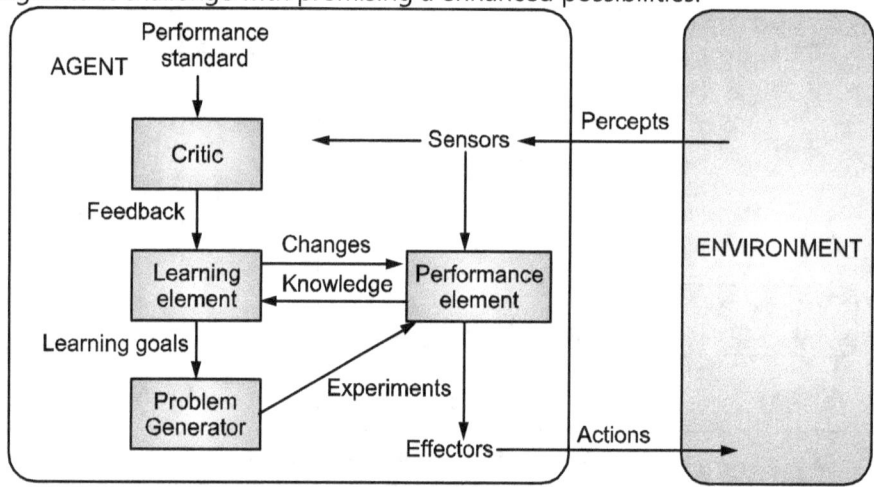

Fig. 5.13: Learning Agent

Growing use of AI in the prospective social behavior researchers and practitioners have realized that single agent systems, multi-agent systems, and distributed AI are widespread attractive, ranging from human– computer interaction over distributed problem solving to the simulation of social systems. Multi-agent principles, are ideal for building a wide range of computer applications, ranging from complex and time critical systems to quite simple e-mail supervisors, which gives it an appropriate choice for traffic control system.

By modeling the separate instruments as intelligent agents, it might be possible to tune the actions of the individual instruments through the agent concept of collaboration. Letting the individual instruments handle the most basic forms of coordination automatically might also relieve the traffic operator.

There are two basic ideas:

1. Consecutive ramp monitoring installations coordinate their actions to promote the flow at a downstream bottleneck.
2. Traffic management instruments coordinate their actions to attain a common goal on the network level.

Reinforcement learning, an AI method for machine learning, is used to provide a single, multiple, or integrated optimal control agent for both recurrent and non-recurrent congestion.

The study involved testing the methodology in three different applications:

1. Highway control using multiple ramp controls
2. Integrated corridor control with a single ramp
3. Variable message sign (VMS), and integrated corridor control with multiple ramps and VMS.

The microsimulation tool Paramics, which has been used to train and evaluate the agent in an offline mode within a simulated environment, is described. Results from various simulation case studies are encouraging and have demonstrated the effectiveness and superiority of the technique.

Fuzzy Logic Based Algorithms

Fuzzy logic algorithms appear well suited to highway entrance ramp monitoring because they can utilize inaccurate or imprecise information and allow smooth transition between monitoring rates. Inputs and outputs are descriptive (e.g., —no congestion,□ —light congestion,□and —medium congestion□ to allow for imprecise data.

Fuzzy logic systems use rule-based logic to incorporate human expertise. This way, it can balance several performance objectives simultaneously and consider many types of information, such as traffic conditions downstream, occupancy, flow rate, speed, and ramp queue. These capabilities allow fuzzy logic to anticipate the problem and take temperate and corrective action before the congestion occurs.

It has been shown that control of an urban expressway depends upon a skilled operator's judgment and decisions. The premier goal of the research was to investigate the effectiveness of fuzzy logic-based models in describing the operator's judgment process. A simple fuzzy reasoning model for on-ramp control and its performance were presented in their papers.

A fuzzy controller for highway entrance ramp monitoring and controlling that uses rules of the form: IF —freeway condition□ THEN —control action.□ The controller has been designed to consider varied levels of congestion, a downstream control area, changing occupancy levels, upstream flows, and a distributed detector array in its rule base. Through fuzzy implication, the inference of each rule is used to the degree to which the condition is true.

Using a dynamic simulation model of conditions at the San Francisco –

Oakland Bay Bridge, the action of the fuzzy controller is compared to the existing —crisp control scheme, and an idealized controller. Tests under a variety of scenarios with different incident locations and capacity reductions show that the fuzzy controller is able to extract 40% to 100% of the possible savings in passenger-hours. In general, the fuzzy algorithm displays smooth and rapid response to incidents, and significantly reduces the minute-miles of congestion.

3. Conclusions

This paper has surveyed the application of some AI paradigms to the problem of highway entrance ramp monitoring and provided the control strategies using fuzzy logic based algorithms and agent-based algorithms. Results from the studies performed to evaluate such algorithms seem to indicate the promise of AI when applied in such a context.

Note: Case study is taken from: http://www.ijritcc.org/download/IJRITCC_1364.pdf.

5.2.4 Mobile Computing   [April 16, Oct. 16]

Mobile Computing is a technology that allows transmission of data, via a computer, without having to be connected to a fixed physical link. It is a process of computation on a mobile device.

Mobile voice communication is widely established throughout the world and has had a very rapid increase in the number of subscribers to the various cellular networks over the last few years. An extension of this technology is the ability to send and receive data across these cellular networks. This is the principle of mobile computing.

Mobile data communication has become a very important and rapidly evolving technology as it allows users to transmit data from remote locations to other remote or fixed locations. This proves to be the solution to the biggest problem of business people on the move - mobility.

Pervasive means 'existing in all parts of a place or thing'. Pervasive computing is the next generation of computing which takes into account the environment in which information and communication technology is used everywhere, by everyone, and at all times.

Mobile computing is also called pervasive computing when a set of computing devices, systems, or networks have the characteristics of transparency, application-aware adaptation, and have an environment sensing ability.

There are two kinds of mobility's.

(a) **User mobility:** In user mobility a user can access the same or similar services at different places. That is the user can be mobile, and services will follow him.

(b) **Device mobility:** The communication device moves with or without help of a user. Several techniques in communication network guarantees that communication is even possible while device is being moved.

Characteristics of Mobile Computing:

Some of the characteristics of mobile computing are based on following:

1. **Hardware:** The characteristics of mobile computing hardware are defined by the size and form factor, weight, microprocessor, primary storage, secondary storage, screen size and type, means of input, means of output, battery life, communications capabilities, expandability and durability of the device.

2. **Software:** Mobile computers make use of a wide variety of system and application software. The most common system software and operating environments used on mobile computers includes MSDOS, Windows 3.1/3.11/95/98/NT, UNIX, Android etc. These operating environments range in capabilities from a minimalist graphically-enhanced- penenabled DOS environment to the powerful capabilities of Windows NT. Each operating system/environment has some form of integrated development environment (IDE) for application development. Most of the operating environments provide more than one development environment option for custom application development.

3. **Communication:** The ability of a mobile computer to communicate in some fashion with a fixed information system is a defining characteristic of mobile computing. The type and availability of communication medium significantly impacts the type of mobile computing application that can be created.

   The way a mobile computing device communicates with a fixed information system can be categorized as:

   (a) Connected: The connected category implies a continuously available high-speed connection.

   (b) Weakly Connected: The ability to communicate continuously, but at slow speeds, allows mobile computers to be weakly connected to the fixed information system.

   (c) Batch: A batch connection means that the mobile computer is not continuously available for communication with the fixed information system. In the batch mode, communication is established randomly or periodically to exchange and update information between the mobile computer and fixed information systems. Mobile computers may operate in batch mode over communication mediums that are capable of continuous operation, reducing the wireless airtime and associated fees.

   (d) Disconnected: Disconnected mobile computers allow users to improve efficiency by making calculations, storing contact information, keeping a schedule, and other non- communications oriented tasks. This mode of operation is of little interest because the mobile device is incapable of electronically interacting and exchanging information with the fixed organizational information system.

   Data Communications is the exchange of data using existing communication networks. The term data covers a wide range of applications including File Transfer, interconnection between Wide-Area-Networks (WAN), facsimile (fax), electronic mail, access to the internet and the World Wide Web (WWW).

Working of Mobile Computing

In mobile computing platform information between processing units flows through wireless channels. The processing unit (client) is free to move about in the space while being connected to the server. This capability allows organizations to set their offices at any location. The discipline of mobile computing has its origin in Personal Communications Services (PCS). PCS refers to a wide variety of wireless access and personal mobility services provided through a small terminal (e.g., cell phone), with the goal of enabling communications at any time, at any place, and in any form. These PCS are connected to Public Switched Telephone Network (PSTN) to provide access to wired telephones.

PCS include high-tier digital cellular systems for widespread vehicular and pedestrian services and low-tier telecommunication system standards for residential, business, and public cordless access applications.

Several wideband wireless systems and special data systems have been developed to accommodate internet and multimedia services. Mobile computing is not one technology. It is a range of solutions that enable user mobility by providing access to data anytime, from anywhere.

Fig. 5.14: Components of Mobile Computing

As shown in figure, mobile computing has three components
1. Handheld, mobile computing device.
2. Connecting technology that allows information to pass back and forth between the site's centralized information system and the handheld device and back.
3. Centralized information system

Here is how Mobile Computing Works:
1. The user enters or access data using the application on handheld computing device.
2. Using one of several connecting technologies, the new data are transmitted from handheld to site's information system where files are updated and the new data are accessible to other system user.
3. Now both systems (handheld and site's computer) have the same information and are in sync.
4. The process work the same way starting from the other direction. The process is similar to the way a worker's desktop PC access the organization's applications, except that user's device is not physically connected to the organization's system. The communication between the user device and site's information systems uses different methods for transferring and synchronizing data, some involving the use of radio frequency (RF) technology.

In today's market, the three most commonly used wireless data transfer methods are:

1. Wireless local area network (Wireless LAN).
2. Wireless Internet or wireless Web.
3. Data syncing or "hot syncing".

This is not a wireless data transfer method, although it is often reference as wireless. Data syncing used docking cradles or docking stations that are connected to a LAN to transfer data from the device to the organization's information system.

Wireless LAN:

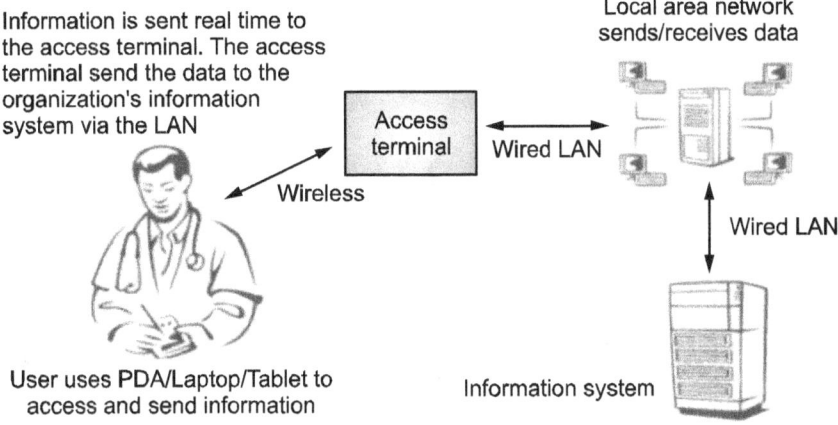

Fig. 5.15: Wireless LAN

Wireless LAN is a flexible data and communication system used in addition to, or instead of, a wired LAN. Using radio frequency (RF) technology, wireless LANs transmit and receive data over air, minimizing the need for wired connection and enable user mobility. Unlike such technologies such as infrared, wireless LAN is not a "line of sight" technology. Therefore the handheld device can operate anywhere within the coverage area. In a wireless LAN user enters data into a handheld device such as personal digital assistant (PDA), laptop or tablet that has a special wireless LAN card. This card has an antenna that transmits the data in real time using radio frequency technology to an access terminal, usually connected to a ceiling or wall. The access terminal is connected to the local area network and sends the data-received or request for data- from the handheld to site's information system. Conversely, data from site's information system can be sending to the handheld using same technology.

Wireless Internet:

Wireless Internet, also known as the wireless web, provides mobile computing access to data using the Internet and specially equipped handheld device. Using a web phone or a latest PDA phone with micro web browser, the user can display data accessible from the internet. The mobile device connected to the cellular system sends the request to computer link server. This server act as a gateway that translates signal from the handheld device into language the web can understand, using an access and communication protocol. One of the leading protocols is WAP (Wireless application protocol). The server also forwards the request over the internet to a web site, such as Yahoo, Google or the organization's site information system. The web site response to the request and forwards the information back through the link server. Again the response is translated into a Wireless Markup Language (WML) so it is viewable on the small cell phone screen. This translated response is then sent to the cellular system and finally to the Web-enable mobile computing device. Example for the current uses of wireless internet include accessing short emails, quick look up capabilities (stocks, weather, flights, movies, restaurants, retail transaction, alert messaging etc.

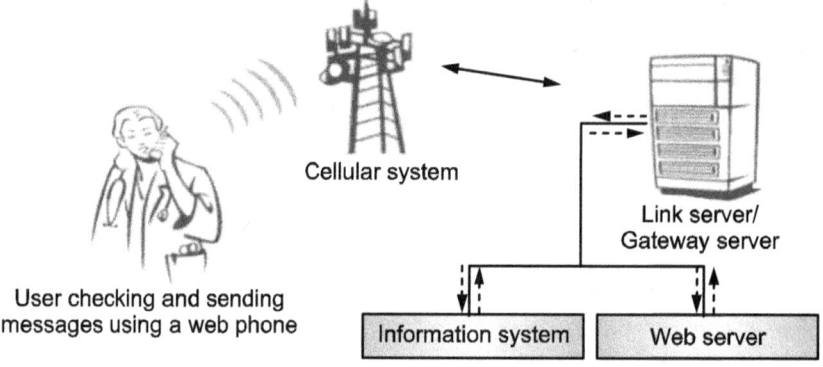

Fig. 5.16: Wireless Internet

Data Synchronization:

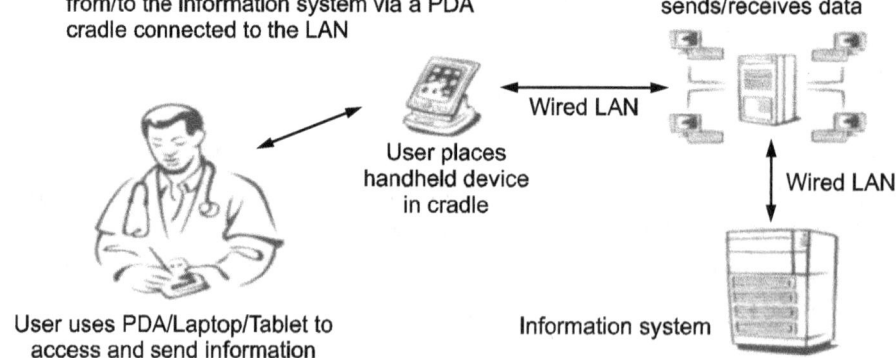

Fig. 5.17: Data Synchronization

Data Synchronization provides many of the benefits of mobile computing without the cost of installing wireless LAN equipment or needing access to the Internet. Information is periodically downloaded from the organization's information system to the handheld device and then uploads from the device to organization's information system. Updating of information is available in both the sides. The major drawback of data synchronization is that it does not provide real time access to data. Data syncing is not a wireless data transfer method because data are transferred from the mobile computing device to the site's information system through a docking (or syncing) cradle wired to the LAN. It is commonly grouped under the general term of "wireless" because the user's device is physically attached to the LAN only during the batch data transfers.

Data Synchronization solutions have been used widely in health care and are typically the first use of wireless because of the low cost to implement and the wide range of application that deliver real value to the organization. Generally, data syncing solutions work best in health care settings where 1. Mobile user has access to the LAN for periodic data updates and 2. The work being performed does not require access to the most current information.

Importance of Mobile Computing

The importance of Mobile Computers has been highlighted in many fields of which a few are described below:

For Estate Agents

With mobile computers they can be more productive. They can obtain current real estate information by accessing multiple listing services, which they can do from home, office or car when out with clients. They can provide clients with immediate feedback regarding specific homes or neighborhoods, and with faster loan approvals, since applications can be submitted on the spot. Therefore, mobile computers allow them to devote more time to clients.

Emergency Services

Ability to recieve information on the move is vital where the emergency services are involved. Information regarding the address, type and other details of an incident can be dispatched quickly, via a CDPD (Cellular Digital Packet Data) system using mobile computers, to one or several appropriate mobile units which are in the vicinity of the incident.

In courts

Defense counsels can take mobile computers in court. When the opposing counsel references a case which they are not familiar, they can use the computer to get direct, real-time access to on-line legal database services, where they can gather information on the case and related precedents. Therefore mobile computers allow immediate access to a wealth of information, making people better informed and prepared.

In companies

Managers can use mobile computers in, say, critical presentations to major customers. They can access the latest market share information. At a small recess, they can revise the presentation to take advantage of this information. They can communicate with the office about possible new offers and call meetings for discussing responds to the new proposals. Therefore, mobile computers can leverage competitive advantages.

Stock Information Collation/Control

In environments where access to stock is very limited ie: factory warehouses. The use of small portable electronic databases accessed via a mobile computer would be ideal.

Data collated could be directly written to a central database, via a CDPD network, which holds all stock information hence the need for transfer of data to the central computer at a later date is not necessary. This ensures that from the time that a stock count is completed, there is no inconsistency between the data input on the portable computers and the central database.

Credit Card Verification

At Point of Sale (POS) terminals in shops and supermarkets, when customers use credit cards for transactions, the intercommunication required between the bank central computer and the POS terminal, in order to effect verification of the card usage, can take place quickly and securely over cellular channels using a mobile computer unit. This can speed up the transaction process and relieve blockage at the POS terminals.

Taxi/Truck Dispatch

Using the idea of a centrally controlled dispatcher with several mobile units (taxis), mobile computing allows the taxis to be given full details of the dispatched job as well as allowing the taxis to communicate information about their whereabouts back to the central dispatch office. This system is also extremely useful in secure deliveries ie: Securicor. This allows a central computer to be able to track and recieve status information from all of its mobile secure delivery vans. Again, the security and reliabilty properties of the CDPD system shine through.

Electronic Mail/Paging

Usage of a mobile unit to send and read emails is a very useful asset for any business individual, as it allows him/her to keep in touch with any colleagues as well as any urgent developments that may affect their work. Access to the Internet, using mobile computing technology, allows the individual to have vast arrays of knowledge at his/her fingertips.

Paging is also achievable here, giving even more intercommunication capability between individuals, using a single mobile computer device.

In student learning process:

Mobile computing is being used in education mainly for teaching and learning and also administration and research.

E-learning: E-learning is defined as instruction delivered via an electronic media including the Internet, Intranets, extranets, satellite broadcast, audio/videotapes, interactive TV and CD-ROM E-learning can be implemented in the classroom or outside the classroom. It is best suited for distance learning but it can also be used together with face to face learning .Students have access to course materials online anytime and in any place and they can work at their own pace.

M-learning: Mobile learning is the term used to describe any form of training that uses mobile devices such as mobile phones. Hand held devices are used in M-learning. The e-Learning Guild describe m-learning as "any activity that allows individuals to be more productive when consuming, interacting with, or creating information, mediated through a compact digital portable device that the individual carries on a regular basis, has reliable connectivity, and fits in a pocket or purse." Technological changes are driving the use of mobile devices in education. Students has own mobile device and use them at a higher rate than the older generation. With M-learning, students can access content including quizzes and other assessments, balance sheets and other data, learning games, and other content delivered via different applications from anywhere. Students can work together and share and get immediate tips and feedback from others.

Limitations of Mobile Computing:

1. **Insufficient Bandwidth:** Mobile Internet access is generally slower than direct cable connections, using technologies such as GPRS and EDGE, and more recently 3G networks. These networks are usually available within range of commercial cell phone towers. Higher speed wireless LANs are inexpensive but have very limited range.

2. **Security Standards:** When working mobile, one is dependent on public networks, requiring careful use of Virtual Private Network (VPN). Security is a major concern while concerning the mobile computing standards on the fleet. One can easily attack the VPN through a huge number of networks interconnected through the line.

3. **Power Consumption:** When a power outlet or portable generator is not available, mobile computers must rely entirely on battery power. Combined with the compact size of many mobile devices, this often means unusually expensive batteries must be used to obtain the necessary battery life. Mobile computing should also look into Greener IT, in such a way that it saves the power or increases the battery life.

4. **Transmission Interferences:** Weather, land and the range from the nearest signal point can all interfere with signal reception. Reception in tunnels, some buildings, and rural areas is often poor.

5. **Potential Health Hazards:** People who use mobile devices while driving are often distracted from driving are thus assumed more likely to be involved in traffic accidents. Cell phones may interfere with sensitive medical devices. There are allegations that cell phone signals may cause health problems.

6. **Human Interface with Device:** Screens and keyboards tend to be small, which may make them hard to use. Alternate input methods such as speech or handwriting recognition require training.

Although wireless technology is maturing rapidly, several limitations stand in the way of widespread adoption. Good decision about technology need to be based on a realistic understanding of current performance and how limitations can be addressed.

Technology	Current Issue and Limitation
Mobile Computing Devices	• Handheld device such as PDAs and pocket PCs have small screens, short battery life, limited processing power, and rudimentary data integration capability. • Laptop and tablets provide greater processing, battery life and data viewing power, but are considerably larger heavier, with limited data interfacing capabilities.

contd. ...

Wireless LANs	• Data transfer speed is currently slower than traditional LANs. • Real Time interfaces between mobile computing and LAN based applications are custom developed for each site and therefore expensive to create and maintain.
Wireless Internet	• Wireless Internet technology faces similar issues with data transfer speed. • Additional problem of multiple connectivity standards.
Data Synchronization	• Same device limitations as described above plus the need for application specific cradles wired throughout the service area. • Supports only batch data updates.

The Future

With the rapid technological advancements in Artificial Intelligence, Integrated Circuitry and increases in Computer Processor speeds, the future of mobile computing looks increasingly exciting.

With the emphasis increasingly on compact, small mobile computers, it may also be possible to have all the practicality of a mobile computer in the size of a hand held organizer or even smaller.

Indeed, technologies such as Interactive Television and Video Image Compression already imply a certain degree of mobility in the home, ie. home shopping etc. Using the mobile data communication technologies discussed, this mobility may be pushed to extreme.

The future of Mobile Computing is very promising indeed, although technology may go too far, causing detriment to society.

Case study

Authentic Learning of Mobile Security with Case Studies

Minzhe Guo, Prabir Bhattacharya
School of Computing Sciences and Informatics
University of Cincinnati
Cincinnati, OH

Kai Qian
Department of Computer Science
Southern Polytechnic State University,
Marietta, GA

Li Yang
Department of Computer Science
University of Tennessee at Chattanooga
Chattanooga, TN

Abstract: This work-in-progress paper presents an approach to authentic learning of mobile security through real-world-scenario case studies. Five sets of case studies are being developed to cover the state-of-the-art of mobile security knowledge and practices. Some of the developed case studies are being implemented in related courses and the preliminary feedback is positive.

Keywords- Authentic Learning, Case Study, Mobile Security

I. Introduction:

Owing to their ultra-portability, enriched functionality, and ease of use, smart mobile devices, such as Android and iOS based smartphones and tablets, play more and more important roles in many aspects of our society. Users increasingly use their mobile devices to access to the wealth of information available on the Internet, to store sensitive data, to communicate and entertain, and to process many of their daily tasks. These, however, also attract attackers to extend their targets to mobile platforms, resulting in a rapidly increasing number of mobile threats and a growing sophistication of mobile attacks . In this work, we use the notion of mobile security to cover the topics of security and privacy issues, attacks, and defenses involved in the use of smart mobile devices. The mobile security is at the intersection of wireless communication, mobile computing, and computer security; and has its unique characteristics, such as introducing new and unique mobile security threats. Few existing security courses cover the full spectrum of mobile security topics; in addition, dedicated courses and effective materials on mobile security are sparse. This calls for efforts to promote mobile security education and to foster qualified mobile security professionals.

This work-in-progress paper presents an approach to authentic learning of mobile security through real-worldscenario case studies. Authentic learning situates students in learning contexts where they encounter activities that involve problems and investigations reflective of those they are likely to face in their real world professional contexts . A recent report pointed out that rather than only teaching students abstract concepts and assigning students abstract exercises, engaging students in real-world settings will benefit student effective learning in security education. In this work, we approach to authentic learning of mobile security via the design of learning materials into real-world scenario cases, and take advantage of mobile device as the authentic learning platform, which will also help create a portable and affordable security learning tool.

Courses focused on mobile security remain sparse in most computing curricula. Tague offered a mobile security course at the Carnegie Mellon University ; however, it was a project-based course that provided students with topics for discuss and explore. In contrast, our work emphasizes on learning mobile security through real-world case analysis and hands-on experience, and we develop the materials for the learning. The application of Android in the education of various computer science subjects is obtaining increasing interests. For example, Andrus and Nieh developed a series of five Android kernel programming projects and an Android virtual laboratory to teach an introductory operating system course; Kurkovsky used mobile game development as a motivational tool to engage students early in the curriculum; and Loveland described the use of Google Android mobile platform and Google's Web Toolkit to provide students with experience in designing and implementing user interfaces for mobile and web applications. The above works showed that the use of Android engaged students' interests in learning and improved effectiveness. Our work focuses on using Android to promote the study of mobile security and we directly use mobile devices and applications for security analysis and practice.

II. Case Study Design

To implement the authentic learning for mobile security, this work employs the following strategies in the development of the case studies, including: 1) connecting the abstract security concepts to real-world mobile security cases so that students can better understand the concepts and can work more actively and effectively with facts and realistic problems; 2) designing each case from both of the attack and defense perspectives so that students can gain more insights and can design better defense solutions via the experience with actual attacks; 3) infusing hands-on practices in the course of case studies and designing most of the practices in such a way that they can be performed on mobile devices directly; 4) encouraging students to identify for themselves the mobile security issues; and 5) providing students with opportunity of reflection in action so that they can learn how and when to use particular strategies for problem solving. Following the above strategies, we are developing five sets of case studies, including:

- **Mobile Malware:** Case studies that (1) discuss the mobile malware attacking strategies and demonstrate instances of real-world Android malware; and (2) discuss the defense methods and instruct on practicing defense solutions.
- **Secure Mobile Coding:** Case studies that (1) use code examples to demonstrate the security weakness or unsecure coding patterns in the development of different Android app components, including Activity, Intent, Service, Content Provider, and Broadcast Receiver; and (2) discuss the best practices for improving the security of the Android app coding, such as using explicit Intent Filter to avoid Intent spoofing.
- **Cryptography on Mobile Devices:** Case studies that (1) discuss how to utilize the built-in cryptography mechanisms (e.g., SSL or VPN settings) to improve the security of data in device (database storage, shared memory, shared preferences, internal and external storage), on Cloud, or in the course of network communications; and (2) discuss how to program with Android/Java cryptography libraries to enhance the security of mobile apps.
- **Access Control.** Case studies that (1) discuss the Android permission model, including its basic concepts, use cases, weaknesses, and enhancements; and (2) discuss other access control and authentication mechanisms for mobile devices and application, including single sign-on and two-factor authentication.
- **Mobile Privacy.** Case studies that demonstrate the leakage of privacy-related data from mobile devices and communications (e.g., location information, user behavior and usage patterns), and discuss the configurations and best practices for mobile privacy enhancement.

As an example, the set of mobile malware case studies consists of an introductory case study and a set of individual malware case studies. The introductory case study summarizes the state-of-the-art mobile malware research and the malware reports from leading mobile security companies. Each individual malware case study introduces a family of realworld mobile malware, covering the topics of the attackers' incentives (e.g., Premium Calls/SMS or Information Stealing), attacking strategies (e.g., repackaging or update attacks), and existing defense solutions. It is observed that the number of new instances and variants of existing mobile malware families increases rapidly, but the number of new malware families grows rather slowly. We will prepare for each case study at least one real instance of mobile malware in the family so that students can experience the actual attacks in a sandbox environment (i.e., an Android emulator on a virtual machine with experimental settings and data) and analyze the malicious behaviors and features. Each individual malware case study will also instruct student on practicing defense methods. Current mobile malware defense methods include app analysis (static/dynamic/permission analysis), configuration of system security settings, watchdogs, and user education. As the mobile malware evolves, the introductory case study will be updated and new cases will be developed and added into our individual malware case study set.

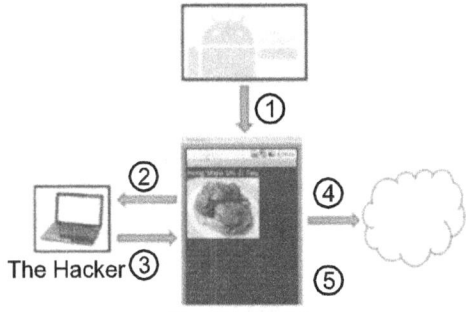

Fig. 5.18: Workflow of Trojan App

Fig. 5.18 Work Flow of a Premium SMS Android Trojan App in Our Mobile Malware Case Studies. (○1 the Trojan app is downloaded and installed on the victim's device; ○2 when the Trojan app is activated by the victim, it sends a notification with the victim's information to the hacker; ○3 the hacker sends the commands to the Trojan app to ○4 send SMS to premium numbers or send Ad SMS to others; and ○5 the trojan app clears messaging history.)

Fig. 5.18 illustrates the work flow of an instance of Android Trojan in one of our individual malware case studies. The Trojan app pretends itself as an Asian Gourmet Android app, performs command and control communication with the hacker, and stealthily sends short messages (SMS) to premium numbers or advertisements to others. In the defense practices, students will be instructed on developing an Android SMS Monitoring App, which monitors the messaging actions in the background and sends notifications to users when suspicious messaging are detected. Note that in the latest version of Android 4.2 (Jelly Bean), Google provides similar kinds of control of premium SMS to enhance the Android security.

III. Conclusion:

This work-in-progress paper presents an approach to authentic learning of mobile security through real-world scenario case studies. We describe our strategies in developing the five sets of mobile security case studies and present more detail design of the set of mobile malware case studies.

Some of the developed case studies are being implemented in CS mobile security class and IT wireless security class. The preliminary feedback from students is positive. Students have gained hands-on real world experiences on mobile security with Android mobile devices, which also greatly promoted students' self-efficacy and confidence in their mobile security learning.

In the future work, we will continue to improve the design of the case studies, complete the case study development, and conduct extensive evaluations.

Acknowledgment

The work is partially supported by the National Science Foundation under award: NSF SFS #1241651. Any opinions, findings, and conclusions or recommendations expressed in this material are those of the authors and do not necessarily reflect the views of the National Science Foundation.

Case Study is taken from:

http://www.utc.edu/center-information-security-assurance/pdfs/paper-fie-mobile-security-2013.pdf

Practice Questions

1. What do you mean by Computing? Explain types of Computing.
2. Define the term
    (a) Computing
    (b) Informatics
    (c) Green IT
3. Difference between Hard Computing & Soft Computing.
4. What is Cloud Computing? Explain types of cloud computing.
5. Write a short note on Service Models of Cloud Computing.
6. What does PaaS means? Explain its characteristics.
7. Define Mobile Computing. Discuss working of Mobile computing.
8. Explain: "Need of Mobile Computing in today's world".
9. What is IaaS? Explain its characteristics.
10. How Cloud Computing works? Explain architecture of Cloud Computing.
11. What is SaaS? Explain its characteristics.
12. List the Importance and Limitations of Mobile Computing.

■■■

April 2016

Time: Three Hours   Maximum Marks: 80

N.B.:   (i)   All questions are compulsory.
        (ii) All questions carry equal marks.
        (iii) Assume suitable data, if necessary.

1.   Attempt any eight of the following: **[8 × 2 = 16]**

(a) Define Software Prototyping.

Ans. Refer to Section 1.11.

(b) What is Varying Arrays?

Ans. Refer to Section 2.7.3.

(c) Define the term 'Data Warehouse'.

Ans. Refer to Section 3.3.

(d) Explain the term 'One-Time-Pads'.

Ans. Refer to Section 4.5.

(e) What are the benefits of Data Cleaning?

Ans. Refer to Section 3.9.

(f) What are the needs of "Green Computing"?

Ans. Refer to Section 5.2.2.

(g) What are the types of Indicators?

Ans. Refer to Section 1.3.

(h) Explain the term Ciphertext.

Ans. Refer to Section 4.3.

(i) What do you mean by Data Integration?

Ans. Refer to Section 3.10.

(j) What is Data Replication?

Ans. Refer to Section 2.4.

2.   Attempt any four of the following: **[4 × 4 = 16]**

(a) State naming convention of objects.

Ans. Refer to Section 2.7.5.

(b) What are the different software prototyping methods and tools?

Ans. Refer to Section 1.11.

(c) Explain the term Public Key Algorithm, RSA.

Ans. Refer to Section 4.11.

(d) Describe centralized and client server based architecture of Database System.

Ans. Refer to Section 2.5.

(e) Describe the role of Requirement Analysis is Software Process.

Ans. Refer to Section 1.8.

3. Attempt any four of the following: [4 × 4 = 16]

(a) Give the advantages and disadvantages of Mobile Computing.

Ans. Refer to Section 5.2.4.

(b) Define OLAP Server Architecture in Data Warehouse.

Ans. Refer to Section 3.4.

(c) Explain Symmetric Key Signature and Public Key Signature.

Ans. Refer to Section 4.14 and 4.15.

(d) Define 'Distributed Database' and reasons for building Distributed Database.

Ans. Refer to Section 2.2.

(e) Explain different types of Ciphertext in cryptography.

Ans. Refer to Section 4.2.

4. Attempt any four of the following: [4 × 4 = 16]

(a) What is Data Mining? Describe its architecture.

Ans. Refer to Section 3.7.

(b) What is Software Quality Assurance (SQA)? State advantages of SQA.

Ans. Refer to Section 1.7.

(c) What is "Green Computing"? Give any example that implements Green Computing.

Ans. Refer to Section 5.2.2.

(d) What is Message Digest in cryptography?

Ans. Refer to Section 4.16.

(e) What is the difference between Standalone and Distributed Database.?

Ans. Refer to Section 2.2.

5. Attempt any four of the following: [4 × 4 = 16]

(a) Explain the term:

　　(i) Homogeneous Distributed Databases.

　　(ii) Heterogeneous Distributed Databases.

Ans. Refer to Section 2.6.

(b) Explain star schema for data warehouse.

Ans. Refer to Section 3.1.

(c) Describe client server architecture in Distributed Database.

Ans. Refer to Section 2.5.

(d) Give the advantages of cloud computing.

Ans. Refer to Section 5.2.

(e) Give the factors that affect software quality.

Ans. Refer to Section 1.6.

■■■

October 2016

Time: Three Hours   Maximum Marks: 80

N.B.: (i)   All questions are compulsory.
          (ii)   All questions carry equal marks.
          (iii) Assume suitable data, if necessary.

1. Attempt any eight of the following: [8 × 2 = 16]
(a) Define the term 'Noisy Data'.
Ans. Refer to Section 3.9.
(b) What are the different characteristics of DDBMS?
Ans. Refer to Section 2.2.
(c) What do you mean by process metrics?
Ans. Refer to Section 1.4.
(d) Write a short note on 'Network Security'.
Ans. Refer to Section 4.1.
(e) What are the advantages of mobile computing?
Ans. Refer to Section 5.2.4.
(f) What is OLTP?
Ans. Refer to Section 3.13.
(g) Explain the term 'Steganography'.
Ans. Refer to Section 4.2.
(h) Define the term 'Function Point'.
Ans. Refer to Section 1.5.
(i) What do you mean by Digital Certificate?
Ans. Refer to Section 4.13.
(j) What are the different types of cloud computing?
Ans. Refer to Section 5.2.1.

2. Attempt any four of the following: [4 × 4 = 16]
(a) Give the advantages and disadvantages of Data Mining.
Ans. Refer to Section 3.7.
(b) What is the difference between Hard Computing and Soft Computing?
Ans. Refer to Section 5.2.3.
(c) Explain Multidimensional Data Model.
Ans. Refer to Section 3.2.
(d) What is Software Quality Assurance (SQA)? State advantages of SQA.
Ans. Refer to Section 1.7.
(e) What is Ciphertext? Explain Substitution Cipher and Transposition Cipher.
Ans. Refer to Sections 4.3 and 4.4.

3. **Attempt any four of the following:**   [4 × 4 = 16]

(a) What is Data Encryption Standard (DES)?

Ans. Refer to Section 4.8.

(b) What is the need of measures in software process?

Ans. Refer to Section 1.1.

(c) State the applications of soft computing.

Ans. Refer to Section 5.2.3.

(d) Explain Data integration and Data Transformation in Data Mining.

Ans. Refer to Sections 3.10 and 3.11.

(e) What is Cryptography? Give different types of cryptography.

Ans. Refer to Section 4.2 and 4.10.

4. **Attempt any four of the following:**   [4 × 4 = 16]

(a) Define concept of Fragmentation. Explain types of fragmentation in Distributed database.

Ans. Refer to Section 2.4.

(b) What are the goals of software prototyping.

Ans. Refer to Section 1.11.

(c) Explain communication techniques for requirement analysis.

Ans. Refer to Section 1.8.

(d) Explain implementation of mobile computing in student learning process.

Ans. Refer to Section 5.2.4.

(e) Explain the concept of Nested tables and its implementation in object relational database.

Ans. Refer to Section 2.7.2.

5. **Attempt any four of the following:**   [4 × 4 = 16]

(a) Explain in brief "Expert System".

Ans. Refer to Section 5.1.

(b) What are the need and advantages of Distributed Database Management System?

Ans. Refer to Section 2.2.

(c) Explain how RSA algorithm works.

Ans. Refer to Section 4.11.

(d) Explain snowflake scheme for multidimensional database.

Ans. Refer to Section 3.2.

(e) What are the different types of Indicators?

Ans. Refer to Section 1.3.

■■■